MIND VIRUS

Charles Kowalski

Literary Wanderlust, LLC | Denver, CO

Published in the United States of America by Literary Wanderlust, Denver, CO.
www.literarywanderlust.com

ISBN print: 978-1-942856-18-4
ISBN digital: 978-1-942856-19-1

Library of Congress Control Number: 2017938664

Cover design: Ruth M'Gonigle

For everyone who has ever been Emily

IN THE BEGINNING

WASHINGTON, D.C.
SUNDAY, MARCH 22

Everything was going according to plan.

The man with blue eyes blended in perfectly with his camouflage: blue jeans, a white T-shirt bearing an American flag with a cross in place of the stars, and just for a touch of extra realism, a "WWJD?" wristband. As he joined the crowd jostling its way into the Verizon Center, he drew no notice beyond a "Welcome, brother! God bless you!" from an usher. Of course, no one asked to inspect his backpack. Even if they had, they would have found nothing more suspicious than a 64-ounce water bottle in an insulating sleeve.

He strategically selected an aisle seat near the central stage. The folding chairs on the stadium floor around him, and then the bleachers, began to fill up with legions of the infected. The stadium could seat thirty thousand, and even this far before starting time, it was beginning to look as though it would be a capacity crowd. He noticed that his breathing had grown shallow, and he found himself wishing for a surgical mask and a bottle of the world's strongest hand sanitizer.

Don't be ridiculous, he admonished himself. *It's all in the mind. There's nothing dangerous in the air here ...yet.*

"Brothers and sisters," came the announcer's voice,

"welcome to *Awaken America!* This place is packed and the Spirit is ready for action! Glory, hallelujah! And now, may I present the man who made it all happen. Brothers and sisters, let's hear it for the Reverend Isaiah Hill!"

To thunderous cheers, he made his grand entrance: Isaiah Hill, super vector, personally responsible for the infection of thousands. The spotlights shone blindingly off his white suit and the white teeth gleaming from his black face, magnified a hundredfold on the four giant screens suspended from the dome.

"Good morning, brothers and sisters!" he greeted the adoring crowd, his voice echoed faintly in Spanish by a simultaneous interpreter. "And do you know what comes in the morning? Joy! 'Weeping may endure for a night, but joy comes in the morning.' And the dawn we've all been waiting for is coming, brothers and sisters! It's time to *Awaken America!*"

Right on the last word, clouds of confetti and columns of laser light shot up from the corners of the stage. The gospel choir burst into song, as dry ice vapor cascaded from the risers to make it look as though they were ascending to heaven. Yes, Hill had clearly gotten where he was because he knew how to play on the emotions like a virtuoso organist, while keeping the stops on the brain pushed firmly in.

As the crowd joined their voices to the choir, the man with blue eyes clapped and swayed along with the others, mouthing the words that scrolled across waterfalls and Rocky Mountain landscapes on the screens. As one speaker after another took the microphone, he added an occasional "Hallelujah!" or "Praise the Lord!" to the answering chorus. The words left a slimy, evil-tasting residue in his mouth, but he consoled himself with the thought that this was the last time he would ever be in a place like this. And it was an even greater consolation to be the only one who knew that the same was true for hundreds, hopefully even thousands, of the others here.

Then came the cue, exactly according to plan.

"Dear brothers and sisters," came the Reverend Hill's voice over the loudspeakers, "are any of you sick? Are any of you weary? Are any of you carrying heavy burdens? Come to one of our prayer stations, and our ministers will lay hands on you and pray for the healing of everything that harms you. Come unto Him, dear brothers and sisters! Come unto Him!"

A soprano soloist from the choir started to belt out a gospel-style rendition of "Come unto Him" from *The Messiah,* backed by an array of instruments that Handel could never have imagined. All around the stadium, people began to rise from their seats and make their way into the aisles.

That was the cue. He reached into his backpack, uncapped the drinking tube on the water bottle, and pressed the button in a pocket of the sleeve. He heard a muffled beep.

The countdown had begun.

He zipped the backpack closed, leaving the end of the drinking tube protruding from between the zipper tabs. He set the backpack on his chair, taking care to keep the bottle upright. And stepped into the aisle.

That was when things stopped going according to plan.

A few places in line ahead of him, one of the healing ministers was laying his hands on the head of a young woman kneeling before him. Suddenly, she let out a piercing scream, fell over backward, and began to shake as if she were in the throes of an epileptic seizure.

The people around her stood back, and one cushioned her head with a folded sweatshirt. "Oh, God! Oh, dear God!" she cried when she could speak again, tears streaming down her cheeks as she kicked her feet and clapped her hands. "Yes, Lord! Thank you, Jesus!" To the blue-eyed observer, she looked as though she were simultaneously coming to a climax and watching her number come up for Mega Millions.

She showed no sign of stopping, and the people around her, either staring at her or with eyes turned heavenward in prayer, kept him from moving forward. He turned around to look for another escape route. Behind him was another young woman, in a wheelchair. Her parents stood behind her, diverting their gaze from the spectacle in front of them just long enough to exchange a glance that said, *Dare we hope*? They filled the aisle, there was no getting around them.

Trying to pass through the row of seats across the aisle would only take him farther from his goal of the exit. The only remaining option was to go back through the row he had just left. He tried to squeeze past the young couple next to him, but the woman stopped him with a friendly hand on his shoulder.

"It's all right, brother!" she said with a reassuring smile. "You've never seen anyone slain in the Spirit before? I know, it's a little unnerving the first time. But there's nothing to be frightened of. It's a great blessing, to be touched by the Holy Spirit. If you like, I'll pray with you, so that the Spirit can touch you and heal you too.

Can I?"

He shook his head, and tried even more urgently to squeeze past. He took an involuntary glance at the backpack he had left on his seat.

The woman's eyes followed his. "Aren't you forgetting your bag?"

Now he was in a full state of panic. His heart cried out for oxygen, no matter how sternly his brain ordered his body to hold its breath. He gave her a shove that sent her tumbling over the folding chairs into the row behind her. He tried to run, but her boyfriend blocked him and tackled him to the floor.

"Security! We need security here!"

THE FIRST BOOK

1

WASHINGTON, D.C.
THURSDAY, MARCH 26

"Which of these looks most like a jihadi to you?"
Professor Robin Fox projected three pictures onto the screen, and aimed his laser pointer at the first. "Number one?" This was of a black-clad militant glaring menacingly through a ski mask, a Kalashnikov slung over his shoulder.

"Number two?" An old man kneeling on a prayer rug, poring over a well-worn Qur'an.

"Number three?" A suicide bomber in an explosive-laden vest, photographed just before setting off on his final mission.

The show of hands was fairly evenly divided between numbers one and three, except for a few who were correctly anticipating a curve ball.

"Now, if I were to put the same question to Mohammed, may peace be upon him, here's how he would probably answer." He highlighted the first picture. "This one—well, maybe, as long as he was following the law: 'Defend yourselves against those who fight you, but commit not aggression, for Allah loves not the aggressor.' "

Fox highlighted the old man. "This one—definitely. According to one hadith, when Mohammed's troops came home after a victory on the battlefield, he said to them: 'Now that we've returned from the lesser jihad, we can go back to the greater jihad.' By which he meant the daily struggle to learn, to grow in the faith, to be a better person. And he might add that anyone engaged in the pursuit of knowledge has a greater reward than a martyr."

He highlighted the suicide bomber. "This one—definitely not. All the hadith agree that Mohammed always condemned suicide in the strongest terms. According to one story, a group of soldiers in his army once made their commander so angry that he ordered them to kindle a fire and burn themselves in it. They refused, and when Mohammed heard about it, he said, 'If they had gone into the fire, they would have continued to burn in it until the Day of Judgment. Obedience to your commander is no virtue if it means disobedience to Allah.' "

A murmur ran through the room, and he allowed it a moment to run its course. "Maybe this misguided soul sees himself as a martyr," he continued when it was quiet again, "but I would guess that if Mohammed could have imagined such a thing as suicide bombing, he would probably have seen it as the spiritual equivalent of burning down your own house to collect insurance money."

A muttered comment reached his ears. "I wonder how many people know that story."

He didn't have to look to know that the voice came from Arnie. Fox had never quite understood what he was doing in a seminar in Religion and Peace. If he was looking for an audience for his belief that the United States was God's chosen nation, and the only path to peace was for its armed forces to intimidate the rest of the world into submission, he should have figured out long ago that he was in the wrong class.

"You're quite right," Fox said. "These stories need to be more widely known. That's why I tell them, and..." he turned around and spread his hands to include everyone in the room, "...that's why I count on you to pass them on."

He was willing to let that be his exit line, but Arnie spoke up again, in a louder voice. "I mean, you should go over there and tell *them*," he said, waving a hand in a vaguely eastward direction. "To all those people hell-bent on making the whole world into one big caliphate."

The rest of the class was oddly still. Usually, when Arnie started one of his diatribes, it was the cue for a few sighs and rolled eyes from the others. But in the wake of the Verizon Center attack, the tension in the air all over Washington had pervaded the George Washington University campus as well. No one knew anything yet about the attacker or his motivation, but speculation was already rife, and most of the accusing fingers were pointing toward Mecca.

Fox toyed with a card in his hand, debating whether to play it. It was something he usually kept very quiet, a chapter in his life on which he devoutly hoped he had turned the final page. But for some people, it was the only thing that gave him any credibility, and he was sure that Arnie was one of those.

"They probably wouldn't listen to me," he said. "But they might be more receptive to people like the one who first told me these stories—an imam in Iraq."

Arnie's confrontational look gave way to surprise. "What were you doing in Iraq?"

"I could tell you, but then I'd have to...do something that might cost me my job in the Peace Studies program."

Arnie's eyes widened even further. "Intelligence?"

"Military intelligence, to be exact. And if anyone wants to make the old wisecrack about that being an oxymoron, you'll get no argument from me."

Arnie straightened up in his seat. "I'm sorry, Mr. Fox. I didn't know."

"There was no reason why you should. And just so we're clear, anyone I catch saluting or calling me 'sir' fails the course."

He turned to address the whole class. "That's all for today. Thank you very much, ladies and gentlemen, and..." he pressed his palms together and inclined his head, "...peace be with you."

They returned his signature greeting and made their way out, shouldering their backpacks and chatting about their weekend plans. Fox was left alone in the room, surrounded by the ghosts that the mention of Iraq had conjured from their graves across the sea.

Another day, he told them. *Another day teaching peace, in the heart of the country that sent us to kill you. How many more will it take, before you consider my debt paid? Before you can finally rest?*

The ghosts didn't answer, of course. They never did.

Fox headed out of Corcoran Hall into a glorious spring afternoon. The fabled Washington cherry trees had mostly traded their blossoms for leaves by now, although there were a few branches where some puffs of pink still held their own against the steadily encroaching green. In Japanese, a cherry tree in this transitional state could be described by a single word, *hazakura*. For Fox, the sight of cherry trees in bloom always brought on a wave of nostalgia for Japan, a touch of homesickness for one of the half-dozen countries he had called "home" over the course of a childhood spent following his father to diplomatic postings around the globe.

University Yard was eerily deserted for such a beautiful day. Ordinarily, he would have expected to see all the cheerful signs of spring on a college campus: picnics, outdoor study sessions, half-naked frat boys raising funds by inviting passersby to slather them with chocolate syrup and whipped cream. Today, though, everyone was moving briskly from one building to another, spending as little time in the open air as possible. Some of them were wearing surgical masks. The Verizon Center attack had been quickly stopped, and there was nothing to suggest that any contamination had escaped, but fear had infected the air as effectively as any virus.

Fox had to hurry, too, but for a different reason. He

was scheduled to meet someone who had called earlier that morning, asking urgently for an appointment—a John Adler, from NBC. Fox had already been approached once by the National Geographic Channel about serving as a consultant for a miniseries they were planning about sacred sites around the world, and he was curious about what interest a mainstream network could have in him.

He arrived at the red-brick building on G Street that housed his office. The mulberry tree beside the entrance was faithfully performing its self-appointed duty of marking the liturgical seasons, its branches decked with flowers in the deep purple of Lent. In a few weeks, it would trade them for the green leaves of Ordinary Time.

Once inside, he stuck his head into the department office, and greeted the administrative assistant. "Hi, Mirage." Her name was actually Maya, but the name her Indian father and American Jewish mother had settled on meant "wellspring" in Hebrew and "illusion" in Sanskrit, leaving her an easy mark for the nickname.

She returned the greeting with a good-humored smile. "Hi, Mr. Fox."

"Mr. Adler hasn't arrived yet, has he?"

"Not yet." She glanced at the clock. "You made it with five minutes to spare. Oh, and while I've got you, do you know whether you can make it to the Passover seder next week?"

"If you're bringing something, I sure hope so." Fox knew that the blend of cultures and religions in her family was not always smooth, but it had its compensations, one of which was the invention of chocolate macaroons with a touch of cardamom.

The study of other religions, Fox always told his

students, requires you to examine the world from new angles. Whether by design or simply age, this building lent architectural credence to his point. After a glance at his mailbox, he climbed stairs not quite straight, with a tread not quite even, to a door not quite flush with jambs not quite plumb under a lintel not quite level. It bore a wooden plaque, a gift from a former student, with a cartoon fox and the inscription, "The Fox Hole."

He barely had time to sit down and catch his breath before the knock on the door came. In walked a man in gray slacks and a blue blazer, with less hair than he had once had, and the bulk of someone who had once been muscular but had let himself go in recent years—specifically, since getting married, judging from the way the flesh of his finger bulged around his wedding band.

"Robin Fox, I presume?"

"Mr. Adler, thank you for coming." Fox rose to greet him, and the visitor extended his hand. At shoulder height, palm down, so that Fox had to turn his up to meet it—a less than subtle way of trying to establish yourself as the dominant, and the other as the submissive partner. Fox took a step closer to him, and turned his hand vertically as he shook it, restoring things to an equal footing.

"Please, have a seat. What can I offer you? Coffee, tea, espresso, cappuccino, hot chocolate?"

Adler directed a slightly amused glance at the Barista machine perched atop a dorm fridge in the corner. "Are you running a Starbucks here, or what?"

"My students sometimes call it that."

"Black coffee would be just fine, thank you."

Adler took a seat in the armchair. Fox put in enough

coffee for four cups, in case the interview went on long enough to require refills. As he prepared it, Adler glanced around the room at the Tibetan tanka scrolls, Russian icons, Arabic calligraphy, and other ornaments that Fox had acquired during his wanderings.

For a moment, Fox struggled to recall whether he had seen him somewhere before. Then he realized that it was not the man himself who looked familiar, but his eyes. They bore the look he had often seen in military interrogators, a mixture of remorse and defiance, which came from spending years inflicting more cruelty under orders than they ever would of their own volition, and a lifetime afterwards trying to justify it. The lines around the eyes spelled out the words, "I did what I had to do."

Fox wondered what a television executive had had to do.

"Now, how can I be of assistance?" Fox asked, as he set the cups on the small table. "Is it my research in world religions you're interested in, or my work with USPRI?" He referred to the United States Peace Research Institute, where he served part-time as a research fellow.

Adler shifted slightly. "Actually, Mr. Fox, it's the expertise you gained in your previous career."

Fox's smile abruptly deserted him. He suddenly regretted making so much coffee, because three cups was more than he could drink by himself, and this was going to be a very short interview.

"You aren't representing a television network, I take it."

"Sorry for the deception. The fact is, I'm representing your country."

Well, Fox thought, if Adler was a specialist in

weapons of mass destruction, the "NBC" hadn't exactly been a lie: Nuclear, Biological, and Chemical.

"What do you want with me?" Fox's voice had lost its cordial tone.

"Do you know about the HIG?"

Fox shook his head.

"The High-Value Detainee Interrogation Group."

Fox supposed there was really no way to make an elegant acronym for that.

"A joint task force run by the FBI, CIA, and military intelligence," Adler went on. "We've been working on the Verizon Center suspect for three days now, and he hasn't said a word. We can't even tell whether he speaks English. No pocket litter except a few dollars in cash— no passport, driver's license, credit cards, nothing that could identify him. His biometrics don't match anything in our database. We've sent his picture to the news networks and offered a reward to anyone who could give us any information about him. You must have seen it."

Fox had. The picture had been reappearing endlessly on CNN: a pasty white face, with scraggly blond hair, and piercing, ice-blue eyes.

"So, what does this have to do with me?"

Adler leaned forward in the armchair. "CDC has confirmed that the virus used in the attack was encephalitis Z," he said, giving Fox a significant look. "The Zagorsk virus."

Fox winced internally. The name of Zagorsk used to be a pleasant one for him, evoking the hauntingly beautiful chants from the fourteenth-century Russian Orthodox monastery. Now, he could no longer hear it without recalling an episode in Iraq that he wished he could forget.

"And so," Adler continued, "we would like you to join us as a consultant on this case."

Fox had seen the blow coming, but that did nothing to soften its impact.

"Mr. Adler, as you've no doubt noticed by now, I'm no longer in the military. There must be plenty of expert interrogators on active duty who can help you."

"But none who have experience with Zagorsk. As far as anyone knows, only once before has anyone attempted to use that as a weapon. It could have started a terrible epidemic...but fortunately for us, a certain sharp-eyed intelligence officer caught it in time."

"Clearly, you know my record," Fox said. "So you must also know that I left the service as a conscientious objector."

"With a Bronze Star."

"And before I had been out of the service a month, I would gladly have traded all the stars in the Pentagon for a single night of sleep without nightmares."

"I'm sorry, Mr. Fox...but if ever your country needed you, it's now. Not just because of your skill as an interrogator, but because your perspective on any intel we get just might supply the missing piece that allows us to stop the next one."

To stop the next one. That was a phrase Fox had heard too often, to justify too many barbarities. "Please, Mr. Adler. *24* is off the air now—and your 'ticking bomb' scenario has never materialized outside of the TV screen anyway. What makes you so sure there's going to be a next one?"

"Well, consider this: With the crazy guys acting

alone, usually you can't get them to shut up. They leave behind videotaped messages or write thousand-page manifestos. They want the world to know why they did what they did. Our suspect, on the other hand, hasn't said a word. He has something to hide. What else do you suppose it might be?"

Fox had to admit the justice of the question. He said nothing.

"Mr. Fox," Adler went on in a gentler tone, "it's not as though we're asking you to put your uniform back on and hop aboard a C-130 to Iraq. All you need to do is take a short ride on the Metro to the Hoover Building, and spend some time with him. You realize it's not every day that we consult civilians on such a sensitive matter. You must understand what an honor it is. And if you say yes, you would be doing a great service for your country."

He gave Fox his card, with the CIA emblem in the corner. It seemed the time for cover stories was past. "Think it over. Whenever you come to a decision, call me on my cell phone."

He stood up to leave. "Just one request, Mr. Fox: Don't think too long."

Emily Harper lifted her eyes to the window, several stories tall, that offered a commanding view of the Tidal Basin and the cherry trees still in bloom around it. The architects of USPRI's bright and airy headquarters had designed it to take full advantage of this vista, presumably to help the staff to feel more peaceful. Most days, it worked. But not today.

She turned her eyes back to the monitor, and typed

the final sentence of her e-mail.

> *The United States Peace Research Institute urgently requests your cooperation in locating her and ensuring her safe travel to the United States.*

She pressed the "send" button, then printed out a hard copy to send by fax, unable to stop herself from wondering whether any of it was going to do any good.

She took a deep breath, and touched the pendant that hung around her neck, the one Robin Fox had given her at their graduation. A cross and circle, Celtic style, to remind her: *Let your faith bring you peace, and it will spread out from you to the entire world.*

The two of them had been such close friends in college that everyone assumed they were a couple. And they probably could have become a very happy one, had he not been in the ROTC. A childhood spent watching her father struggle with his demons from Vietnam had convinced her that one military man was enough for one lifetime. When he graduated and got his commission, they gradually drifted apart, until a miracle brought them both to USPRI years later.

"Emily." As if the universe had been reading her thoughts, she heard his voice behind her.

She turned, and gave him as much of a smile as she could manage. "Hi, Robin."

He took a seat next to her. "You feeling all right?"

She ran her fingers through her long red hair, and massaged her temples. "Yeah, OK, I guess. How about you?"

"If I said yes, then we could both be liars together."

She allowed herself a chuckle. "What's up?"

"Ladies first."

She sighed. "Leila has disappeared."

Leila Halabi was a Palestinian peace educator whom USPRI had invited as a panelist for their upcoming symposium, Reaching Across the Wall: Peacemakers of Israel and Palestine. Miriam Haddad, from the Middle East section, had left Tuesday on what should have been the routine errand of escorting her to Amman, and then to Washington.

"How could that happen?" Fox asked.

"It seems they got separated at the Rachel's Tomb checkpoint, on the way to Jerusalem. Miriam waited around for hours, but Leila never made it through. She tried and tried to find out what happened, but they pushed back so hard she started to worry that if she tried any harder, they would deport her—or else disappear her too."

Miriam was the daughter of a Jewish mother and Arab father. With her Jewish faith, American passport, dark complexion, and Arabic-sounding name, she never knew from one visit to the next whether the Israeli authorities would decide to treat her as an honored guest or a suspected terrorist. This time, it evidently suited their purposes to choose the latter.

"Snatching her out from under the nose of a USPRI observer?" asked an incredulous Fox. "What did the Israelis expect to accomplish by that, other than stepping on Washington's toes?"

"The way things have been going lately, I think they've stopped caring whose toes they step on."

Fox sighed and ran his fingers through his hair. "Do you suppose Rick could help? Find some way to put pressure on them?"

Emily shook her head. Naturally, her husband had been the first person she asked. "He said that USPRI was a non-governmental organization, and a member of Congress couldn't intervene on its behalf."

"That didn't stop him in Colombia."

"Crossing swords with Colombia wouldn't cost him any votes. With Israel, it's another matter."

Fox's mouth contracted, in the way it usually did when politeness was preventing him from speaking his mind. Emily continued: "I'll just keep calling the Israeli embassy, sending faxes, and generally making myself as much of a nuisance as possible. Miriam is doing everything she can over there, and Rabbi Sternberg has been a huge help. I'll do what I can, wait to hear from Miriam, and hope for the best."

She looked at her monitor with a sigh, then turned back to him. "Your turn."

For a moment, his eyes took on the hunted look that she had often seen in her father's. The one that saw the house, the yard, all of suburban America only as canvas stage sets, which the slightest push might topple over to reveal a jungle full of snipers.

"I've been called back to Nineveh."

The capital of the ancient Assyrian Empire, where Jonah had been sent to prophesy, was also the site of Mosul in Iraq, where Fox had been stationed. It had become their code word for anything having to do with the military or intelligence work.

Her horror must have been visible in her face, because he hastened to add: "Not physically. It's just that the Feds and the Agency together haven't been getting anywhere with the Verizon Center suspect, so they asked me to come in as a consultant."

She suddenly felt the same chill she had when she first saw him in uniform, and remembered the thought that had flown through her mind that day. *There goes a sheep into the midst of wolves. Please, dear God, keep him safe. Protect his body from the enemy, and his soul from his fellow soldiers.*

"Why is the CIA involved? And why, in heaven's name, do they want you involved?"

He hesitated long enough that she answered herself: "I suppose you're not at liberty to tell me. Oh, God! You'd think that when you left, you had sent them a clear enough message."

"You'd think so. But it looks like they just couldn't manage without me." He managed a wry smile. "Ordinarily, I'd be flattered that someone thinks I'm indispensable."

"Someone already does. So be careful, all right? And remember, just in case they try to make you forget: you're a free civilian this time. If they ever ask you to do anything against your conscience..."

"I know." He glanced at his watch. "Hey, are we still on for Thom's book signing?"

"Oh, my God." Emily looked up at the clock. "I got so wrapped up in this that I completely lost track of time."

"We can still catch the tail end of it. Come on. You need something to change your mood."

Fox and Emily slipped unobtrusively through the door of Barnes & Noble Downtown and merged with the standing-room-only crowd. The face that beamed from the lectern, and from the poster for *Common Good: What Humanism and Religion Can Learn from Each Other*, had scarcely changed since they last saw him, at their graduation from Harvard. The rings in the ears and eyebrows were still there, as was the sparkle behind the glasses. The main difference was that his collection of tattoos had grown, the most conspicuous addition being the Japanese character *mu*, "nothingness," just visible through the V-neck of his shirt. Fox guessed that he had acquired it during his flirtation with Buddhism, but it still suited him in his present incarnation as a born again humanist.

"...in terms of what we *do* believe. Life is just too short to spend it tearing things down. The question that we all need to ask ourselves is: what do we want to build? And personally, what I'd like to build is a world where each one of us, no matter who we love or what we believe, can find a place where we're accepted, valued, and loved. I finally found mine, and I hope you find yours. Thank you."

He acknowledged the applause with a bright smile and a theatrical bow. As a long line formed at the signing table, Fox and Emily hung back, intentionally taking the tail end. It took the better part of an hour before Fox reached the head of the line and laid his copy of Thom's book on the table.

"You meant to say '*whom* we love.'"

Thom looked up. "Oh, my *cosmos*!" He jumped up from his chair with a force that knocked it over, and looked as though he were about to vault over the table and do the same to the stack of books beside him, but decided at the last second to take the more earthbound route around the table. "Could it be? Robin Hood and Maid Marian?" He flung his arms wide to embrace them both, and planted a noisy kiss on each cheek.

"Thom-with-an-H!" Emily returned, laughing.

He let go, but kept a hand on each of their shoulders. "It's been for-*ev*-er! How are you?" He gave Emily an admiring up-and-down glance. "Emily, you're more beautiful than ever! So I guess you've decided that aging is for lesser mortals? I..." His gaze suddenly fell on her ring, and his mouth opened wide enough to reveal his tongue piercing as he looked from one of them to the other. "OMC! Did you two finally end up getting *married*?"

"One of us did," they said in unison.

After a slightly embarrassed pause, Thom turned to Fox. "And Robin! What have you been up to?"

"Long story." *Tours of duty in Guantanamo, Afghanistan, and Iraq, followed by a dark night of the soul that took me from mountain temples in the Himalayas to island abbeys in the Hebrides, from sitting with Zen monks to whirling with Sufi dervishes, all in search of something I'm still not at all sure I've found.* "But it eventually brought me to GWU, to the religion and peace studies departments."

"That's fan-*tas*-tic. I always knew you would be a teacher. To inspire and enlighten the world, that's what you were born to do. So have you finally figured out what you believe?"

Fox gave a wry chuckle. "If I had a dime for every time someone asked me that question, I could retire next year. Or even this year, if you made it a quarter for every time it came from some sweet Southern girl who looked as though I'd break her heart if I didn't say, 'That the one and only way to salvation is to accept Jesus Christ as your personal savior.'"

Thom displayed his tongue piercing again as he let out a laugh that reverberated through the store. "So how *do* you answer?"

Fox glanced over his shoulder. Although they had been last in line, there was still a tall, dark-haired man standing by the door, watching them and clearly waiting for them to finish. "The ten-second version? First John chapter four pretty much sums it up for all faiths, as far as I'm concerned. God is love. Anyone who loves is in God. Anyone who hates and claims to be in God is a liar."

"That John dude's a trip sometimes, but he really nailed it with that one, didn't he? I only wish more Christians would actually read that far into their Bibles."

"Are you doing anything after this?" Emily asked.

"I am, I'm afraid," he said with a regretful downturn in the corners of his mouth, although his eyes twinkled with anticipation as they flicked briefly to the tall figure by the door. "And I'm taking off for Chicago at God o'clock tomorrow morning. But I'll be back for the American Humanist Association convention. Believe it or not, I'm one of the keynote speakers! We'll have to catch up then."

"Definitely. When is it?"

"May first. National Day of Reason. Mark your calendars."

"Congratulations, Thom," Emily said. "I'm so happy for you. I know it's been a long, hard journey for you, and I'm glad to see everything's finally been coming together."

"It so has. It couldn't possibly be any better." He stretched out his arms for another group hug, and his face took on the rapturous expression they had often seen when he was enjoying a glass of fine wine, a Bach concerto, or a bite of *fusilli integrale al pesto* at their favorite restaurant in Cambridge: the one that said there was nowhere in the universe he would rather be than right here.

"Ah, with moments like these, who needs Heaven?"

2

WASHINGTON, D.C.
FRIDAY, MARCH 27

The clock was approaching pick-up time as quickly as the bacon, eggs, pancakes and coffee were approaching room temperature. Emily had just started to head for the bedroom to fetch her husband when he burst into the kitchen, pulling on his suit jacket as he went, and skidded into his chair, his fork in his right hand, his anxious eyes on the Omega on his left.

"Thanks, Em." He looked wistfully at his plate. "My last American breakfast for ten days."

She took her seat opposite him. "I wonder what you'll get for breakfast in China."

He grimaced, and grunted around a mouthful of pancake. "Last time, it was waterlogged rice with seaweed and crap coffee. On the bright side, maybe I'll lose some weight."

"Have a safe trip. And let me know what kind of

progress you make."

He washed down his half-chewed mouthful with a swig of coffee. "On?"

She gave him a look from under raised eyebrows. "Tibet, of course."

"Oh, right." He suddenly focused on his pancakes with rapt concentration, as though it were vital to national security that his next forkful be cut at an angle of precisely sixty degrees. "Yes. Yes, of course."

Emily set down her fork. "It *is* on the agenda, right? You said you would make sure it was."

"I said I'd try. And I did, Em, I really did. But the committee leadership feels—and I can't really argue with them—that with so much at stake, the time isn't right for us to be poking our noses into such a sensitive issue."

"According to them, the time hasn't been right for the past fifty years. When *will* they feel it's right?"

The honk of a car horn outside cut the discussion short. Rick stood up, took one last gulp of coffee, and grabbed his suitcase as Emily followed him to the door. He leaned over for a kiss, which Emily took on her cheek, along with a particle of scrambled egg. "Take care, Em. Love you."

All members of Congress, it had often been said, had surgery to remove their backbones as soon as they took office. While working on Rick's campaign, she would have sworn he was different. And so he was. In his case, it was a series of keyhole operations, one vertebra at a time, so skillfully done that he never felt a thing.

She watched him out of sight, went back to the table to finish her breakfast, and turned on the TV for company. But with the first headline she saw on CNN, the coffee in her mouth suddenly turned to liquid nitrogen, so cold it burned.

As always, the first thing Fox did upon waking was to seat himself on a cushion in the corner of his room, light a stick of incense, and pick up a Buddhist rosary he had acquired in Kathmandu, a hundred and eight sandalwood beads. 108, the number of ways in which the world conspires to distract the seeker with illusions: Pleasant, unpleasant, or neutral sensations, real or imagined, times the past, present, and future, times the five senses plus the consciousness. The goal of meditation was to pierce through them, one by one, until only the Real was left.

If only it were that easy. Meditation, like an overdue cleaning of a messy desk, had a way of revealing things that had long lay half-forgotten, and it was a constant struggle against the temptation to stop and take a closer look. In this case, the images that kept surfacing included many that he wished would stay buried.

But when he finished his meditation, his knew what he had to do, as much as he dreaded it. He had an egg on rice and a cup of coffee, and when he judged it was a reasonable time, picked up the phone and dialed.

"Adler here."

"Mr. Adler, this is Robin Fox."

"Ah, Fox. Good to hear from you. Have you made up your mind?"

"Yes. I'll do it. I'll act as a consultant for you, in whatever way I'm able—with the understanding that my first duty is still to my teaching."

"Of course."

"There's one thing I ask in return. I'm sure you must have contacts in the Israeli intelligence services."

Adler paused. "Our office does, certainly."

"USPRI was planning to bring a Palestinian peace educator to the States, but she has unaccountably disappeared. If we have an empty chair on the panel because the Israelis grabbed her for no reason, it will be a huge embarrassment all around. So as a favor to USPRI, I'm sure you can go through some back channels and find out what happened to Leila Halabi."

There was another pause on the end of the line, then: "OK, I'll see what I can do."

Fox thought he detected a slight rise in Adler's voice stress, but he was willing to put it down to a patchy cell phone signal.

"And for the time being, the first name I would suggest you look into is Venera Goridze, from the Republic of Georgia."

"Venera..."

"Goridze." He spelled it.

Fox was mildly surprised that, even though Adler knew about the episode in Iraq, he was hearing this name for the first time. But on the other hand, it was typical. Intelligence agencies were notorious for stovepipe organization, each one pursuing its own goals, sharing no more with the others than absolutely necessary. He recalled excruciating hours in the interrogation booth, using every trick at his command to extract some vital piece of information, only to learn later that the CIA had been sitting on it all the while. And military intelligence, for its part, saw no reason to be any more forthcoming with the Agency. The joint task force where Adler served sounded like an attempt to break down these barriers, but the old ways died hard.

"And just to confirm, the person we're looking for is Leila Halabi. Last seen yesterday at the Rachel's Tomb checkpoint, between Bethlehem and Jerusalem. Do you need me to spell her name for you, too?"

"No, I've got it."

"I'll see you this afternoon, then."

He had barely disconnected the phone when it rang again.

"Emily?"

"Robin." The tension in her voice as she said his name sent a chill through him. "Have you seen the news?"

"No."

"It's Thom."

Those two words were enough to stop all the clocks. But Emily's voice went on: "They're saying he was murdered."

"My God." With a hand gone numb, Fox picked up the remote and switched on CNN.

"...tour of Thom DiDio, humanist chaplain at Oberlin College, came to a tragic end this morning, when his publicist found him dead in his Washington hotel room. The Bible placed in the room by the Gideons was found on the body, with two verses highlighted. One was from the book of Leviticus, chapter 20, verse 13: 'If a man lies with a man as one lies with a woman, both of them have done what is detestable. They must be put to death; their blood will be on their own heads.' The other was Psalm 14, verse 1: 'The fool says in his heart, "There is no God." They are corrupt, their deeds are vile; there is no one who does good.' The incident has been reported to the Civil Rights Unit of the FBI's Criminal Investigative Division as a hate crime."

A hole opened in Fox's chest, sucking all the air out of his lungs. "Oh, Emily," he said. "Oh, God, Emily, I'm sorry."

There was silence at the other end, except for muffled sobs. Fox's gaze stayed on the screen, which now showed the portrait from Thom's book jacket. The awed smile that said "Oh my cosmos, is this for real?" The eyes that radiated goodwill to all, the light inside them beckoning a bright future that now would never come. Who, Fox wondered, could look at that face and see anything to provoke a murder? Only someone who refused to see the face at all.

"I hope you were wrong, Thom," Fox said softly to an unseen presence. "I hope you've found there really is a Heaven."

Miraculously, Fox made it through the day's classes without breaking down. When he went to USPRI headquarters and saw Emily, neither of them said a word. She simply stood, walked into his waiting arms, and laid her head on his shoulder as tears flowed from the eyes of both. As he held her, stroking her hair, only minimally conscious of the curious glances from the other staff members, he could almost feel the touch of another arm on his shoulder, as though Thom were there with him, doing his incorporeal best to comfort them.

"He loved everyone," she finally said. "I often felt he was a better Christian than I was. Who could do such a thing?"

"Whoever it was," Fox said, "I can't believe they read the same Bible that we do."

An image of their last meeting with Thom came to Fox's mind, and he asked: "Emily, do you remember the man standing by the door at the book signing? Did you get a look at him?"

She shook her head. "Just a glimpse. I remember thinking that if they made another 007 movie, he could play the leading man. Tall, dark, handsome in a cold way."

"Do you think you could help make a sketch of him, or pick him out of a line-up?"

"I can try." Emily closed her eyes for a moment, then opened them again and looked up to the ceiling. "Forgive me, Father."

"What for?"

"You once told me something you had heard from a priest in Northern Ireland. How did it go? In the language of heaven..."

"There is no word for 'revenge,'" Fox finished for her.

"I'm trying hard to remind myself of that." She swallowed, and her gaze hardened. "At the same time, a part of me wants to see them nail the bastard who did this."

A desert in the heart of Washington.

This was Fox's impression of the J. Edgar Hoover building as he approached its stark facade, designed in the style known as "Brutalist"—a philosophy which he hoped applied only to the building and not to what went on inside. Row upon row of smoked-glass windows looked out over the city from walls the color of Iraqi sand. A ring of concrete planters surrounded the entire block, but while their twins across the street sported green domes, these held only dirt, cigarette butts, and a few brave blades of grass.

A chill ran through him and his heart began to beat faster, a sensation that had been a constant companion in Iraq. He had to take a surreptitious glance down to reassure himself that he was still wearing a suit and not desert camouflage, before passing under the row of flags and through the "Business Appointments" entrance.

He showed his identification to the police officer on duty, passed through a metal detector, signed at the escort desk for his badge, and passed through a turnstile to find Adler waiting to take him to his first briefing. Adler was representing the CIA on this case, so he would observe interrogations from the monitor room, but stay out of the interview room until they could determine the suspect's nationality. If it turned out to be American, then the presence of a CIA agent at his interrogation would open a can of jurisdictional worms that a defense attorney would love.

The room that served as their headquarters was windowless. The walls were covered with whiteboards, with a cluster of desks in the center, and a small conference table where two women in dark suits were waiting.

Adler made the introductions. "Ladies, I'd like you to welcome Professor Robin Fox, who earned a Bronze Star for his work with military intelligence in Iraq. Robin, this is Estrella Kato, representing the FBI..."

Kato was dark-skinned, with an Asian cast to her eyes, and black hair down to her collar. Fox took note of her name. Father Japanese, and mother Latina, or perhaps Filipina? She shook his hand, keeping her eyes on him the way a house cat might regard a new guest consenting for the moment to tolerate his presence, but reserving judgment about whether to make him truly welcome.

"...and Malika Abramova, our linguist." The next was a blond-haired, blue-eyed Slavic beauty. The days when she could have played the femme fatale in a James Bond film were a bit past her, but in her younger days, the CIA might have had to outbid Hollywood for her talents.

"A pleasure," she said, shaking his hand with a warmer smile than her colleague's.

Fox turned back to Adler. "Have you managed to get anything on him yet?"

Adler shook his head. "Nothing, not even a name. For the time being, we're calling him Harpo."

"Harpo?" Fox raised his eyebrows in mock alarm. "How many other Marx fans are there in the CIA?"

"Very funny. When he was arrested, he only had a few dollars in his pocket, and the aerosol device in his backpack."

"What avenues are you pursuing?"

"Two main possibilities that we can see. One, he's a Jihad Joe—an American convert to Islam who went to a terrorist training camp somewhere overseas."

"Two?"

"He could be Eastern European—most likely Chechen. A few years ago, we had intelligence that al-Qaeda made overtures to the Chechen mafia, offering them tons of high-grade Afghani heroin in exchange for expertise from the old Soviet WMD operations."

"Did anything come of that?"

"Not as far as we could learn at the time. But maybe they were just waiting for the right moment."

Adler's theory sounded frighteningly plausible, but there was still a piece missing.

"If he's an American citizen, then surely his data would have turned up a hit somewhere—driver's license, passport, military records, or at least someone, somewhere, who recognized his picture. And if he came in from another country, then Customs and Border Patrol would have taken his photo and prints when he arrived, wouldn't they?"

"Unless he entered illegally."

"I suppose he's been given his Miranda warning?"

"Yes," said Kato, "and also his Berghuis warning."

"What's that?"

"Berghuis v. Thompkins. That's a Supreme Court decision that says that if you want to take the Fifth, you have to say so. You have to say, 'I invoke my right of silence.'"

"But he still hasn't said a word."

"No."

"What do we know about the Reverend Hill? Any sense of what might have made him a target?"

"Only that he has a big mouth," she replied. "He's made some very public comments that've made some very influential people very upset. Most recently, the leader of the Nation of Islam. What was it he said? Something like, 'If our young people feel that they need to turn to some political fringe group dressed up in Muslim clothes to find a purpose in life, then we ministers of the true faith have failed them.' "

"Impressive. One slap for NOI and one for his fellow Christian ministers, in a single sentence."

"You can see how this could cause an uproar within the black community. But as you've no doubt noticed, our subject is extremely white. And if they thought this was a domestic incident, they wouldn't have called you in."

"They," not "we." She was disavowing any part in the decision to invite him.

"How were you planning to introduce me?" Fox asked. This was the delicate part. In Iraq, whenever they brought a new person into an interrogation in progress, they used the Third-Party Introduction technique, ratcheting things up a notch by making the subject believe that the new arrival was someone with higher authority to determine incentives or punishments. But Fox had no authority at all.

"We'll say you're from military intelligence," said Adler. "It's not a lie, and there's no need to mention that you're retired from the service. So, are you ready to meet Harpo?"

"Ready as I can be."

"Give him hell."

Adler stayed behind as Kato and Malika led the way into the interview room. Fox followed behind them, trying not to betray any nervousness. The subject was supposed to be the nervous one, while the interrogator was the one who held all the cards, or at least needed to give that appearance. But first impressions were as important in a first interrogation as in a first date, and it was a long time since Fox had last been in either situation.

They had the room set up right, Fox noted. "Harpo" sat in a chair that looked none too comfortable, with a small table by his side, and nothing between him and the interrogators' chairs. Too often, interrogation rooms were set up with chairs on opposite sides of a table, which kept the interrogator from having a head-to-toe view of the subject, and could conceal important clues.

Fox looked over the subject. His face was as it had appeared on CNN, except a little thinner: long, unkempt blond hair and pale white skin. His cold blue eyes stared fixedly at the line where the door met the floor. When Fox came in, they flicked up briefly, but stopped short of meeting his.

Fox sat in one of the two chairs facing Harpo. Kato took the other, and Malika seated herself behind and to one side of the suspect, out of his field of view. The rule for interpreters in interrogations was that they should be heard and not seen.

"Hello," Fox greeted him. When he made no response, Fox placed a hand over his heart with a slight bow. "*Assalam aleikum.*"

This greeting usually helped to break the ice with subjects from anywhere in the Muslim world. But Harpo simply continued staring ahead, making no acknowledgment of his presence.

"What would you like me to call you?"

Malika interpreted the question into Russian, and then Chechen. Harpo remained silent and motionless.

"Do you speak English?"

No response, to either the question or Malika's

interpretation. Fox tried a few more of his own: "*Parlez-vous français? Sprechen Sie Deutsch?*" Harpo showed no reaction to any.

"Come on, we've been over this before," Kato said. "Anyone who's ever watched TV knows that when you're arrested, you have the right to remain silent. The thing is, in order to claim it, you have to speak up. You have to say, 'I invoke my right of silence.'"

The prisoner gave no sign that he was aware of her existence.

"I'm interested in your choice of weapons," Fox said. "The Zagorsk virus. You really know your stuff. None of this off-the-rack anthrax or smallpox for you. No, it had to be a top-of-the-line designer virus. Tell me, how is Dr. Goridze doing these days?"

He gave no sign that he recognized the name.

"You're good at playing dumb," Fox said, "but I can tell that you're really quite smart. Smart enough to understand that talking can only help you. You realize that these people aren't trying to get a confession out of you. Nothing you can say will incriminate you any more than the evidence already has. We've established the who, what, when, where and how already. All we're missing is the why. Don't you want people to understand why?"

Silence.

"Are you angry about something the United States government has done?"

Silence.

"Are you angry with the Reverend Hill personally?"

Silence.

"Or do you have something against black people in

general?"

Silence.

"Come on now, there must have been some message you were trying to send by doing this. What's the point of it all, if no one knows what the message was supposed to be?"

Silence.

"Or is there another who, when, and where that we don't know about yet?"

Harpo's face was as impassive as ever, but his breathing quickened slightly.

"Are there more of you out there? Is there one more? Are there three more? Two? Five? Four?" Fox called the numbers out of sequence, to keep him off balance.

He thought he observed a slight twitch on the number "five."

"If there are, you know how it works," Kato said. "The first one to talk gets the best deal."

Silence.

"Very well," Fox said. "We can keep playing this game for as long as you like. But you've noticed that there are several of us and only one of you. We can take turns. We can keep this up night and day until you finally get tired of it."

He nodded to Kato. She rose.

"Think it over," she said to him. "I'll see you later."

They left the interview room and went back to the conference room, where Adler was waiting.

"You weren't kidding," Fox sighed. "That's the toughest nut I've ever seen in my life."

"Me, too. And I've seen a few."

"So what happens now?"

"He goes back to his cell and has dinner."

"Can you order in from some local take-out place? Give him a menu and let him make a choice. Even if he only points, at least you'll have gotten him to communicate."

"All right, we can try that."

"Can you put a hidden camera in his cell?"

"It's already equipped with one."

Of course. "Let's give him a box of books tonight, then. Copies of the Qur'an in Arabic and English, and some novels in English, Russian, any other languages you can get your hands on. See what he chooses. Find out something about where his interests lie—or, at the very least, what language he speaks."

Adler nodded. "That's a good idea."

"Have you given him a polygraph test?"

"We have. Of course, he didn't say anything, but we gave him the Silent Response Test. And got nothing measurable."

"We had a video camera on him," Kato interjected, "so that I could run a FACS analysis later. If you're not familiar, that means..."

"The Facial Action Coding System," Fox finished for her.

She looked at him with a slightly surprised expression. "You know it, then?"

"I learned the rudiments of it in interrogation training, but that was a decade ago. I'm sure your knowledge is much more up-to-date."

"But we got nowhere with that either," Adler continued. "And besides, that system was designed in America. If he turns out to be from some other country, all bets are off."

"Not necessarily," Fox said, noticing out the corner of his eye that Kato was just drawing a breath, presumably to make a similar reply. "Facial expressions of emotion are pretty much the same everywhere. Different cultures have different rules about what you can show and what you should hide, of course, but just about everyone reacts the same way when they think no one's watching. Am I right about that, Agent Kato?"

"Exactly." She favored him with a slight nod.

"Can we run another polygraph on him?" Fox asked.

"If you like," Adler said with a shrug. "We can set it up tomorrow."

"And when we do, can we have a guard in the room?"

"What for?"

"I have an idea. But if I'm to put it into practice, I'll want some extra protection."

"All right. And speaking of protection, I'm recommending that everyone on this team be vaccinated against Zagorsk, just as a precautionary measure. I can arrange a shot for you if you want."

Fox grimaced. He had always been wary of the side effects of vaccines for exotic diseases, and thoughts of a certain individual in Iraq made him more so.

"Has the vaccine been proven effective?" he asked Adler.

"It's bound to be better than nothing."

"And just out of idle curiosity, is there any treatment for Zagorsk?"

"Rid has been working on an antiserum, but..."

"Who has?"

"Sorry. USAMRIID—the U.S. Army Medical

Research Institute for Infectious Diseases. But as I was saying, it's still in the experimental stage. They've gotten good results with monkeys if they got the treatment before symptoms started to appear. But the incubation time for Zagorsk is very short, so the window could be as narrow as a day. And they've never had the chance to test it on humans."

"I'll take my chances."

"As you like."

"Oh, and Agent Kato? Did I hear right that the FBI was investigating the murder of Thom DiDio?"

"The Civil Rights Division is handling that, jointly with the Metro Police."

"My friend and I were at his book signing, the last night before he died. We had a look at someone there who might be of interest to you. We can probably give you a description or help you create a composite sketch. We'll gladly offer any help we can. Thom was a good friend of ours."

"Thank you. I'll pass that on to them." She nodded again, hesitated a moment, and added: "I'm sorry for your loss."

"Yeah, sorry to hear that," Adler chimed in. "And by the way, thanks for the tip about Venera Goridze. We've been in touch with the Georgian Intelligence Service, and they've launched a full-on search for her."

"Good luck to them in finding her. She's managed to stay under their radar for the past ten years."

"Oh, you'd be surprised at what they can do when they put their minds to it."

3

MOSUL, IRAQ
2005

When Fox first heard the name of Venera Goridze, it was an ordinary afternoon, or as close as they came in Iraq. He was sitting at his desk in the "gator pit," the interrogators' bullpen, a cavernous octagonal room in a base that had once been one of Saddam Hussein's palaces. With the marble walls, fluted columns supporting the high ceiling, and Qur'anic inscriptions around the inlaid dome, it could have been a copy of the Taj Mahal, if not for the plasma screens and mismatched desks that the U.S. Army had contributed to the decor.

He had just refilled his coffee cup, to keep himself awake as he slogged through the mind-numbing task that occupied most of his time: writing IIRs, Interrogation Intelligence Reports, and then rewriting them when they were sent back for breaking one of the myriad rules in the Army's byzantine style manual, such as using quotation marks around anything other than the name of a ship. Years later, his dissertation review board would prove lenient by comparison.

Corporal Mendes stormed into the gator pit, slammed a file down on his desk, and collapsed into his chair. "Asshole!" he muttered to no one in particular.

"Ibrahim?" asked Staff Sergeant Newcomb.

Fox could think of several words to describe Ibrahim, but that one would not have made the list. A mild-mannered imam who spoke English like an Oxford don, he was one of Fox's favorite detainees, someone he could always count on for a stimulating discussion over the chessboard—although so far, he had managed neither to extract any useful intelligence from him nor to win a single game.

"You've got to show him who's boss," Newcomb told the fuming Mendes. "Break him down. Interrogation is all about control. Power is the only language these hajjis understand."

Fox looked over at him. "How did you know about his pilgrimage?" he asked. "Did he tell you?"

"Huh?"

"You referred to him as a hajji. How did you know that he had made the pilgrimage to Mecca?"

"Is that what it means?" Mendes asked.

Fox resisted the urge to roll his eyes. "Breaking a detainee," he said, "is like breaking a wild horse. You have to get him to trust you—make him want to cooperate with you. Trying to get his cooperation by force only makes him dig his heels in harder."

"Breaking a horse," snorted Newcomb. "I can just see the movie now. *The Hajji Whisperer*."

"Well, guys, let me ask you this. You've been on the receiving end of this stuff, at the Schoolhouse." He used the common nickname for the Army's interrogation training facility at Fort Huachuca, Arizona. "Did it make you want to open up and tell your interrogators all you knew?"

Newcomb scoffed. "Those pussies didn't dare dial it up on me anywhere near as hard as I would on a real hajji."

Fox debated whether it was worth pressing the issue any further, and decided it wasn't. Newcomb was an old hand who had enlisted straight out of high school during the first Gulf War, and Fox, a young captain fresh out of an Ivy League school, was exactly the kind of person he most resented having to salute and call "sir." It didn't help matters that he was built like one of the steamrollers his father drove, and could probably flatten Fox with the same ease.

Neither for the first nor the last time, Fox thought to himself: *There must have been a simpler way to piss the old man off.* His father, an Annapolis graduate and Navy officer before he joined the Foreign Service, had refused to put up any money for his college education unless he joined ROTC, insisting that he "give something back to the country that's given so much to you"—and in his mind, the only way to do that was in uniform. Seeing no alternative, Fox had given in, and chosen the Army out of spite.

At the time, it hadn't seemed to make much difference which branch of the service he chose. When he was commissioned, the most action he expected to see was a UN peacekeeping mission somewhere—maybe in Bosnia where, rumor had it, the soldiers were allowed two beers a day and the civilian interpreters were all young and beautiful.

And then the bolt came out of the blue, in the form of four planes diving out of a clear September sky.

Language skills were suddenly at a premium. The Army had promptly packed Fox off to the Defense Language Institute in Monterey to whip his Arabic back into shape, and then to the "Schoolhouse" at Fort Huachuca for interrogation training. Then Guantanamo, then Afghanistan, and now here to this mausoleum with Newcomb and Mendes for company.

The arrival of the officer in charge, Major Browning, snapped Fox out of his reflections. He was a mountain of a man with the face of a bulldog, and even though the gator pit was a non-smoking area, all of Fox's later recollections of him inexplicably featured a fat cigar clamped between his teeth.

"We got a call from a concerned citizen," Browning announced. "He was driving by a farmhouse just north of Mosul, one that he thought was abandoned, when he saw a man get out of a blue sedan with three armed bodyguards. The man's face was hidden, with a headscarf and sunglasses."

A stir ran through the gator pit. Fox set down his coffee mug. This news had jolted him out of his afternoon drowsiness more effectively than caffeine.

"Special Forces hit the farmhouse as soon as we heard," Browning continued, "but they came up dry. Aerial surveillance picked up a blue Volkswagen Passat heading south on the road to Kirkuk, and our boys on the ground intercepted it, but there was nothing in it of any interest. We've brought the driver in." He scanned the room for civilian interpreters and saw none. "Looks like all of our terps are busy, so I need an Arabic linguist. Captain Fox, that means you." He held out a manila folder in Fox's direction.

"Yes, sir."

Fox could manage without an interpreter, although he always preferred to use one when he could. The Iraqi dialect was different from both the variety he had picked up during his father's posting in Egypt and the supposedly region-free MSA the Army taught—Modern Standard Arabic, better known by its tongue-in-cheek name of "Monterey Standard Arabic." Besides, there was always the chance that a detainee would make an off-the-record remark to the interpreter, not meant for the interrogator's ears, that would later prove valuable.

He automatically checked to make sure his uniform blouse was properly "sanitized"—name and rank insignia removed—and headed to the interrogation booth, leafing through the file as he went. When he reached the door, he paused for a moment to collect himself, and then walked in, trying to exude reassurance and authority, like a surgeon entering the consultation room.

A balding man with a mustache was waiting inside, and he did indeed look as nervous as a patient before a major operation.

"*Assalam aleikum,*" Fox greeted him, with hand over heart.

"*Wa aleikum assalam,*" came the surprised reply. By speaking to him in his own language, Fox had cleared the first hurdle.

"Hassan al-Tamimi. What would you like me to call

you?"

"I usually go by Abu Hakim."

"That means 'father of Hakim,' doesn't it? How old is your son?"

"Seven."

"Is that right? My boy just turned five." Fox had never been married and had no children. But interrogation was theater, and a good interrogator was a combination of actor, director, and stage manager. His training had included exercises straight out of drama school: mirroring facial expressions and gestures, speaking in synchronicity, and numerous techniques for improvising themselves into whatever role might help them build rapport with the subject. If Abu Hakim was a family man, then Fox would have no trouble becoming one for the duration.

"Your family must miss you when you're away," Fox continued.

"That's what they tell me."

"Don't worry. If you'll answer my questions, we can finish up here and get you home before they start to worry. Do you know why we stopped you?"

Abu Hakim shook his head. "I have no idea."

"Where were you going?"

"Home. To Kirkuk."

"What were you doing in Mosul?"

"Visiting a friend."

"What's your friend's name?"

"Abu Rahim."

"Where did you meet him?"

"At a restaurant."

"You know, I love Iraqi food. I'm always looking for

new places to try when I get the chance to go off base. What's the name of the place? Do you recommend it?"

"It's called Ninawa. It's our favorite place to meet, right on the bank of the Tigris. They do great kibbeh, and pretty cheap too."

Fox quizzed him for a while on details: what they had ordered, how they had liked it, what they had been talking about, which table they had been sitting at, who was in which seat. Abu Hakim answered all the questions confidently, but often paused longer than necessary to recall details that should still have been fresh in his mind. Soon, Fox had heard enough to satisfy him that Abu Hakim was describing a meeting that had actually happened...but a good deal longer ago than this afternoon.

"All right, Abu Hakim," Fox said with an air of finality, "sorry to take up so much of your time."

Abu Hakim smiled broadly. His shoulders slumped and he breathed a sigh of relief.

Truthful subjects always brightened up a little when they heard that the ordeal was over and they were free to get on with their lives. The ones who looked excessively relieved were the ones who had been lying and thought they had made it through the interview without being caught.

"Now all I need from you is a way to get in touch with Abu Rahim. Once we confirm your story with him, and with the owner of Ninawa, you'll be a free man."

Abu Hakim's smile flagged.

"Or," Fox continued, his voice taking on a graver tone, "you could save us both a lot of time and trouble by simply telling me the truth. Four men, three of them armed, were seen getting out of your car at a farmhouse just north of Mosul."

He shook his head. "That wasn't my car."

"Our eyes in the sky followed it all the way from the farmhouse to the place where the soldiers stopped you."

"I swear on my life and on the lives of my family and on my eyes, you have me confused with someone else!"

The subject doth protest too much, Fox thought. In particular, the last oath seemed superfluous in light of the first. If he were to forfeit his life, what use would he have for eyes?

"Give it up, Abu Hakim! I don't know which makes me angrier: your lying, or your thinking I'm stupid enough to fall for such a clumsy lie. Do you want to go home to your family, or don't you?"

Abu Hakim broke into a sweat, and started trembling and breathing harder. His fear of Americans was entirely understandable, and it was common practice for interrogators to exploit it, but Fox had always found that subjects who were too frightened to think clearly were unreliable. He needed to do something to put the subject's mind at ease.

"Abu Hakim," he said in a softer voice, "I don't know what you've heard about us, but I want you to understand that as far as we're concerned, you haven't done anything wrong. It's the men who were riding with you that we're interested in. Answer our questions about them, and you'll be on your way home to your wife and son."

In spite of these reassurances, Abu Hakim's fear showed no signs of diminishing. Something else was frightening him more than the Americans.

"Abu Hakim," Fox asked in as gentle a voice as he could, "did they threaten your family?"

He kept his eyes downcast, but gave an almost imperceptible nod.

"We can protect them."

Abu Hakim scoffed. "Do you have any idea how many people I've known who worked with you and ended up dead? You can't even protect the people on your own payroll! How could you keep them from getting to my family?"

"By getting to them first."

Abu Hakim shook his head. "You'll never get them all. And they would know I was the one who gave them away."

"That doesn't have to be true. No one needs to know that you talked to us."

"They would find out."

"Well, Abu Hakim, the way I see it, you have two options. Option one: You tell us what you know. You'll be home by dinnertime, and the men who threatened you will be out of the picture by morning. Option two: You keep lying and stalling, and we'll have no choice but to keep you here for however long it takes—days, weeks, months. In the meantime, we'll have to move based on the intelligence we've gathered ourselves. Of course, it will be much less accurate. And if we strike at them and miss, they *will* howl for blood and they *will* know you've been with us. I know, it's not much of a choice, but it's what you've got."

Abu Hakim was quiet for a long time. His expression of fear had changed to the despondency of a man resigned to choosing the lesser of two evils.

When he spoke again, he said: "I was told that I could make some good money just by giving them a ride and asking no questions."

"Can you describe them?"

"Three of them were young men. They were carrying machine guns. The fourth was maybe a little older, but I'm not sure. I didn't see his face."

"The whole way, you never got a look at his face?"

"He was wearing sunglasses, and a kaffiyeh wrapped all the way around his head. Also gloves. White cotton gloves."

"What did he sound like? Could you describe his voice?"

Abu Hakim shook his head. "He didn't speak. It was the guard, riding up front with me, who gave me directions."

"Is there anything else you can tell me about him? Anything distinctive about the way he moved? How he smelled? Anything you can remember."

Fox thought he was grasping at straws, but the word "smell" seemed to jog Abu Hakim's memory. "Yes. He smelled like some kind of lotion."

"Lotion?"

"He applied it on the way. He took off his gloves and undid his kaffiyeh long enough to smear it on his hands and face. I still didn't get a good look at his face in the mirror—he was looking down, and I had to keep my eyes on the road—but I remember that."

Fox's mind began to race. The kaffiyeh and sunglasses might simply have been to keep his identity a secret, but the gloves and the lotion suggested another possibility: abnormally sensitive skin.

And there was one card in the "Most Wanted" deck with that affliction: Saif al-Jaffari, a.k.a. "Germ Jaffari," once a leader in Saddam Hussein's biological weapons project, now a prominent figure in al-Queda in Iraq and a close lieutenant of Zuhairi's. He was known to have a wide range of allergies, including hypersensitivity to sunlight and dust, caused by repeated vaccinations against anthrax, tularemia, smallpox, and the devil only knew what else.

Jaffari was a native son of Mosul, but had made himself anathema in his old hometown by helping Saddam Hussein crush the Kurdish uprisings twenty years ago, so returning to the northern provinces meant taking his life in his hands. What errand could be so important that he would incur such a risk to himself, rather than delegating it to some lackey?

"Where did you take them?"

"From Mosul to Zakho and back."

Zakho was a border town, the kind of place that existed primarily for people to pass through on their way to and from Turkey. The only reason Fox could see for his being there was to meet someone coming across from the Turkish side. A short meeting—he had made the round trip in half a day—but important enough for Jaffari to attend to it personally.

"What did he do in Zakho?"

"I don't know. I was just waiting in the car, like he told me."

"Where did you drop him off?"

"At a hotel. I think it was the Hotel Bazaaz."

"Was he carrying anything?"

"Yes, a briefcase. When he came back, he was

carrying a smaller case, made of metal."

A briefcase full of cash, exchanged for a small metal case full of...what?

"What happened after that?"

"I drove them back to Mosul. Then they paid me and sent me home."

"Who was waiting for you when you arrived at the farmhouse?"

"Just Abu Rahim."

The farmhouse had been empty when Special Forces arrived. Most likely, Jaffari had sent Abu Hakim ahead as a decoy, and left soon after him in Abu Rahim's car.

"Did Abu Rahim drive? Was his car there?"

"Yes."

"What kind of car is it? Can you describe it?"

"It's a Toyota Corona. White."

Of course, it would have to be the most common kind of car in Iraq. "What else can you tell me about it? Does it have any distinguishing features?"

He looked down and to his right for a moment. "No, nothing else."

Most people, if they were right-handed, would look up and to their left when searching their visual memory. Down and to the right was the "internal dialogue" direction. Abu Hakim had something in mind, but he was debating: "Should I tell him or not?"

"Abu Hakim," Fox said, "I promise you, your friend will come to no harm. He took a job for a little extra money, without knowing who he was working for, just like you. That's no crime. But the man riding with him is very important to us. Now, when I asked you about the car just now, something came into your mind that you chose not to tell me. That was a poor decision. I'll ask you one more time: What is the distinguishing mark on that car?"

Abu Hakim stared in astonishment. Fox held his gaze, keeping his face impassive. If Abu Hakim wanted to believe his interrogator had supernatural mind-reading powers, Fox was perfectly willing to let him.

His voice finally came out in a near whisper, as though he was afraid his friend might hear him:

"The passenger's side mirror is missing."

When Fox got back to the gator pit, he saw that one of the civilian interpreters, the one they called MJ, was back at his desk. His full name was Muhannad Jibrail, but when the soldiers gave him his nickname, he took the joke and ran with it, affecting a black fedora and aviator sunglasses. With his naturally fair skin, and curly hair grown long, he needed only a sequined white glove for the resemblance to the self-proclaimed King of Pop to be complete.

"MJ," he said, "I need you to contact the border patrol at the Ibrahim Khalil crossing, and get a list of everyone who entered from Turkey yesterday. We also need last night's guest list from the Hotel Bazaaz in Zakho. Highlight any names that appear on both lists."

"Consider it done, Cap."

While he was working on that, Fox took out a map, ruler, and compass, and tried to determine the routes Jaffari might have taken and how far he could have gone. If he had left Mosul at the same time as Abu Hakim— which would have been around 1400—and taken the highway toward Baghdad, he would be nearing Samarra now.

After a while, MJ handed Fox a faxed list with three names highlighted. Two were Italian: Andrea Dellisanti and Chiara Peretti. They appeared together on both lists, and "Andrea" in Italian was a man's name. Fox wrote them off as a backpacking couple who had taken a quick hop across the border for Iraqi entry stamps and bragging rights.

The third name was Venera Goridze.

Fox searched for her name in all the classified databases he had access to. Goridze, Venera (née Tsiklauri). Born in a small town near Tbilisi, present-day Republic of Georgia. Graduated from the Institute of Epidemiology and Microbiology in Moscow. During the Soviet era, she had worked as a researcher for Vector, the State Research Institute for Virology and Technology, in Siberia. She had also been a supervisor at a vaccine plant in Zagorsk, near Moscow.

He ran another search for the town. Famous since the fourteenth century as home to one of the holiest monasteries for the Russian Orthodox faith, it had taken on a darker shade of notoriety fifteen years ago, when an outbreak of viral encephalitis infected three hundred people. Two hundred had died. Among those that lived, some went into a coma, while others were afflicted with permanent paralysis or brain damage.

Most of the victims lived close to what was ostensibly a veterinary vaccine plant, run by the Ministry of Agriculture. The accident brought to light that it was really a research and production facility for Biopreparat, the Soviet Union's vast and top-secret biological weapons program.

The official explanation, which Moscow still insisted on, was that it had been a particularly bad outbreak of Russian spring-summer encephalitis, carried by milk from infected cows. And just to lend an extra touch of authenticity to the cover story, the government had ordered the managers of several nearby pasteurizing plants thrown into prison.

Venera Goridze had been working there at the time.

Fox glanced across the room. Stephanie Vasily was at her desk. "Steph, could I ask your help with something?"

"Sure, Robin." She stood up and made her way to his desk, with the lithe, catlike movements characteristic of her.

The daughter of a Russian defector who may have been involved in some shady weapons work himself, Stephanie was the most knowledgeable person Fox knew about biological weapons. They had arrived in Iraq at the same time, and had soon become friends, perhaps because he was one of the few who never subjected her to bawdy remarks or clumsy pick-up attempts.

"I've just been reading about the Zagorsk outbreak. What can you tell me about that virus?"

Her green eyes brightened. "Interesting character, that one. Fascinating." One thing that always unnerved Fox about her was the way she spoke of the deadliest viruses with a touch of affection, like a toxicologist who has come to treat the poisonous snakes in the laboratory like pets. "It's what's known as a chimera virus, a genetically engineered hybrid of smallpox and an amplified version of Venezuelan equine encephalitis. It hits the brain and the nervous system, much harder than the natural type, and stays stable longer in the air."

"Is the Zagorsk plant still in operation?"

"Not anymore. All of Biopreparat was shut down when the Soviet Union collapsed. Or so they said."

"Let me guess: Leaving many researchers out of a job? Some of whom mightn't have been above selling a few souvenirs from their former workplace for a bit of hard currency?"

"You got it. And considering that 'security' at old Soviet bio plants usually means one rusty padlock and maybe one fat old guard, it wouldn't be difficult."

And if Venera Goridze had returned to her home of Georgia after losing her job with Biopreparat, it would be a fairly easy overland journey from there across eastern Turkey to the Iraqi border.

"If you were Jaffari, and you got your hands on a sample of Zagorsk, what would you do with it? How would you get the biggest bang for your buck?"

"Let's see..." She raised her eyes to the vaulted ceiling and thought for a while. But before she could reply, they felt a slight tremor, and heard the muffled thud of an incoming mortar shell in the distance. Mortar attacks were a part of daily life on the base, and the soldiers generally reacted to them the way Californians did to earthquakes. You got used to them after a while, but you still automatically checked your escape routes, and you could never quite get free of the adrenaline jolt and the thought of *Is this the one*?

Fox and Stephanie exchanged a wide-eyed glance. American installations were constantly being bombarded by mortars. Recently, the Green Zone in Baghdad and some of the main military bases had been equipped with the CRAM system—Counter Rocket, Artillery and Mortar—which could intercept an incoming shell with a barrage of bullets well before it struck the mark. But if the enemy had filled the shell with a biological agent that could be dispersed in aerosol form, it would fall out better than they could devise.

Fox voiced their shared thought. "Fill a mortar shell with the virus…"

"Lob it into the Green Zone…"

"And either it reaches its target, or the CRAM guns blow it apart in mid-air…"

"Either way, you get the hottest shower you've ever had in your life. And if you could manage to time your attack right before a major transfer of troops, then you have hundreds of soldiers on planes heading back to the States, bringing home an extra souvenir that they won't even know about until symptoms start appearing."

It made ghastly sense. If you were planning to disperse a virus in the United States, why bother with elaborate attempts to smuggle it across the sea, when you had a plentiful supply of walking incubators ready to climb aboard a plane and unwittingly do the job for you?

"Can Zagorsk be transmitted from person to person?"

"That's what it was designed for. We aren't sure exactly how infectious it is, but many of the people infected in the Zagorsk outbreak weren't living in the hot zone themselves. They were family members, or else doctors and nurses who treated infected patients."

The Connect-the-Dots Illustrations for Dante's Inferno.

Fox took a deep breath, and tried to overcome his

rising panic and think logically. "Now, if you were starting from a small sample, you would have to reproduce it at scale and put it into weapons, right? What would you need for that job?"

"You would want to do it at a high-containment facility—biosafety level three at least, four if you had the means. Ideally, you would want a viral reactor, but those are hard to come by, and the sale would raise all kinds of red flags."

"Suppose you were a terrorist cell, operating with the support of al-Qaeda. Money can be had, but you wouldn't have the connections to get fancy equipment like that. You would need to stay under the radar."

She thought for a moment. "Eggs."

"I'm sorry?"

"Ordinary chicken eggs. All you would need to do is inject them with a tiny amount of the virus, and warm them in a thermostatic oven for a couple of days. Then mix the yolks with a stabilizing agent, and voilà, you've got your weapon."

"And to put it into artillery shells?"

"That you could do with equipment from a Coke bottling plant."

"Do we know anywhere in Iraq where this has been tried?"

She leaned over to look at the map on his desk. "We know of several sites linked with Saddam's bio program, but most of them were destroyed after the first Gulf War." She drew a circle on the map with her finger. "They're concentrated in the area around Baghdad, mostly south of the city. The main sites were Salman Pak, here, and al-Hakam, right here. Both of them were bombed, but some of the equipment is still unaccounted for."

She tapped another spot on the map, just southwest of Baghdad. "The al-Daura veterinary vaccine plant would be around here. UNSCOM suspected they might be tinkering with anthrax and viral agents there, but there was no solid proof, so it didn't get bombed. So my bet would be either there, or…"

"Or?"

"Or some other site we don't know about."

Fox called across the room: "MJ!"

"Sir!"

"This might sound like a strange request, but I need you to get in touch with the Ministry of Agriculture. See if anyone has recently been making unaccountably large orders for eggs."

"I'll get right on it, Cap."

Fox sighed, leaned back in his chair, and rubbed his temples. Stephanie reached out a hand, and her strong fingers massaged the back of his neck. "Well, Robin, look at it this way. The Commander in Chief will be very happy with you. You've discovered weapons of mass destruction in Iraq. That should definitely be good for a commendation."

"Right," Fox said dryly. "And if I could somehow arrange to have them postmarked before the invasion, I might have a shot at the Medal of Honor."

4

WASHINGTON, D.C.
SATURDAY, MARCH 28

The coroner's report confirmed that Thom had died of cyanide poisoning. The news claimed the top spot on all the networks, and even the BBC gave it airtime, right after a fire in the chapel of Windsor Castle. Thom's name had clearly been known far beyond the Oberlin College campus.

The president of USAtheists called a press conference. "The murder of Thom DiDio is a tragedy and an outrage. Whether he was killed because of what he believed, or because of whom he loved, is irrelevant. What matters is that the world has lost a great intellect and a great humanitarian, and his blood is on the hands of religious fanatics."

Fox flinched at the incendiary last line. *That's not how Thom would talk.* But if the man needed to lash out, Fox could scarcely blame him.

He and Emily had worked with the FBI to help create a composite sketch, which was now being broadcast regularly on television. But so far, it had yet to yield any leads.

"Any progress with Harpo?" Fox asked once he was back in the incident room at FBI headquarters.

Adler shook his head. "We kept him under observation last night. Gave him a box of books, as you suggested, but he didn't read any."

"What did he do?"

"Just lay on his bed."

"The whole time? You never saw him perform *salat*?"

"Sorry?"

"Say his prayers facing Mecca?"

"Well, he's been in a cell without windows. He has no way of knowing what time it is, or which way Mecca is."

"John, even at Gitmo, we showed the detainees at least that much courtesy. We gave them copies of the Qur'an, a qibla sign to point the way to Mecca, and even played a recording of the adhaan at the proper times."

Adler shrugged. "If you want, you can take it up with the FBI; this is their turf. Now, the technician has him all hooked up, and they're waiting for you in the interview room."

The room held Harpo, Kato, Malika, the technician, Fox, and the extra guard he had requested. The polygraph apparatus, the projector, and a tripod-mounted video camera were crammed into the little space that remained. There was barely room to take a deep breath.

Fox kept a close eye on Harpo, and the readout from

the polygraph. Harpo's breathing was very steady and regular, three seconds in, five seconds out. Fox suspected that he had been trained in ways to "beat the box," to fool a lie detector.

"Do you speak English?"

Fox watched the readout. It showed no variation in his blood pressure, heart rate, or galvanic skin response, either then or when Malika tried him in Russian and Chechen.

"Are there six people in this room?" This was a control question, to show what his vital signs looked like at baseline, after he was over his initial nervousness.

"Are you an American citizen?" No change in his vitals for that either, nor for the Eastern European equivalents.

"Can you hear me? Testing? One, two, three? Four, five? Six, seven?" Then, with a little extra emphasis: "Eight, eight?"

No variation. That diminished the likelihood that he was a white supremacist. The number 88, if letters were substituted for the numerals, became "HH"—a code for "Heil Hitler."

"All right, let's try some names. Do you know A.J. Muste? George Fox? Gene Hoffman?" These were control questions. All those names were peace philosophers, whom Fox thought it highly unlikely that he had ever heard of.

"Venera Goridze?"

No change in the readout. No flicker of recognition on his face.

"Do you realize that if you answer our questions, the prosecutors will be much less likely to ask for the death penalty?"

That finally got to him. The readout showed a slight increase in his vital signs. A normal fear reaction to the threat of death? Or excitement at the prospect of martyrdom?

And they had also established that he understood English. They would have no further need of Malika's services. It was just as well; the smell of her perfume in that confined space had been a little overpowering.

"You know, it must be awfully boring for you, cooped up in a cell all that time," Fox continued. "I've put together a little video for you. I'm curious to see how you'll like it."

He put in a DVD that he had made, a montage of various clips garnered from the Internet. It began with innocuous natural scenes—flowers, mountains, waterfalls—with a background of soothing classical music.

Then came the scenes meant to show his reaction at times of emotional arousal. A battle scene from a movie, with loud explosions and bursts of gunfire. There was a slight rise in his vitals—the startle reflex—but he soon reverted to baseline, and stayed there as the video switched back to the control images.

A clip of a shapely blonde model sliding a gossamer silk robe off her shoulders to reveal her lingerie, and then reaching behind her back to unfasten her brassiere. Fox kept his eyes fixed on the readout, ignoring the stern look he got from Kato and the blush on Malika's face.

Such an image would usually provoke an involuntary response in any red-blooded young male, but Harpo showed no more reaction than at baseline. Clearly, he was very well trained.

The control images again, this time alternating with others meant to provoke an emotional response. A sermon by the Reverend Hill. A cross being set alight by white-robed Klansmen. A muezzin intoning the call to prayer from a minaret. The second plane crashing into the World Trade Center. A speech by Osama bin Laden. A speech by President Obama, announcing the death of Osama bin Laden.

Then came the part that Fox had wanted extra protection for: a clip from a back-alley YouTube video making a mockery of the prophet Mohammed. For this one, he stepped out of Harpo's reach, anticipating that he might jump up and attack even if he had to drag the entire polygraph apparatus behind him.

Harpo showed no inclination to move. The readout showed no reaction. If he was indeed a fanatical Muslim, he had a level of mental discipline worthy of a Zen master.

Fox stepped out of Harpo's field of view again. "All right, we're done. You can turn it off now," he told the technician, while gesturing that he should keep it going. "Very interesting, don't you think? These results indicate..." He put in a dramatic pause, then looked at Harpo and enunciated ominously: "N-S-R."

Harpo's shoulders relaxed slightly, and he let out a long breath. It was barely visible when you looked at him, but it showed up on the readout. A well-concealed sigh of relief.

Fox's suspicions were confirmed. "NSR" meant "No Significant Response," but there was no way Harpo could know that unless he had studied polygraphy.

Even so, the results were remarkable. The most common technique for beating a lie detector involved focusing on some frightening or exciting image after every question, to cause an artificial jump in the vital signs. The goal was to bring up the baseline, creating so many false positives that the polygrapher would have trouble distinguishing them from significant responses. Harpo had done the opposite, bringing everything down to a level where hardly any reaction was perceptible. How much mental training had he had to undergo in order to do that?

When Harpo had been disconnected and returned to his cell, Fox went back to the conference room to watch the video, together with Kato and Adler. The first time through, Fox kept his eyes on the readout. Neither the Klansmen nor President Obama did anything for Harpo; he appeared to feel no particular animosity or affinity toward either. The most noticeable reactions came with the images of the Reverend Hill's sermon, the muezzin, and the Twin Towers.

They played the video again, this time concentrating on his face, looking for microexpressions—facial reactions that may be as brief as one twenty-fifth of a second, but are almost impossible to suppress. Harpo was very good at keeping his face impassive, but not perfect. He could have won big at poker but was not quite ready to stand guard at Buckingham Palace. With the Reverend Hill's sermon, his upper lip curled in a slight but unmistakable expression of scorn.

Fox thought he noticed a very slight microexpression at one point, during the clip mocking Mohammed. It was so unexpected that he thought he must be imagining it, and backed up the video a couple of times to make sure.

"Are you seeing what I'm seeing?" he asked.

"Maybe," Kato said in a voice that sounded as mystified as he felt. "That looks like Action Unit 12A, neutralized."

"Which means?" asked Adler.

"A trace contraction, quickly suppressed, of the zygomaticus major and risorius."

"In English, please?"

"She said," Fox translated, "that he was hiding a smile."

5

WASHINGTON, D.C.
SUNDAY, MARCH 29
PALM SUNDAY

The Reverend Hill divided his time between Arlington Bible Church, "ABC," a megachurch in an affluent Virginia suburb where he served as associate pastor, and the church he had recently founded in a run-down neighborhood in Anacostia, playfully named "Hill City Church." Fox took the Metro to Anacostia, climbed a staircase masquerading shamelessly as an escalator, and followed the directions from the church's website.

The faces Fox saw around him were of many hues, but his own was the palest among them. This was unusual. His grandfather had come back from the Pacific Theater with a Filipina bride, and Fox carried enough of her legacy in his face that whichever country he went to, people tended to assume that he was from one of its neighbors. This trait had often come in handy

in countries where white visitors were the favorite
targets of thieves and con artists, where the prevailing
rule was "fair hair, fair skin, fair game." Even so, he felt
conspicuous, and the suspicious stares he drew made
him feel that he was somehow trespassing.

The church grounds were surrounded by a brick wall,
decorated with an elaborate graffiti mural of Biblical
scenes. Fox joined the line at the gate, which extended
a good way down the block. He wondered whether the
line was always this long, but then saw the reason: two
ushers at the gate, in double-breasted suits that were
bulky enough, even on their already burly frames, to
suggest bulletproof vests underneath. They greeted
every arrival with a polite smile and a "Good morning,
brother! Good morning, sister!" as they subjected each
person's bag to a thorough inspection.

At how many other churches across America, Fox
wondered, would this be happening today? And how
far would it escalate? How long would it be before
the Department of Homeland Security established a
second TSA—a Temple Security Authority, tasked with
defending every place of worship in the country?

If Harpo had been hoping to diminish either the size
or the enthusiasm of the Reverend Hill's following, his
plan had backfired dramatically. Spacious as it was, the
church was filled to capacity with men in suits, women
in elegant dresses, and young people in blue jeans and
white hoodies silkscreened with wings, a halo, and the
words "Hill's Angels."

Now that, Fox thought, was just a bit much.

After the service, Fox found the pastor's office, which
took up most of the top floor of the parish hall. The

dark wooden walls were covered with banners bearing Scripture verses, and a line of portraits: Frederick Douglass, Martin Luther King, and the Reverend Hill. Evidently, he had already decided on his place in the pantheon.

The Reverend Hill rose from behind the massive desk. "Professor Fox. Thanks for coming." He had shed his voluminous black robe embellished with strips of Ghanaian kente cloth, and was now wearing a gray suit, wine-colored shirt, and gold cross.

"Thank you for agreeing to meet me, Reverend." Fox shook his hand. "You must be very busy, and I appreciate your making the time for me." He looked around. "This is quite impressive, I must say."

"Well, the Lord has looked with favor on the works of my hands. Please, have a seat."

"Thank you." Fox sat down in one of the leather chairs facing the desk. "You're also associate pastor at Arlington Bible Church, right?"

"That's right."

"That sounds like a pretty big job in itself. And yet, you seem to be spending most of your energy these days on this church."

He nodded and smiled. "ABC would be a thriving church with or without me. But this one..." he spread his hands, "...is my baby."

"Hence the name, Hill City Church?"

"You know what the Bible says. 'A city on a hill cannot be hid.' "

" 'Neither do men light a candle and put it under a bushel,' " Fox finished for him. "Can I ask what inspired you to choose this neighborhood for your baby to grow up in?"

"I was born not too far from here, in Washington Highlands. If you've seen the church's website, you probably know my story. I hung with a bad crowd, took some wrong turns, landed in jail. And I probably would have stayed there if my uncle, who was a pastor, hadn't kept coming to visit me. Thanks to him, I ended up going to college instead. Ever since then, I've had a dream of starting a church like this one back in my old neighborhood, hoping that I'll be able to do for some of the young people here what my uncle did for me."

"From the looks of things, you've been succeeding."

He nodded. "Our outreach programs..."

"Like Hill's Angels?"

The Reverend smiled. "Yeah, like that. During the day, they run our after-school programs, make visits and deliveries to shut-ins, that sort of thing. And at night, they go in groups on night patrols. The police tell me that crime in Ward 8 has gone down almost twenty percent since we started that program. You know, Jesus told us to visit the sick and the prisoners, all of that, but I've always felt that He'll be even happier if we can keep people out of the hospital or prison in the first place. Don't you think so?"

Fox nodded agreement.

"Reverend, I'm sure the FBI has been over this with you already, but can you think of any reason why you might have been targeted? Has anyone been making threats against you lately?"

He replied with a chuckle and a shake of the head. "I could show you a whole drawer full of fan mail. Of course, there are always the skinhead types that have nothing better to do than try to keep the black man down. When I talk about how being born again is the only way to salvation, I hear from the Jews and Catholics. When I talk about marriage and the family, I hear from gay rights groups. But you know what Jesus said, right? 'Blessed are you, when men shall revile and persecute you, and utter all manner of evil against you falsely for my sake.' By that standard, I must be the blessedest brother this side of the river!"

They shared a laugh.

"I was interested in your choice of texts this morning," Fox said. The Reverend Hill had preached on the story of Joseph at the end of Genesis, and how his abduction into slavery at the hands of his brothers was a necessary first step on the road to saving both Egypt and Israel from a devastating famine. "Do you feel like Joseph? What good do you see coming out of this evil?"

He spread his hands. "Well, we can't answer that question while we're still prisoners, can we? All we can do is to have faith that it will, someday, somehow."

Fox nodded, rose, and extended his hand. "Thank you for your time, Reverend. It was a pleasure meeting you."

"Likewise."

Fox's hand was on the doorknob when Hill called after him, "Professor Fox. Any chance that I can see him? The suspect."

Fox paused. "Why?"

The look Hill gave him over the rims of his glasses said, *Do you really have to ask?*

"I'll see what I can arrange," he promised.

Thom's family in Missouri had expressed the hope for a small, quiet funeral, but that proved to be no more possible than bringing him back to life. The ubiquitous "God Hates Fags" brigade, showing detective skills worthy of the FBI, had found out the time and place and shown up at the cemetery, with signs ranging from the wearyingly predictable No TEARS FOR QUEERS to a devil gleefully proclaiming THOM IS IN "H."

Anticipating them, atheist and gay rights demonstrators had also flocked to the site from as near as St. Louis and as far as Boston. The police erected a barrier between the protestors and counter-protestors, but the tension was palpable, and not just across the line. Relations between the atheist and LGBT camps were not always cordial, and angry words flew even between some on the same side, such as when a couple bearing the signs HOMOPHOBIA IS A SIN and JESUS HAD TWO DADS TOO passed too close to an atheist whose No GOD, NO HATE sign was somewhat belied by his neighbor's EUTHANIZE CHRISTIANS.

Watching the drama unfold on CNN, Fox hoped that Thom could at least be laid to rest without bloodshed. But that hope, too, was dashed when the bearer of a sign reading WHOEVER IS WITHOUT SIN, LET HIM CAST THE FIRST STONE sustained a scalp wound as someone on the other side took him up on it.

Fox's phone rang. He pressed the mute button on the TV remote and picked it up.

"Robin Fox."

"Mr. Fox, this is Agent Kato. Sorry to bother you on a Sunday. Is this a good time?"

Not remotely. "Sure, go ahead."

"Mr. Adler just called and said he had some important news. Can you come in?"

Fox looked back at the screen, and switched it off before the chaos got any worse. "I'm on my way."

He arrived at the Hoover Building to find Kato alone in the conference room. "Evening, Mr. Fox. Sorry to interrupt your day off."

"That's all right. You saved me from having to watch Thom DiDio's funeral become the flashpoint for a second Civil War." He collapsed into a chair. "And let the record show that I was working today. This morning, I went to Anacostia to interview the Reverend Hill."

"Really. You actually caught him there? Not fleecing his flock in Arlington, or jetting off to some fundraiser in Beverly Hills?"

"I'm not sure that's quite fair. Yes, it's clear that he loves the spotlight, and seems a little more fond of the sound of his own name than you would expect from a spiritual leader. But still, he's serious about helping his community..."

"Oh, please. He's branded himself as the miracle man of the mean streets—'I found Jesus in jail, and look at me now'—but if he's so serious about this one-man Harlem Renaissance he's planning for Anacostia, then why isn't he living there instead of a McMansion in McLean?"

"I take it this touches a nerve with you."

"I've seen his type before. He's no different from the one who conned my mother out of money that should have gone for my brother's and my education, and did nothing for her in return except keep her terrified that my father was going to hell. In a way, I suppose I should be grateful to him. Thanks to him, I decided that I'd rather live my life one hundred percent natural, no added fear, no added guilt. And everything I've seen since has only confirmed me in that. If there really is a God up there, sitting back and allowing people to do all the things they do to one another, then I'd want to see him indicted as an accessory on about a trillion counts."

A whistle came from the door. "And I thought the docket was crowded now."

Fox turned toward Adler. "Evening, John."

"Am I interrupting a theological discussion?"

"Not exactly. Agent Kato was just debriefing me about my visit to the Reverend Hill's church this morning."

"What did you find out?"

Fox gave him a brief recap of the interview. "He said he wants to see Harpo."

"What for?"

"Presumably, he wants to offer forgiveness."

"First things first," said Adler. "We need to figure out who the hell Harpo is and where he's from, and then start building a case against him. Once he's been tried and sentenced, then there'll be plenty of time for pastoral visits. *Plenty* of time."

"And I hope," said Fox, "you're going to tell us we've just come a big step closer to doing that."

"Would you believe we have? I've just gotten word from the Georgian Intelligence Service." He beat a drum roll on the table. "They've caught Venera Goridze."

Kato and Fox both applauded, and Adler acknowledged it with a theatrical bow. They exchanged high fives all around.

"They got her to admit that..."

"Got her to admit?" Fox suddenly remembered hearing that the Republic of Georgia, despite many vehement denials, was suspected of hosting a "black site," a secret detention and torture facility for the CIA.

"Do you want to hear this, or don't you? She freely chose to reveal, if you like, that she had stolen samples of Zagorsk from her old workplace. And last year, she made a little hop across the border to Turkey to make a sale, to someone by the name of Rashid Renclaw. The description she gave matched Harpo on nearly all points: age, height, hair color, eye color. The only difference was that she said he was handsome. But hey, maybe to a sixty-year-old Georgian woman, anyone looks good. And she said he spoke English with a British accent."

"You don't look quite as excited as I'd have expected."

"Well, I've told you the good news. The bad news is that so far, we haven't been able to get anything else on him. Even supposing that the first name is one he gave himself when he converted to Islam, we haven't been able to track the surname down anywhere. Our best guess is that it's a shortened form of this Polish name, which I can't even pronounce." He showed Fox on a piece of paper: *Renclawowicz.* "But in any case, no leads on it."

Kato and Fox headed back into the interview room. Fox noticed that Harpo's eyes looked less defiant than they had last time, and more dazed, as though he had gone through the night without any sleep. He also saw that some of the hair around his temples had been shaved.

"Good evening, Mr. Renclaw. Or may I call you Rashid?"

He continued to stare dully into the middle distance. Fox's hopes sank a notch. Either Harpo was too exhausted to show any reaction, or that was not his name.

"Or should I say: *Dzien dobry, Pan Renclawowicz?*"

He showed no sign of comprehension. It was just as well; that greeting had all but exhausted Fox's store of Polish.

"How was your trip to Turkey?"

No reaction. Fox's hope began to evaporate. The We Know All approach was getting them nowhere. Either Harpo had been working hard at perfecting his poker face since their last interview, or nothing Fox was saying struck any chords with him.

Very well, he thought: if this was a case of mistaken identity, he would take it and run with it.

"Did those Syrians bother to tell you what they were planning to do with the sample you sold them?"

He said nothing, but looked slightly puzzled. Understandably so, since Fox had made that up on the spot.

"Or maybe you haven't heard. You must not get much news in here," he continued. "This morning, there was an attack during Divine Liturgy at the main Orthodox church in Aleppo. Using—you guessed it—the Zagorsk virus."

He watched Harpo's face very closely. Anyone faced with a groundless accusation like this would naturally proclaim his innocence, by facial expression if no other way. But once Harpo's initial curiosity had passed, he showed no further reaction. Fox's story was completely improvised, but it seemed to be coming as no surprise to Harpo.

"ISIS claimed responsibility," he went on, "and Syrian intelligence is very anxious to know who supplied them." He gave Harpo a hard stare. "What do you think we should tell them?"

Kato laid a hand on Fox's arm. His mind raced to think of a subtle way to signal to her: *Just play along.*

She leaned toward him. "You can't be serious. Threatening him with rendition to Syria?" She said this in a whisper calculated to be overheard, while giving his arm a conspiratorial squeeze. There had been no need to worry about her. She was a seasoned interrogator too.

"Hey, who's threatening anyone with anything?" he countered. "All they're asking for is information. Now, of course it's possible that the two incidents are unconnected. But still, two attacks on Christian worship services, one week apart, both using Zagorsk—does that sound like a coincidence to you?"

This was supposed to be Harpo's cue to protest: *You're making a mistake! I'm not Rashid Renclaw! I don't know anything about any Syrians!* But he kept his gaze on its accustomed spot on the floor.

"But if he won't confirm or deny it," Fox went on, "then all we can do is get back to the Syrians with what we've managed to find out on our own. We have a suspect caught trying to disperse Zagorsk at an American prayer rally, and we have Venera Goridze's admission that she sold a sample to a Rashid Renclaw, who by her description sounds a lot like our boy here. They can make the call themselves."

Once they were out of the interview room, Kato gave Fox a sidelong glance. "I would never have thought you'd be such a good liar."

"I guess I should take that as a compliment," he replied as they entered the conference room. "You're not such a bad actress yourself. But unfortunately, we're no further ahead."

Adler was looking expectantly in their direction as they came through the door. They briefed him. "I'd say it's a safe bet that Harpo is not Rashid Renclaw," Fox concluded. "He didn't even seem to recognize the name."

Adler heaved a sigh of disappointment. "Well, at least now we have the name of someone else in his network."

As intelligence went, it was a mixed blessing. It was something, but if Harpo truly had never heard the name before, it meant at least two degrees of separation between him and Renclaw. The network was suddenly starting to look bigger.

"He didn't look like he had gotten much sleep last night," Fox added.

"Well, I don't imagine any of us did."

"And another thing: Why was he missing hair around his temples?"

"We had the psych team in to give him an evaluation. They had to rule out the possibility that he was catatonic."

"Rule it out how?"

"Electroconvulsive therapy."

Fox jumped as though the same treatment had just been administered to him. "Shock treatment? Did they not tell you that plays havoc with a person's memory? What good is it if we get him to talk, and he's forgotten everything he's done?"

"It only affects short-term memory. It's long-term we're interested in."

"John, I'm a little bit unclear about the rules of

engagement for HIG, but we haven't established that Harpo is not an American citizen. If he turns out to be, and it gets out that these...'enhanced interrogation techniques' have been used on him, under the supervision of a CIA agent, no less..."

Adler waved a hand. "It wasn't an interrogation technique. It was a psychological diagnostic tool. Now, if it happened to have the unintended side effect of softening him up a little..."

Softening him up. The words opened a door to a long-disused closet in Fox's brain, releasing a cascade of images and a whiff of a stench that he could perceive as clearly as if it were right there in the room. His stomach contracted at the memory.

"John!" Fox cut him off. "Just so we're clear, if you're going to be using torture, by whatever name you choose to call it, I want no part of it."

"Well, thanks for letting me know. I'll make sure you don't have any."

6

MOSUL, IRAQ
2005

As the sun set, loudspeakers crackled to life on minarets all over the city. The call to prayer floated through the evening air, mingling with smoke fragrant with meat and spices, ascending to heaven like a thousand burnt offerings.

On the base, all eyes were glued to the live feed from an RQ-1 Predator over Samarra. Thanks to the information Abu Hakim had provided, aerial surveillance had managed to identify a white Toyota Corona with the passenger-side mirror missing, just as it was heading into downtown Samarra, and track it until it turned into a parking garage under a large apartment building.

Browning swore as he watched it disappear.

"This looks like a job for the door-kickers," Newcomb suggested.

Browning started to nod, but the prospect made

Fox uneasy. A cordon-and-search operation might provoke Jaffari and his crew to do something desperate. Desperate terrorists with a live virus in the middle of a densely populated city would make a fearsome combination.

Before Browning could voice his agreement, Fox spoke up. "Can I offer an alternative suggestion, sir?"

Newcomb glared at him. Browning said, "Go ahead."

"They're likely going to hole up in that apartment block for the night, and move on to their final destination in the morning. Keep the building under surveillance tonight, and follow them when they move out tomorrow. If all goes well, we can track them to their processing plant. Maybe even to Zuhairi."

Browning nodded. "Let's do it. Recommendation for Abu Hakim?"

"NFIV," Fox replied. No Further Intelligence Value. "We should get him home as quickly as possible."

"He located Germ Jaffari for us, right?" Browning asked.

"That's right, sir. He's been very cooperative."

"Then he must know something more. Keep working on him. If you can't get any more out of him, then maybe they'll have better luck at Abu Ghraib."

Fox looked hard at Browning's face for any sign that this was some kind of joke. He saw none.

"What if he really has told us all he knows, sir?"

Browning gave him the look of condescending amusement that hard-bitten veterans like to use on naive young recruits. Fox's thoughts flew to Abu Hakim and his wife and son. Who would have the duty of telling them that there was no knowing when, or whether, he would be coming home again?

"How about Ibrahim? Get anything more out of him?" Browning continued.

"Nothing yet, sir," Fox had to admit.

Browning sighed and glanced at Newcomb and Mendes. "Well, maybe the next shift will have better luck. We're adjourned."

Fox went back to his IIRs. After a while, he saw Newcomb and Mendes exchange a glance, and stand up from their desks as if in response to an unspoken signal.

Fox did the same, hoping he could get to the cages ahead of them, but a private appeared from nowhere, stood directly in his path, and saluted. He was barely eighteen, freckle-faced, too small for his uniform, and generally looked much better suited to holding the console of a PlayStation than a rifle.

"Honor bound!" he shouted in a voice that ricocheted painfully from the marble walls.

"What?" Fox replied, caught off guard, before he remembered a memo that they had received a few weeks ago. He was astonished that anyone had actually paid attention to it. "To defend freedom," he replied while returning the salute, completing the prescribed call-and-response routine. "What do you need?"

He handed Fox a manila folder. "Sir, three new detainees for inprocessing, sir!"

"Take it down a notch, private. I was never a drill instructor. I still have my sense of hearing." Fox took the file and examined the first page. "You're kidding. This one was taken in for getting off a bus at the stop before a checkpoint? That's all?"

"Sir, yes, sir. Our leader thought that if she was

so anxious to avoid the checkpoint, she must have something to hide, sir."

Fox turned to the next one. "And this one. Ten years old? Taken in for throwing a rock at a tank?"

"Sir, yes, sir. We figured he must either be an insurgent or know someone who was, sir."

"And this last one? The owner of a kebab stand? How did he become a person of interest?"

"Sir, he was seen consorting with a known insurgent, sir."

"Consorting how?"

"Sir, he served him lunch, sir."

"For God's sake!" Fox flung the folder down on his desk. "Can't you see that we're trying to run a high-priority investigation here? And every detainee you bring in for ridiculous reasons like these takes manpower away from that! Now get back to your patrol leader and tell him to stop wasting our time!"

He flinched. Fox immediately felt guilty for losing his temper. After all, this private was only the messenger.

"Sir, yes, sir." He finally stepped aside, and Fox ran down the passage to the cages.

He never envied the guards at the cages their duty. The cell block was a makeshift construction, a decidedly less than palatial addition to the original palace. The odors of sweat, human waste, and military-strength pepper spray combined to form a smell like a toilet inside a locker room where someone had just vomited after downing a bottle of Tabasco sauce.

As it always did when he walked into the cages, the assault on his ears came a moment behind the one on his nostrils. Hands pounded on bars, or reached between them in pleading gestures, and supplicating voices shouted, "*Sayyidi! Min fadhlik!* Sir! Please!" The detainees knew that he spoke their language, would be sympathetic to their concerns, and had at least some small measure of authority to get something done about them, so his appearances here always occasioned a welcoming chorus like this. Which was why he tried to keep them infrequent.

"Sir! Help me! I'm sick, and the guards won't let me see a doctor!"

"Sir! Why am I here? How long am I going to be here? Am I going to die here?"

"Sir! You'll take care of my family, right? Please! You promised!"

Fox looked in the direction of the last voice, and immediately wished he hadn't. It was Abu Hakim. He had undoubtedly figured out what was going to happen to him, and what had become of Fox's promise that he would soon be released. But there was no tone of accusation in his voice, only anxiety for his family's safety.

Fox looked away, his face burning as he did. He resolved to make sure Abu Hakim's family was properly looked after. At the moment, though, he had more pressing concerns.

He hurried to the end of the row of cells, where another corridor branched off from the main one. He motioned to the guard, and shouted to make himself heard over the clamor: "What's down there?"

"Those cells have just been built, sir," he answered. "They're not in use yet. They haven't even had lights put in, sir."

Fox headed down the corridor.

"Sir!" The guard called after him. "I said there's nothing down there! Sir!"

Without lights, the hall soon grew so dark that Fox had trouble seeing the walls. But at the far end of the corridor, he saw light emerging from behind one of the cell doors. And as he approached, he heard a voice behind the door.

"Still think you're so smart, hajji? You don't start talking soon, this is going to be your bed every night from now on."

Fox had no doubt about whose voice it was.

He looked through the bars. By the dim light of a battery-operated lantern, he saw three uniformed figures: Newcomb, Mendes, and a stranger. Newcomb sat at a small table, on which lay some kind of machine. Cables ran from it to a metal bed frame, and connected to the wrists and ankles of the detainee strapped spread-eagled onto it. A gaunt, elderly man, naked except for a hood over his head.

The moment Fox looked in, Newcomb pressed a switch on the machine. The detainee convulsed, and went on writhing until Newcomb released the switch.

"*Allahuma, agferlehom*," said the voice from within the hood. "Allah, forgive them."

It was Ibrahim's voice.

Fox pounded on the door. "Open up!"

Mendes and the medic gave a guilty start, and the medic, after a moment's hesitation, opened the door. Newcomb only turned his broad face toward Fox with a malevolent grin.

"What the hell is going on here?" Fox barked in his

best officer's voice.

"Just softening him up for you," Newcomb replied placidly. "And your timing was perfect. Now that hajji-lover Fox has come to his rescue, tomorrow he'll probably tell you everything he knows."

Fox turned to face the stranger. "Specialist! Is that or is that not a medic's insignia I see on your sleeve? What the hell got into you to be a part of this?"

The medic took a step back. "Just...just checking to make sure they aren't doing any severe and lasting damage, sir."

"Do the words 'first do no harm' mean nothing to you?"

"Attention," Newcomb commanded, and Mendes and the medic obeyed. Fox was about to point out that they were a little late in showing due honor to an officer, when he saw that their eyes were not on him, but on the door.

"Get anything out of him yet?" asked Major Browning.

Fox stood there, dumbstruck, as Browning's eyes turned to meet his. He slowly raised his hand in salute, his arm feeling as though a ten-pound weight were strapped to it.

"Fox, what a surprise," Browning said. "What brings you here?"

Mendes answered for him. "He was a little confused about whose authority it was that set this up, sir."

"Well, now we've cleared that up, haven't we? But as long as you're here..." He gestured to the chair. "Care to do the honors?"

Fox looked at the chair as though it, rather than the

bed frame, were wired with electrodes. "No, thank you, sir."

"Let me rephrase that." Browning dropped his tone of mock courtesy. "Have a seat and take your turn. That's an order."

"Sir, that order is illegal."

"Want to take your chances arguing that in front of a court martial?" Mendes asked.

"You want me to tell a court martial everything I've seen here?" Fox said, still addressing Browning. "If that's the way you feel, bring it on."

"Oh, I don't think it needs to come to that," Browning replied. "All of us are witnesses that he disobeyed a direct order from a superior officer, aren't we? Just that would be enough to knock him down a couple of pay grades and have him reassigned to some infantry unit in the Triangle of Death."

Fox looked from one to another of their faces. "I can't believe what's happening here. Look at this man. Look at him!"

He thrust his finger at the bound, naked, hooded figure. Their eyes followed his point for the briefest of moments, barely long enough for him to reach behind his back and make an adjustment to the machine. There was no time to check whether it was the right one.

"Sir, is this the image of your command you want the world to see?" he went on. "Are you trying to make this place into another Abu Ghraib?"

"The world will never see it," Browning answered. "No one outside this room will ever know what happened here." He leaned toward Fox and continued menacingly, "If they do, we'll know exactly who leaked it, won't we?

Now, sit—your—ass—down."

Fox lowered himself into the chair, wondering if this was how a condemned criminal felt when he took the seat from which he would never stand up.

"Ibrahim," he said, "this is your last chance. Do you really want me to use this machine? Remember how it felt when they were using it on you. Remember how you writhed. Remember how you screamed."

He paused for a reply, as everything in him silently entreated: *Ibrahim, please! Say something! Save yourself and me!* But no voice issued from under the hood.

Fox's face contorted, as he spat out angry words in Arabic.

"Speak English!" Browning demanded. "What did you just say?"

Fox glared at him. "I thought that even you could understand. I called him a worthless scumbag hajji."

And he threw the switch.

Ibrahim's body convulsed. "*Allahuma, agferlehom!*"

"Where is Mehdi al-Zuhairi?" Browning demanded. When he got no reply, he jerked his head in Fox's direction. "Dial it up."

Fox did as ordered. "Come on, make it easy on yourself, hajji."

He threw the switch.

"*Allahuma, agferlehom!*" The words came out even louder, and his thrashing became more violent.

"Where is Zuhairi?"

The hooded figure was silent. Browning gestured to Fox.

"Still going to play tough guy, are you, hajji?" He

threw the switch.

"*Allahuma, agferlehom!*" His cry chilled Fox to the bone, but what penetrated all the way to the marrow was the grin that Browning, Newcomb, and Mendes were sharing among themselves—a solidarity of sadism that cut across rank distinctions. Had they all been this way before they joined the Army? Or had Iraq done it to them?

"Dial it up."

The medic was watching the dial with growing alarm. "Sir, it's getting to the point where it could be dangerous. He's an old man; those muscle contractions could break his bones."

"I said dial it up!"

"Sir, you heard what he said!" Fox shouted. "Are you..."

"Captain!"

With trembling fingers, Fox turned the dial.

"If you don't start talking soon, you'll see Allah face to face...hajji!"

The sound that tore from Ibrahim's throat went beyond words to a pure primal scream, that echoed down the hall and into the corners of Fox's bowels.

"That's right, hajji," Browning said. "Scream as loud as you can. Keep everyone in the cells awake all night wondering what we're doing to you, and who's going to be next."

Ibrahim's pleas for divine mercy had faded away into a low moan. "*Allah, Allah, Allah.*"

Fox jumped up, yanked the cables out of their jacks, and threw them to the floor. "That does it! Sir, I refuse to go along with this any longer. If you want to court martial me, or ship me off somewhere to get shot at, then you go right ahead."

Browning gave him a long look, with the faint hint of a self-satisfied smile on his face.

"No need," he finally said. "You did your best, Fox. Like a good soldier."

He clapped Fox on the shoulder and left. Newcomb followed behind him, and Mendes brought up the rear, pausing at the door long enough to look back with a leer.

"Good luck learning how to walk without your wings, Mr. Fallen Angel."

7

WASHINGTON, D.C.
MONDAY, MARCH 30

"All right, ladies and gentlemen, let's see your unforgivables."

Amid a few startled giggles, Fox went around the classroom to collect the slips on which the students had written their answers to his question: "What is one thing you could never forgive?" In exchange, he passed out laminated cards, blue on one side, red on the other.

As he was sorting the papers into order, he instructed his students: "As I read these out, please hold up the blue side of your card if you think you could forgive this if it happened to you, and the red side if you think you couldn't."

He read the cards out, starting with the comical ones: "Farting in an elevator."

Then the ones of most immediate interest to college students: "Stealing my boyfriend or girlfriend."

And finally, the truly serious ones: "Killing my child." As he went through the stack, the number of blue cards decreased and red ones increased.

"You may have heard the argument," Fox went on, "that if religion and the concepts of heaven and hell were taken away, the world would plunge into chaos. Everyone would be killing and stealing and raping to their wicked hearts' content. How many of you would agree with that?"

A few hands went up.

"All right, some. But personally, I'm glad to see that more of us have more faith in humanity than that. Don't kill your enemies? There are a hundred good reasons not to do that, so even if you take God out of the picture, you'll still have ninety-nine. Our list of 'Thou shalt nots' would probably be more or less the same, with or without God's signature. What religion brings to the table is the 'Thou shalts.' Forgive your enemies? Love your enemies? That goes beyond anything that secular law or morality has any right to demand."

A scoff came from Arnie. Fox turned to face him. "Do you have a different opinion?"

"It's easy to sit here and talk," he answered. "But if someone killed you, your friend, or your family, how forgiving would you feel?"

Fox took a deep breath, held it for a moment, and let it go slowly.

"Well, let me answer those in order. First of all, if someone killed me, I suppose I'd be too dead to feel much of anything."

He let the laughter subside, before going on more seriously: "About someone killing my friend, as of last

Friday, that's not an academic question for me. Thom DiDio was a good friend of mine." He paused for effect. "If I ever met the killer, I hope I would be able to act like the woman whose testimony you're about to hear."

He booted up his laptop, saying a silent prayer of thanks for the invention of video, to which he often found himself resorting these days as his side job in counterterror took more and more time away from his class preparation.

"She actually experienced the last of the 'unforgivables' we just heard. Her child was kidnapped and killed. Be honest, now: if that happened to you, how many of you would want to see the killer die?"

Nearly all the hands in the room went up.

"Most of us would. That's the natural human reaction, and she felt it too. But you'll see how her faith allowed her to go beyond the natural human desire for revenge, and try to contact the killer personally and listen to his story. And in the course of talking with her, he gave away enough information for the police to identify him. When he was arrested, and she finally met him face to face, she told him that in the spirit of forgiveness, she would decline to ask the prosecutors for the death penalty. And it was only then that..."

His voice suddenly trailed off, leaving the room full of expectant silence.

A tentative voice broke it. "Mr. Fox?"

Fox shook his head and tried to refocus.

"...that he confessed to his crime, and two other murders as well."

He started the video, then slipped out of the room and called Adler.

"Adler here."

"John, this is Robin Fox. You remember I told you yesterday that the Reverend Hill said he wanted to see Harpo. We need to let him."

"I thought we already decided that..."

"We did. I know this is way outside protocol, but trust me, this is my area of expertise. And besides, what else has worked?"

There was a pause on the other end. "All right, then. Let's set up a time to bring him in. And how soon can you come in today?"

"As soon as class is over."

"Good. There's something you need to see."

When Fox arrived at the Hoover Building, he saw a bigger smile on Adler's face than he had ever seen before. "Ah, there you are, Robin. Tell me, do you ever play the lottery?"

"Not really."

"I'm thinking I might just hop on a train to Pennsylvania and pick up some tickets. How many would you like?"

"Feeling lucky today, are you?"

He presented a folder with a dramatic flourish. "The Metro Police have come through for us. Someone found a paper bag with a money belt in it, taped behind one of the newspaper vending machines at the Gallery Square Metro station. Clever hiding place. There's enough space between them and the wall that he could reach in, but if no one saw him doing it, it's unlikely they'd think to check there. This is what was in it."

He opened the folder to reveal photographs of a British passport, a credit card, and a plane ticket from Washington to London for the day of the incident. The plan had been simple: get in, plant the device, get out, recover the stash, and be halfway across the Atlantic before anyone knew what he had done.

Fox read the name aloud. "Thaddeus James Moresby-Stokes?"

"I know," Adler said. "Who the hell has a name like that?"

"So where has he been lately?"

"Wouldn't we like to know." Adler pointed at the issue date, which was less than a month ago. "He must have renewed it just for this trip, so that there would be no visas in it to raise red flags. Nothing from Turkey— or Syria, Pakistan, or any other likely spot for jihadi summer camp. The only stamps in it are an exit from London, and an arrival in Montreal."

That explained why CBP had no record of him. The United States photographed and fingerprinted all non-citizens on arrival, but Canadian immigration was not as strict. And there were any number of places where he could have slipped across the border undetected.

"Well," Adler went on with a slightly malicious grin, "now we've officially established he's not an American citizen. So, I get to take my turn with him. Care to join me?"

They went into the interview room together. Harpo raised his eyes briefly to register this new arrival.

"Thaddeus James Moresby-Stokes," Adler said.

Harpo started, and his eyes widened.

"Yes, I know your name," Adler continued. "You

don't need to know mine. All you need to know are my initials. Here's a hint: the first one is C, and the last one is A."

Harpo—Fox continued to think of him by his code name, which was definitely less unwieldy than his real one—kept his silence. His eyes still stayed on the floor, but they were wide with fear. His breath began to come more quickly.

"Yes, that's right," Adler went on. "I get a crack at you now. Don't much like that idea? I don't blame you. I know I'm not as easy on the eyes as those two ladies who've been working with you. And I'm nowhere near as nice and polite as this gentleman here. I've never been much for social pleasantries. I like to stay focused on my job. And my job is to get you to tell me what you know. By—any—means—necessary."

Harpo was beginning to sweat, but still he kept his silence.

"Remember what that lovely lady told you about the right to remain silent, the right to the presence of an attorney, and all that?" Adler pressed on. "Forget it all. All you need to know about your rights is that when I ask you a question, you had better answer right. Who sent you? Who are you working for?"

His gaze remained fixed ahead, as beads of sweat appeared on his face.

"Where is the next target? When are you going to hit it?"

Harpo was gasping audibly for breath, but he made no other sound.

"Damn it!" Adler shouted, pounding his fist on the table next to Harpo and leaning over him until their faces were only a few inches apart. "You listen to me! The gloves are about to come off. You think that what you've been through in here is the worst that can happen to you? Think again! We've been going easy on you, because this is America, and we play by the rules here. But if you keep holding out on us, we can take you to a place where the rules don't apply. Where nobody will have any idea where you are. Where there are no video cameras to monitor us, and no one to tell us what we can and can't do. So what's it going to be? Talk now, or scream later?"

Fox was devoutly hoping Adler was a better analyst than he was an interrogator. In the theater of interrogation, the interrogator was often called on to play the heavy, but even under the mask of rage, it was essential to stay in control. When the interrogator lost his temper, things went bad very quickly, both for the subject and for their chances of gleaning any useful intelligence. And by jumping straight into full-on Fear Up Harsh mode, Adler had left himself no room for gradual escalation. Everything in Fox was telling him to intervene, but he had no authority here. He was only a consultant, a guest in the Agency's house.

Harpo looked up at Adler, making eye contact for the first time.

"I can endure all things, through Allah who gives me strength."

His words, spoken in an accent that Fox placed somewhere around Bristol, electrified the air like the first click underfoot that tells a platoon they are marching through a minefield. Adler flashed Fox a triumphant smile that combined "We did it!" with "I told you so."

Fox stood still, barely breathing. *Oh, no. Please, no.*

Adler turned back to the subject. "Who are you? Who are you working for?"

"American Sharia State. What you have seen is only the beginning. The attacks will continue, in times and places that you least expect, until you infidels repent of your wicked ways and make Sharia the law of the land."

"By which you mean?" Fox managed to ask.

"Death to unbelievers. Death to homosexuals. Death to anyone who dares insult the Prophet. All boys will be taught the Qur'an in schools, and girls will never see the inside of a classroom. They are to be the property of their fathers until they become the property of their husbands. Any woman seen outdoors without a burqa and a male escort will be stoned. Eighty lashes for drinking alcohol or listening to music. No pork on supermarket shelves. No..."

There was a knock on the door. Without waiting for a reply, a staff member opened it and stuck his head in. "Agent Kato, you have a call from London."

Kato left. Fox glanced inquiringly at Adler, and after receiving an assenting nod, turned to Harpo.

"This movement of yours," Fox said. "Tell me more about it. Are you Sunni or Shi'a?"

"S-unni." There was the merest hint of an indecisive pause on the first "s."

"Now, this whole business of imposing your version of Sharia throughout the United States," Fox went on. "I'm curious: How do you reconcile that with the Qur'an, Sura two, verse 256, and the precepts of Umar bin Abdulaziz?" He referred to scriptures that spoke against compulsion in religion and imposition of the laws of

Islam on non-Muslims.

Harpo kept up his defiant expression, but underneath, his face took on the look of a student caught without his homework.

Fox let him sit in silence for a while before pressing on: "And if you believe that all music is haram, how do you interpret the hadith of the Two Festivals in al-Bukhari?"

Harpo's mouth worked hesitantly for a few moments before he finally spoke. "I would be wasting my breath, debating theology with an infidel like you."

"Somehow I thought you would say that."

Fox's phone vibrated. He stole a glance at the screen. The message from Emily read, "Urgent news from Miriam."

"I'm sorry, John," he said, "I'll have to excuse myself."

Adler nodded. "We'll take it from here."

Fox stood, then turned back to Harpo. "Oh, by the way: You left out turning the Capitol into a mosque and draping a burqa over the Statue of Liberty."

When Fox arrived at USPRI headquarters and rushed to Emily's desk, a minuscule upturn of the corners of her mouth was as close as she could come to a smile.

"You've heard from Miriam," he said. "And it's not good news."

Emily nodded. "She got a call from Leila's mother, in tears—completely devastated. Leila somehow managed to get a message smuggled out to her. She's been arrested, and they're holding her at HaSharon Prison."

Fox wondered at the efficiency of the underground

network that could convey information through channels the CIA missed. "What could they possibly be charging her with?"

She gave him an impatient look that said, *At other times, I might find your naiveté charming.* "You know how it works over there. She's in administrative detention. They can hold her for six months without needing to charge her with anything."

"What can we do?"

"I'm going over there."

"To Israel?"

"Yes. Miriam is sounding like she's at the end of her resources. She and Rabbi Sternberg have been organizing protests at the prison, but they're starting to worry that things could turn violent. If I go, at least I can flash Rick's card, and put some pressure on the Israelis by giving them the idea that they've crossed the American government and touched off an international incident. It's worth a try."

"When are you leaving?"

"On the first flight I could get. Wednesday morning."

"Hell of a time for this to happen. Friday is the first day of Passover. At sunset, the entire State of Israel will shut down."

"That's why I have to leave right away. The symposium starts next week. And you have some idea what prison in Israel is like, especially for a Palestinian woman. If there's a chance we can get her out of there even one day early, it's worth it."

Fox nodded. "God go with you, Emily."

"Thanks."

She stood up, wrapped her arms around him, and

squeezed. The last time she had hugged him like that was the day before he started his military service. Like Jacob's hold on the angel, it was at once an embrace, a prayer, and an act of defiance: *I won't let go until You promise we can see each other again.*

Fox's apartment in Arlington was a short Metro ride from campus, with a wide choice of cuisines within easy walking distance, and a rooftop patio designed especially for enjoying the view of the Washington Monument and the Capitol dome with a glass of pinot noir in hand. He liked everything except the name of the street, Army Navy Drive, and the nearest station, Pentagon City. It was as though the universe were conspiring to keep him from ever forgetting that chapter in his life.

He stopped at Nando's Peri Peri for take-out chicken, and started to head home with it when the feeling struck him that something was out of place. It took a moment to realize what it was. Usually, on his way home from the station, he would pass by what his neighbor liked to call "the United Nations of Children." At all hours of the evening, long after what most Americans would consider bedtime, he would see children splashing in the fountains until they were soaked to the skin, while their mothers, in hijabs and abayas, laughed and chatted over frozen yogurt from Yogi Castle. Tonight, however, the lounge chairs on the Astroturf were vacant. Only once did he spy two veiled women, emerging from the Lebanese Taverna and walking swiftly and purposefully away, eyes fixed straight ahead but still scanning the surroundings. The attitude of a traveler in a dangerous place.

Overcome by a sudden feeling of foreboding, he rushed home and switched on CNN.

"...a group calling itself American Sharia State. Moresby-Stokes pledged that attacks would continue until the group's interpretation of Islamic Sharia law was implemented throughout the United States. His demands included..."

"Oh, God," Fox said aloud. "Oh, John. Tell me you didn't."

He grabbed his phone and dialed.

"Adler here."

"John, what the hell?"

"What the hell what?"

"What the hell do you think what the hell what? How did the garbage Harpo was spouting get onto CNN?"

"What do you mean? We finally have a name for him, an organization, and a motive. The American people deserve to know. Don't you think they've waited long enough?"

"Oh, perfect. That is just brilliant. Except for one thing: Did it somehow escape your notice that every word out of his mouth was a lie?"

"What are you talking about?"

Fox's palm made forceful contact with his face. "I can't believe this! You were there. You heard me interview him. He's no more a Muslim than you are."

"Well, of course he couldn't hold his own in a scholarly discussion with you. Do you have any idea how many wannabe jihadis set off for the sunny shores of Syria with copies of *Islam for Dummies* in their carry-ons? None of them know the first thing about Islam, beyond what they hear from fire-breathing preachers on

YouTube."

"For God's sake, can't you tell when you're being played? His whole manifesto could have been lifted straight from some right-wing scaremongering website. He even gave it a ridiculous name, and you still fell for it."

"What?"

"American Sharia State. What are the initials?"

There was a crestfallen silence at the other end. Fox went on: "That's exactly what he was trying to make out of us. And you played your part like a you-know-what at the lyre."

Another long pause. "If he isn't a Muslim," Adler finally replied, "why would he want us to think he was?"

"I don't know." Fox looked back at the screen, with Harpo's talking points still scrolling across it. "But whatever message he was trying to send, we've just become his press secretaries."

8

WASHINGTON, D.C.
TUESDAY, MARCH 31

The Muslim community braced for a backlash. The chief imam at the Washington Islamic Center called a press conference. "We condemn this attack as the work of a twisted soul, and we urge anyone with any further information about the suspect or his group to make it known at once to the FBI. We mourn with our city, and our thoughts and prayers are with the families of the victims." The dean of the National Cathedral, the Catholic Archbishop of Washington, and the senior rabbi of the Washington Hebrew Congregation each took the microphone in turn after him, urging members of their own faiths to show restraint.

The president of USAtheists felt the need to weigh in with a press conference of his own. "Be honest, America: does this news come as any surprise to anyone? The barbaric attack on the Verizon Center by fanatical

Muslims, and the senseless murder of Thom DiDio by fanatical Christians, are just the two latest additions to the unending list of ways religion incites good people to do bad, and bad people to do the unspeakable. Religious violence is the scourge of the modern world."

The Metro Police had set up a round-the-clock watch at the Islamic Center. Predictably, a crowd had already gathered, chanting "Islam is evil!" and waving American flags and placards. Never bow to Islam and No Sharia in America were among the more repeatable ones.

Forgive us, Fox pleaded silently to the Great Unknowable as he watched the spectacle on television. *We knew not what we were doing.*

But the cameras showed other demonstrators there, also with American flags, whose signs read We stand with our Muslim neighbors and America loves everyone. They also showed a vandalized mosque in Brooklyn, where volunteers from a local church and synagogue were hard at work repairing the damage.

Fox switched off the television and headed to the Metro station. On the way, he saw men and women in green shirts, holding signs reading I'll walk with you, offering a protective escort to any Muslim wary of walking through Washington alone.

There's hope for us yet, he thought.

The Reverend Hill was scheduled to meet Harpo that afternoon. As soon as Fox finished his last class, he headed directly to the Hoover Building. Adler briefly glanced toward the doorway as he came in, then lowered his gaze without acknowledging him, just as Harpo often did.

Kato cleared her throat and broke the awkward silence. "I didn't get the chance to fill you in on what I heard from Scotland Yard yesterday," she said. "Our boy is a first-year student at—if you please—Oxford, majoring in biochemistry. One arrest last year, when he got into a drunken fight and broke a window in a pub, but no other priors. And something else weird."

"What's that?"

"After we first contacted them, they called his parents to tell them their son had been arrested in America. They said, 'We have no son,' and hung up."

"Are they sure they had the right people?"

"Come on!" said Adler. "How many people named Moresby-Stokes can there be, even in England?"

Fox had to admit he had a point. And even assuming it was a case of mistaken identity, polite puzzlement— *I'm sorry, you must be confusing me with someone else*—would be a more natural reaction than a brusque rebuff of the kind Kato had described.

"His prior arrest," Fox said. "Did it say where it was?"

Kato leafed through the file. "Yes. It happened at the Admiral Duncan Pub, on Old Compton Street, in the Soho district of London."

"I see." And Fox did see, a little more clearly now.

The intercom rang, and Kato picked it up. "Incident room, Kato...All right, send him up." She set down the receiver. "Hill's here."

An agent escorted Hill to the interview room, and Kato accompanied him inside. Adler and Fox retired to the observation area to watch him through the one-way glass.

"This strategy of yours had better work," Adler muttered.

"Like yours has?"

Adler shot him a glare, then turned his attention back to the interview room.

"Mr. Moresby-Stokes," Kato said, "you have a visitor."

She opened the door wider to let Hill in. As soon as Harpo saw him, his eyes widened, and he pressed himself harder against the back of his chair.

Hill sat down in the chair opposite Harpo, while Kato remained standing.

"Hello," he said. "We haven't met. I'm Isaiah Hill."

He extended his hand. Harpo regarded it as if it had just come from foraging in an overripe garbage bin. After an awkward pause, Hill withdrew it.

"You came a long way, just to hurt me," he went on. "You must really feel that I've done something bad. If you'll tell me what it was, I'll try to make it right."

He paused to give Harpo an opening, but got only a venomous glare. Fox began to feel that Hill truly had to be under divine protection. An ordinary mortal might have withered before the death rays emanating from Harpo's eyes.

"And I want you to know that I forgive you," he continued. "I know you're feeling a lot of pain, and every day, I've been praying for you, and for the healing of whatever it is that's eating you up inside. Can I say a prayer for you now?"

Harpo looked as though he were facing a centipede the size of a boa constrictor.

The Reverend Hill took his silence as consent, turned

his face and palms toward heaven, and began to pray. "Father God, I just want to pray to you, have mercy upon this young man. Heal whatever sickness in his heart led him to do this, Father God. Forgive him, Father God, for he knew not what he was doing."

He turned his palms to Harpo, and his voice took on an authoritarian tone. "And I cast you out, Satan! Any evil spirits that are lurking in this man's heart, I charge you right now in the name of the Lord Jesus Christ..." he reached out and laid a hand on Harpo's head, "come out of him!"

"Get your bloody hands off me!"

Harpo's hands flew up to sweep the Reverend Hill's aside. Kato moved swiftly to restrain him. Adler and Fox ran out of the observation room and burst into the interview room.

"Don't touch me!" Harpo roared, in a voice that resounded piercingly in the confines of the tiny room. "Don't come in here gabbling about Satan and evil spirits and all that rubbish! I've had enough hands laid on me, and enough Bibles waved over me, to last a bloody lifetime. And don't patronize me with your 'he knew not what he was doing.' I knew exactly what I was doing!"

A moment of silence ensued, during which all the air in the room seemed to be rushing toward Harpo to fill the void after his explosion. Fox broke it by asking gently, "What exactly were you doing?"

"Using one virus to cure another."

"I beg your pardon?"

"Do you know what the deadliest virus in the world is?"

"Enlighten me."

"Zagorsk, Ebola, smallpox—nasty little buggers all, but the worst they can do is kill their host. There's only one virus that propagates itself by making its host kill anyone who isn't similarly infected."

"And that is?"

"The virus of the mind called *religion*!" He thrust a quivering finger at Reverend Hill. "You and your kind belong to the infancy of our species! The time has come for the rubbish you preach to fall out and be thrown away like a baby tooth. And I'm sorry to shatter yet another infantile fantasy, but there's no Tooth Fairy to turn it into anything of value!"

Adler laid a hand on Reverend Hill's shoulder. "Reverend, maybe you've done all you can here today?"

Reverend Hill nodded agreement, and allowed Adler to escort him out. Kato and Fox were left there with the subject.

"Thaddeus," Kato began. "Or do you go by something like Tad, or TJ? All right, TJ it is. I understand where you're coming from. Believe me, I have no use for anyone who tries to force their idea of God down my throat."

"And yet, you thought it would be a bloody brilliant idea to bring *that* here to talk to me!" TJ retorted, with a jerk of his head toward the hall. "Let me ask you something, agent. Do you believe there's room in this world for religion?"

She shrugged. "I suppose there are some people who need it."

"Bloody accommodationist!" TJ spat the word at her in the tone of voice most people reserve for words like "murderer." "Then there's no room in this world for the likes of you either! There's a virus ravaging the human species, and if you're not helping us to eradicate it, you're compromising our immune system. I'm sorry, agent, but I have nothing more to say to you."

He returned his gaze to its usual spot on the floor. Fox was afraid he would withdraw into himself again and they would lose their window of opportunity.

"Agent, could you give us the room for a minute?" he asked.

Kato nodded and left. TJ fixed Fox in a defiant glare. "And what do you have to say, Mr. Qur'anic Scholar?"

In the theater of interrogation, Fox had been called on to play many different roles, but he had never been cast so completely against type as he was about to be. If he could put on a performance that convinced TJ, he would consider himself entitled to an Oscar, or whatever equivalent there was that could be displayed in some corner of a Langley basement.

"What did you think?" he asked. "That a virologist wouldn't know his job?"

He took an exaggeratedly wary glance at the one-way window, turned his chair so that his back was facing it, and spoke to TJ in a confidential tone.

"I still have the scar," he said, "from when a nun hit me so hard her stick broke, for forgetting one word of my stupid catechism. I can't tell you how many nights I lay awake in my bunk, thinking about what I would do to her if I got the chance. Of course, it never went beyond fantasy. I never thought I would meet someone who had the balls to actually go through with it."

He watched TJ's expression closely, and noticed a slight shift in the proportion of hostility to curiosity.

"You know what you learn at a school like that?" Fox

continued. "You learn that they can control what you say and do, but they can't control what you think. They can make you say the words and sing the hymns, but the only way they can take away your freedom here.. ." he tapped his head, "is if you surrender it yourself. That freedom is the most precious thing you've got."

TJ nodded slowly. "You understand, then."

Fox had to conceal a sigh of relief. His hastily concocted story had gotten him through the outer gate.

"Of course, that was just school," Fox continued. "I could take anything they gave me, because I knew when the term was over, I had a loving home to go back to." He laid a hand on TJ's unresisting shoulder. "But where do you go when your own family betrays you? When they cast you out...rather than let you love the one you want to love?"

TJ looked at Fox through widened eyes, confirming his theory. Fox recalled the polygraph session, and TJ's reaction to the erotic scene. He hadn't averted his eyes, as a strict Muslim might have, but neither had he shown any sign of sexual arousal. And the report from Scotland Yard said that his prior arrest had been on Old Compton Street, which enjoyed a reputation as the center of London's gay nightlife.

"Home must have been like hell for you," he said.

TJ's lip curled. "There wasn't a single wall in that whole bloody house where you could look without some cheap picture of Jesus staring back at you. Church twice every bloody week. Bible readings with every meal. Couldn't watch TV, couldn't go to movies with my mates, and they watched like bloody hawks to see what I was reading. I could barely breathe in that house."

"And then you went to college," Fox continued for him. "And finally, you could breathe. You could start exploring who you really were. But then one day, you were just out having a good time with your mates, things got a little out of hand, the police got involved, called your parents..."

He stopped when he saw TJ's lip beginning to quiver.

"They actually believed," TJ said, "that I was possessed by the Devil. They took me to church, and they did some kind of...*exorcism* on me. They held me down and hit me with Bibles while everyone chanted, 'Pray out the gay!' They put me into freezing cold baths, and shoved gay porn magazines into my face and ammonia under my nose. And when none of that worked, they told me that until I renounced my sinful and wicked ways, I was no longer welcome in their house. Actually, that last was probably the kindest thing they had ever done for me."

"They decided their principles were more important to them than their own son. Well, all I can say is, I hope their principles take good care of them in their old age." Fox paused. "There's someone I wish you could have met. His story was very much like yours. It took him a lot of searching, but eventually, he found a place where he could flourish. He found a way to be happy...until his life was cut short."

A slight smirk appeared on TJ's lips. "Are you by any chance referring to Thom-with-an-H DiDio?"

The interview room began to spin around Fox. TJ had been apprehended before Thom's death, and had no access to news since then. The only way he could know about the murder was if he had been involved in it.

"You know who killed him," Fox said through numb lips.

TJ's smirk expanded. "Yes. And if you haven't caught him by now, you never will."

Control is Interrogation 101. The instructors at the Schoolhouse had drummed this motto into new interrogators endlessly, meaning that they should always project the image of omnipotent figures who held ultimate power over the subjects' destiny. In the field, Fox had discovered their words were true, but not in the way they meant. From his experience, the most important quality in an interrogator was *self*-control. An interrogator who let his emotions get the better of him could undo weeks of painstaking work in a single moment.

Fox now recited that principle over and over in his mind, like a magical incantation that would lose its power at the slightest interruption of the chant. At the moment, every muscle in his body was yearning to pounce on TJ and choke him, kick him, beat him until he confessed everything he knew. But in addition to breaking all the Interrogation Rules of Engagement, that would ruin their chances of getting any more out of him.

"Why?" was the only question he could manage.

"Isn't it obvious? We needed a martyr. And who better for the job than someone who insisted on dimming the Brights?"

"Excuse me?"

"He was a traitor. A *faitheist*! He had a bloody 'Coexist' bumper sticker on his car! Please! As if it were possible for reason to coexist with delusion! For a healthy body to coexist with a virus! The human race will never reach the next stage in its evolution as long as even one specimen of this virus remains. We will eradicate it from the face of the earth...even if everyone infected with it has to die, until only the rational ones are left alive!"

TJ collapsed back into his chair, breathing hard.

This was the moment. His rant had left him exhausted and depleted his blood sugar. His energy, and his resistance, would be at a low ebb. And by listening to him, Fox had created in him a subconscious sense of indebtedness—"transference," the psychologists called it. If TJ was ever going to give up any useful information, it would be now.

But how, Fox wondered, to make the best use of this chance? Which line of questioning to pursue? Police interrogation was backward-looking, with the goal of solving a past crime. Military interrogation was forward-looking, with the goal of planning a future strategy. The two called for different approaches, and Fox felt he was being offered the opportunity either to find justice for Thom or thwart the next attack, but not both.

Fox sat back in the chair, closed his eyes, took a deep breath, and tried to clear his mind.

Robin, he thought he could hear a familiar voice say. *Don't worry about me. As hard as it may be to believe sometimes, we live in a moral universe. One way or another, justice will be served. Leave the affairs of the dead to the next world. Focus on protecting the living in this one.*

He opened his eyes and returned his attention to TJ.

"So what's next? A bomb in the National Cathedral?"

TJ shook his head. "The cathedrals can stay. There

are some brilliant works of architecture among them, it's just too bad that all that genius had to be forced to serve stupidity. One of these days, they can all be turned into museums, just like Auschwitz—to remind us of the evil we left behind."

"So how do you go about eradicating a virus of the mind? In the physical world, you do it by vaccination. But in this case..."

"The only vaccine against this virus is reason," TJ finished for him. "And they haven't yet found a way to put that into injectable form."

"So what does that leave you?"

"Fortunately, we found a cure that can transmit itself along the same vectors as the virus: through families and religious institutions. All we have to do is introduce it into the main viral reservoirs, and it will do the rest of the work for us."

"What do you mean by 'the main viral reservoirs'?"

He gave Fox a long look, with the hint of a smug smile. "That will be revealed if you look in the book that contains all revelations."

"Are you referring to the Bible?"

He nodded.

"Where?"

"Seek and ye shall find."

"Damn it, TJ, if you keep playing games with us..."

"I'm not playing games. There may be a clue in the Bible. If there is, I wasn't the one who put it there."

"Who was?"

He gave Fox a defiant look. "I—invoke—my—right—of—silence."

And no further questions got a reply from him.

"Very well," Fox finally said as he stood up to leave. "Oh, and that whole business about American Sharia State, or should I say ASS? I suppose you were trying to incite a wave of religious violence across the country? Set Christians against Muslims, hoping they would kill one another off and save you the trouble? Something like that?"

TJ kept silent, but his smirk returned.

"Well, I have just one thing to say to you," Fox went on. "You underestimated America."

"He said that there might be a clue in the Bible," Fox told Adler and Kato in the conference room.

Kato sighed. "The Bureau has been over that thing countless times. They've dusted it for fingerprints, looked at each page under ultraviolet light..."

"Has anyone actually tried reading it?"

She shrugged. "If you want to, go ahead. Let me know if, by some miracle, you find anything we missed."

"I will. And next time you're in touch with Scotland Yard, you might want to pass on the description we gave you of the suspect in Thom DiDio's murder. Something tells me they might have better luck with it than we did."

Kato brought an evidence bag, opened it, and took out the Bible. Fox signed the chain-of-custody form, put on the gloves she provided, and began to turn the pages, looking carefully at every line for anything out of the ordinary.

Genesis. The Creation. Adam and Eve. Cain and Abel. The Flood. The Tower of Babel. The calling of Abraham. Sodom and Gomorrah. Abraham and Isaac.

Esau and Jacob. Joseph and the misadventures that led him to Pharaoh's court, the story that Reverend Hill had chosen for his Palm Sunday sermon.

Exodus. The exile in Egypt. The birth of Moses. The burning bush. Moses before Pharaoh. The ten plagues.

And then, there it was.

A black dot, so small that it could easily be overlooked, or mistaken for a stray drop of printer's ink. It appeared under the number 4 that began the fourth verse of Exodus 13:

This day came ye out in the month of Abib.

9

WASHINGTON, D.C.
WEDNESDAY, APRIL 1

At first, America wondered aloud whether this was someone's idea of an April Fool's joke. But as the news outlets went on repeating the story of TJ's confession, the reality began to take hold on the national consciousness: as improbable as it sounded, it was true.

The atheist community braced for a backlash. Already, the owner of a car with a Flying Spaghetti Monster emblem had emerged from a Chevy Chase supermarket to find her windshield covered in tomato sauce. To forestall any worse, the Metro Police had shifted their round-the-clock watch to USAtheists' Washington headquarters. Demonstrators marched outside the building, waving placards with messages like BELIEVE IT OR NOT, YOU WILL BE JUDGED!

The president of USAtheists took his place in front of the cameras once again, looking markedly more subdued. "We unequivocally condemn those who hijacked the name of reason to commit this irrational act. By definition, no one who harms another human being can call himself a humanist. We mourn with our city, and our thoughts are with the victims and their families." Fox almost felt sorry for him, left without recourse even to the standard platitude of "...and prayers."

The group's website had a new page of tips to help its members survive the sudden turn of the tide. "Remove bumper stickers and other identifying insignia from cars. Dress inconspicuously; avoid any clothing with provocative slogans such as 'My Dinosaur Ate Your Jesus Fish.' Do not, under any circumstances, attempt to carry books by Christopher Hitchens or Sam Harris through airport security."

Fox switched off the news, went to campus, and muddled through his classes on autopilot, as a separate compartment in his mind constantly churned over the verse.

This day: The first day of Passover.

Came ye out: The Israelites emerging from their captivity in Egypt.

The whole first half of Exodus 13 dealt with the institution of the Passover tradition. If this was the meaning of the passage, they would have to work fast. Passover would begin at sundown on Friday.

But if that was the message, then why not start at the beginning of the passage? Why verse 4, in particular?

In the month of Abib.

When he finally had a free moment in his office, he looked up the Hebrew word *abib*. It referred to a stage in the growth of barley, when the seeds were fully grown but not yet dry. The time of year when it generally reached that stage, early spring, was the first month in the Jewish liturgical calendar. The King James Version transliterated it as *abib*, but more modern translations rendered it as *aviv*. It could also be used in a general sense for "springtime," and had that meaning in modern Hebrew, as in the city named "Spring Hill"—

Tel Aviv.

He grabbed his phone and called Adler.

"John, I think I've figured it out."

"Let me hear it."

"The passage is talking about the institution of Passover. And *abib*, in modern Hebrew, is *aviv*. I'm betting that the next attack is planned for the Passover holiday, in Tel Aviv."

There was a pause at the other end. "If you're right, that still covers a lot of ground. Do you have any more specific ideas about when and where?"

Fox was asking himself the same question. The seder, the Passover feast, was traditionally observed at home. There would be no large-scale event equivalent to the *Awaken America!* rally, with tens of thousands of believers packed into an enclosed space.

"I'm working on that. But in the meantime, you'll make sure the Israeli authorities are warned?"

"Of course."

"And as long as you've got them on the phone, could you give them a message from me?"

"What message?"

"If this intel proves actionable, they'll owe the States a big favor. And we've just found out—no thanks to the CIA, by the way—that Leila Halabi is being held in administrative detention at HaSharon Prison. The United States Peace Research Institute urgently requests her immediate release."

"I'll see what I can do."

"John, the last time you said that, the results didn't impress me much. I didn't ask you to see what you could do. I asked you to get her out of there."

Adler sighed into the receiver. "Robin, I only wish I had as much clout with Israeli intelligence as you seem to think I have. But I'll pass on your request."

"Thanks."

Fox disconnected him, and then dialed another number. There was someone else who needed to be warned.

He called Emily's cell phone. When it failed to ring, he called USPRI.

"Good afternoon, United States Peace Research Institute, how may I direct your call?"

"Hello, Rachel. This is Robin Fox."

"Oh, hi, Robin! How are you doing?"

"All right, and you?"

Then he bit his tongue, but too late. Those last two polite monosyllables had just slipped out, in violation of one of the cardinal commandments of USPRI: Thou shalt not give Rachel an opening if thou art in a hurry.

"Oh, man, you'd never believe what happened to me this morning! I was doing my yoga, and I was in the Pincha Mayurasana, the peacock pose, with my hands on the floor and my feet in the air, and this bee flies in through the window and gets right up my top! I panicked and fell out of the pose, and the little devil stung me! Right in the..."

"Ouch!" He had no need to know which part of Rachel's yoga-sculpted body the bee had selected as its target. "Are you all right?"

"Oh, yeah. I did Reiki on it, and after about fifteen minutes, the pain and swelling were completely gone. You know, you really ought to get yourself attuned. I'm always amazed at how well it works, like that time when..."

"Rachel, I'm sorry to cut you off, but I'm afraid this is urgent. Is Emily there, by any chance?"

"Emily? She's on her way to Israel."

The bottom fell out of Fox's stomach. "She's left already?"

"Yeah, she left early this morning. This close to Passover, the only itinerary we could get for her was a wicked long one via Montreal and Frankfurt. Twenty-five hours and three different airlines. Brutal. The only time I've seen worse was back when we needed to get Miriam to Amman and there were no flights through Europe because of the volcanic ash cloud from Iceland. Three days stuck at the airport, and she couldn't even claim her baggage!"

"Right, I remember that." Fox was trying to think of a strategy to get off the phone politely, but something brought him up short.

"What did you just say?"

"I said, she couldn't claim her baggage! She had to manage only with what was in her carry-on. Man, I'd go crazy! Can you imagine going three days without even being able to change your..."

"I wouldn't even want to try. Thanks, Rachel."

He hung up and called Adler back.

"Adler here."

"Ben-Gurion Airport."

There was a pause, followed by a scoff. "Are you kidding? No terror attempt against Ben-Gurion has ever succeeded. Security there is the tightest of any airport in the world. Their passenger screening makes TSA look like ushers in a church. And checked luggage has to go through X-ray machines, compression chambers..."

"I know," Fox interrupted him. "But all that is for outbound passengers. What about inbound?"

There was another pause, then: "How would you get a device like that onto an inbound flight? There's no way you could carry it through security, in just about any airport in the world these days. And if you tried to carry it in checked luggage, Israeli customs would catch it at the other end."

"Exactly. Which is why your best bet would be to activate the device after you claimed your checked luggage, but before you got to the customs inspector. In other words, the baggage claim area."

There was silence at Adler's end.

"Not as dramatic as the Twin Towers, maybe," Fox went on, "but it would get the job done. They would start at a small airport, where security screening for checked luggage isn't too tight. Then, once they got to Tel Aviv, they would activate the device and leave it there, in the one part of the airport where an unattended bag wouldn't draw immediate suspicion. An enclosed space, packed with tourists and pilgrims from all over the world. What better target?"

There was a long silence. Finally, Adler said, "You might be on to something. I'll update the Israelis. Oh, speaking of which, the Brits have given us a lead for Thom DiDio's killer."

"Yes?"

"Kenneth Oldman, better known as the 'Portsmouth Poisoner.' Everywhere he worked, his co-workers got sick with strange symptoms, sometimes fatally. Fifteen years in prison, intensive treatment at the psych rehab center in Grendon, and just released this year."

"I guess the treatment didn't work as well as they thought. Well, now that we have an idea who he is, do we have any more of an idea where he is?"

"Not yet, but I'll let you know as soon as I hear anything."

"Please."

After hanging up, he sent an e-mail to Emily, and called her husband's office.

"Hello, you've reached the office of Representative Frederick Paxton."

"This is Robin Fox from USPRI. I need to send an urgent message to the Congressman."

"I'm sorry, the Congressman is away on a congressional delegation until..."

"I know, but this is an emergency. His wife is in danger."

There was a pause at the other end. "Okay, sir, if you'll leave your name and number, I'll pass your message on to the Congressman."

Fox did as requested, feeling like a castaway rolling a message into a bottle and setting it adrift. He hung up, and took a deep cleansing breath in an unsuccessful attempt to slow the pounding of his heart.

Emily had been warned of the danger.

Assuming, of course, that she would have the chance to check e-mail before she landed in Tel Aviv.

Adler was going to notify Israeli intelligence. They would have everything under control.

She had a long flight, with two layovers. It would be theoretically possible to leave after her and still arrive before her.

And do what? He couldn't even be sure his hypothesis was correct.

He ran a search for flights from Washington to Tel Aviv. Purely for purposes of academic research.

His work was here, in Washington. He could serve her and everyone else best by staying and working with the HIG to uncover the rest of the network. To say nothing of his classes, for which his preparation had become increasingly slapdash since Adler came into his life.

The most direct flight would take off from Washington that evening, with one stop in Newark, and land in Tel Aviv thirteen hours later.

Without knowing exactly how it got there, he found the telephone receiver in his hand. He caught the fingers of the other hand in the act of dialing a number.

This was ridiculous.

"Good afternoon, thank you for calling Top Flight Travel. This is Jenny. How can I help you today?"

He heard a voice that sounded remarkably similar to his own, saying: "Hello, this is Robin Fox. I'm wondering if it's possible to make a last-minute booking for the United flight from Washington to Tel Aviv via Newark, leaving tonight." He glanced at his computer screen, and gave her the flight number.

What did he expect to do that the Israeli security forces couldn't? Who the hell did he think he was, a knight in shining armor riding off to rescue a damsel in distress?

"Please hold for a moment while I check availability."

It was two days before the start of Passover. If there were any vacant seats on any route to Israel at all, it would be a miracle. If there was one on this flight, it would be an unmistakable sign from the Universe that this was his divinely appointed mission.

"Thank you for waiting, Mr. Fox. I'm sorry, that flight is fully booked..."

There he had it. The Universe had spoken.

"...in economy class," she went on. "But there's been a cancellation in business class."

He looked at the fare listed on the screen and did some mental multiplication. Somehow he doubted that Adler would take it kindly if he sent him the bill.

He opened his mouth to say something like, "Okay, I knew it was a long shot, but thanks for checking anyway."

The words that actually came out were:

"I'd like to reserve it, please."

THE SECOND BOOK

10

TEL AVIV
THURSDAY, APRIL 2

The one time in Fox's life that he flew business class at his own expense, and he was utterly unable to enjoy it.

Smiling flight attendants served him grilled sea bass on a china plate, but with his stomach feeling as agitated as his mind, all he could do was hope the next patch of turbulence wouldn't propel the award-winning chefs' creations directly into an airsickness bag. He averted his eyes every time the sommeliers came by, not daring to risk being less than fully alert when he landed. He stretched out in his reclining seat and tried to sleep, and when that failed, he brought it upright again and tried to meditate. But he ended up spending most of the journey with his eyes on the flight map, watching the dashed line ahead give way to the solid line behind with agonizing slowness.

Finally, he began to feel the welcome sensation of descent, as the public address system broadcast the usual final-approach routine with an Israeli twist: return seat backs and tray tables to their upright and locked positions, make sure all window shades are raised, do not use cameras or binoculars in Israeli airspace.

As soon as he was off the plane, he charged ahead of the other disembarking passengers, swerved to avoid colliding with an old man in Orthodox garb who had stopped to plant a kiss on the *mezuzah* at the end of the jetway, and sprinted down the corridor to passport control. Having heard that Israeli airport staff are trained to look for any sign of agitation, he tried to keep his impatience from showing as the inspector pored over every page of his passport as if it were the latest bestseller, and her computer screen as if she intended to read all the customer reviews on Amazon.

"What is the purpose of your visit to Israel?" she finally asked him.

To save it from a bioterror attack, if you'll just let me through in time. "Sightseeing."

"Have you been to any Arab countries?"

As if no danger could possibly come from anywhere else. "Not lately."

After scrutinizing his passport a while longer, she slipped in a blue and white entry card. Apparently, enough visitors had asked for it, instead of the stamp that would render their passports invalid for travel in most of the Arab world, that it had become standard procedure. Fox grabbed his passport back and passed into the baggage claim area.

A huge banner greeted arrivals with "Welcome for Passover," in English and Hebrew. The strips of pinpoint lights over the luggage carousels, reflected in the mirror shine of the floors and ceilings, made them look like roulette wheels in a giants' casino. Appropriately, he thought, considering the gamble he was taking by coming here.

Spacious though it was, the hall was as much of a mob scene as any American airport on the eve of Thanksgiving or Christmas. The carousels were surrounded by jostling hordes of visitors from all over the world, with attire ranging from black suits and coats to tank tops and rainbow-colored tights, from fedoras and long sideburns to baseball caps and fluorescent orange headphones, from protruding prayer shawls to protruding boxer shorts. There was no shortage of pilgrims arriving for Holy Week, either: Italian priests, Korean nuns, Africans in tribal costumes, and Americans in black leather vests with patches reading "Bikers for the Lord." The air was filled with a Babel of languages. Fox heard Hebrew, Spanish, Russian, Tagalog, and English with accents ranging from Ireland to his Virginia home—nearly everything, in fact, with the conspicuous exception of Arabic.

Forget about needles and haystacks. Hay was stationary, and a needle would stand out in it. This would be more like searching a teeming hive of honeybees for a single intruding yellowjacket.

He made circuit after circuit of the carousels, shouldering his way through the crowd, occasionally muttering an "Excuse me" that went completely unheeded, and trying to look like any other passenger searching for his luggage, all the while scrutinizing the luggage of the other passengers as closely as he could.

Adler had told him that the airport would be under heightened security, but all he saw were a few guards in their blue uniforms with no visible weapons. He noted the tinted windows set high in the walls, and hoped there was more to the security apparatus here than met the eye.

During one of his circuits, he saw a backpack sitting unattended on one of the benches.

In one of the side pockets, it had a large water bottle in an insulating sleeve.

The cap on the drinking tube was hanging loose.

Fox ran up to the nearest guard, hoping that the information they had furnished to Israeli intelligence had made its way to him, and that he could understand English. Fox knew some biblical Hebrew, but that was no more likely to help him in Tel Aviv than classical Latin would be in Rome.

"Excuse me!" Fox said. "You may have been briefed that someone might be trying to smuggle in a biological weapon. I think that's it, there in that backpack!"

The guard gave him a stare, and then called to his companion. They exchanged a few words in Hebrew, and the other one spoke into his radio.

From some place of concealment somewhere, two police specialists in hazmat suits came running to the bench, carrying a transparent plastic bag with built-in gloves.

A woman ran in front of them and grabbed the

backpack off the bench. As she slung it over her shoulder, she let loose with a machine-gun volley of angry Hebrew first at the officers, and then at Fox. He was glad not to be able to understand the words, but still, her face and voice conveyed her meaning unmistakably.

As she stomped off, one of the guards gave Fox a glare, while two more shared a snicker at his expense. He hadn't even cleared customs yet, but he felt as though Israel had already declared him *persona non grata*.

Face flushing, he resumed his patrol, grateful that the throng of people would at least shield him from the guards' view.

A two-note chime sounded, followed by a recorded announcement in Hebrew and English: "Attention please. Carrying weapon is prohibited in all terminal hall. Thank you." Fox wondered that, for all the money the Israelis had poured into this airport, they couldn't have spent a little extra to have their grammar checked.

The screen above one of the carousels lit up with the number of a flight from Frankfurt. As Fox watched from a distance, he saw a fair-haired young woman fumbling with a duffel bag. She took out a sweatshirt and put it on, then suddenly clutched her abdomen with a grimace, zipped up the bag, and hurried off in the direction of the restroom.

It was well done. Any casual observer would think that she was suffering a sudden bout of traveler's diarrhea. And yet, there was something just slightly overdrawn about the performance. She would have been fine as a stage actress, but she would need to work on subtlety if she wanted to be an Oscar candidate.

He moved in for a closer look at the bag. The two

zipper tabs were linked with a padlock, and a plastic tube protruded from between the tabs.

Next to it, waiting for her bag to appear, stood a woman with long red hair.

"Emily!"

Fox ran toward her, but his path was blocked by a surge of tourists from Brazil, one of them holding a plumed hat that must be part of a samba costume. He tried to shoulder his way through them, but they filled the space between carousels completely.

Fox jumped onto the conveyor and clambered over the oncoming suitcases. "Emily!" he called again.

She looked up. "Robin! What are you doing here?"

He pointed at the bag on the floor next to her. "Move away from that! Quickly!"

Two guards converged on him. "Hey!" one of them shouted in English. "What do you think you're doing?"

Fox jumped off the carousel and pointed at the bag. "There's a suspicious object in there!"

These were different guards than the ones who had witnessed his false alarm, but apparently word traveled fast. The one he had spoken to turned to his colleague, with a shake of his head and a shrug of exasperation, and said something in Hebrew that included a word like *meshuga.*

"Look at it!" Fox urged. "Look at how the zipper is locked around the tube!"

Emily turned back. "He's telling the truth." She pointed to the woman who had left the bag, and was now almost at customs. "I saw her put something in and walk away, leaving it."

Fox whirled to face her. "Emily, for God's sakes,

run!"

They ran for the exit. One of the guards, with another shout, gave chase. The other spoke into his microphone, and to his relief, Fox saw the police specialists reappear in their protective gear. Apparently they had decided the threat was worth taking seriously after all.

The woman who had left the bag was on her way out into the arrivals hall. Fox and Emily charged through the green lane at customs, the guard still hard on their heels. "Nothing to declare!" Fox shouted over his shoulder to the inspectors.

They ran through the door into the arrivals hall. An elliptical ring of "Welcome" signs created a buffer zone, but beyond it was a crowd of greeters, eagerly anticipating the arrival of their loved ones. Among them, Fox saw a hand waving, and a familiar face looking anxiously in their direction: Miriam.

The woman slipped into the crowd, to reappear a moment later on the escalator up to the departure level.

In a moment, Fox understood. She had never intended to leave the airport. Her plan had been to fly in, drop her lethal cargo, and fly right out again. She would have anticipated that, with all the hordes passing through the baggage claim area, it would be hours before anyone discovered what she had done—and by that time, she would be in the air.

"Miriam!" Fox shouted, pointing. "The escalator!"

With no more prompting than that, she grasped the situation. She pushed her way to the escalator, and pressed the emergency stop button.

The elevator lurched to a stop. The suspect lost her balance for a moment, but then recovered and charged up the rest of the way. Leaving Emily with Miriam, Fox took the steps two at a time after her. The guard chasing him now had two more with him as reinforcements.

The suspect reached the top of the escalator, jumped aboard the next one, and ran until her path was blocked by an elderly tourist with his suitcase resting on the step next to him. She jerked the handle from his startled hands, and sent the suitcase tumbling down the escalator as she ran past him. Fox leapt over the obstacle and kept up the chase, the guards behind him doing the same.

The suspect stepped off the escalator on the departures level, and ran toward the giant silver menorah that marked the entrance to the gates. As she passed a bench where a passenger sat sipping a coffee, she snatched the paper cup out of the woman's hand and hurled it down onto the smooth, shining floor behind her, right at Fox's feet. Too late either to dodge or jump over it, he slipped and fell.

The guards caught up with him and seized his arms.

"American intelligence!" he shouted, craning his head in the woman's direction as the guards pulled him to his feet. "She's the one you want!"

Fox sat in a windowless interview room, facing a security agent across a table. *Someone wasn't paying attention in interrogation training*, he thought. *This table is blocking the interrogator's view of the subject's body, and giving the subject a barrier to hide behind. Amateurs.*

"Tell me," the agent said without preamble, "how did you know what was in that bag?"

Fox gave him the look he used on students who came to him with dubious excuses for missing exams. "Do you do interviews often?"

The agent glowered at him. "I'm the one asking the questions here!"

"Then do it right, can't you? You need to start with neutral control questions, build rapport with the subject, establish baseline, observe how he looks when he's relaxed and telling the truth. Otherwise, how could you pick up on changes in his behavior when he's lying? Come on, we did joint training exercises with Shin Bet and Mossad all the time. Didn't they teach you anything?"

The agent jumped up and pounded the table. "Who the hell do you think you are?"

"Robin Fox at your service. Former U.S. Army intelligence, now consultant to the CIA."

This threw the agent off balance. "And the woman who was with you?"

"Is from the office of a U.S. congressman." If Rick had an office in his house, then it was technically the truth.

"The woman you just apprehended," Fox went on before the agent could respond, "we have strong reason to believe, is a member of the same group that recently attempted a biological attack on American soil. She is a person of interest to the United States. I need to question her."

The agent regained his composure. "You're joking, right? I can't let you do that."

"Can't, as in you refuse? Or can't, as in you don't have the authority?"

The agent made no answer.

"Very well," Fox pressed on, "if you don't have the authority, I need to speak to someone who does. Like your superior, Avi Harel."

The agent blinked, undoubtedly wondering how Fox knew the name of the director of Shin Bet. "Any information you have, you can give me."

"This is a high-level investigation. How can we be sure that you have the proper security clearance? Anything further I say on this matter, I can only say directly to Mr. Harel."

The agent hesitated. "Wait here," he said gruffly, in a brave attempt to hold on to his authority. He left the room, and returned after a few minutes.

"Come with me."

To get to FBI headquarters, all Fox had to do was get off the Metro at the Federal Triangle stop, walk to the Hoover Building, push his way through a revolving door, and announce himself. Here, he and Emily were riding in a car with darkened windows to a building whose address was a closely guarded secret. Its agents scoured the Internet continually to detect and strike out anything on satellite maps that might give a clue to its location. And any pedestrian who happened to wander within a hundred yards of it would be accosted by the security forces.

They were given a thorough search and escorted to the office of the director of Shin Bet, Avi Harel. Fox's first impression was that, except for the shaven head, he looked like an Israeli John Adler: the same blazer, the same open-collared shirt under it, and the same pattern of lines around the eyes that had seen too much. Apparently, it was the uniform for senior intelligence agents all over the world.

"Well?" was his greeting. There were two chairs facing his desk, but he made no move to invite them to sit.

"You've heard from your field agents about the biological attack on Ben-Gurion Airport?" Fox asked him.

"Of course."

"Allow me to present," said Emily, "the man who stopped it."

It was kind of her to give him the credit, although not entirely accurate, since she had certainly done her share as well. But the important thing was that Harel had evidently decided they were worth a few minutes of his time, after all. He gestured to the seats facing his desk. They sat.

"My name is Robin Fox. I'm with the High-Value Detainee Interrogation Group, working with the FBI and the CIA to investigate the terrorist cell that your suspect belongs to."

"And I," Emily said, presenting another one of her husband's business cards, "am representing the office of U.S. congressman Frederick Paxton, a member of the House Committee on Foreign Affairs. You know—the one that decides how to allocate the foreign aid budget."

Their introductions might have been more impressive if they had had the chance to freshen up and change into more professional clothes, rather than having to make their case in the unkempt, bleary-eyed condition of travelers just off a transatlantic flight. Still, their words had the desired effect. Now they had his attention.

"We've been questioning one of her accomplices," Fox continued, "and we have some information you might be interested in. There's a strong possibility that the next strike may be somewhere in Israel or the occupied territories."

On the last word, Harel's shoulder rose as the corners of his mouth turned down. Fox pressed on. "Come on, are you really going to sit there and act like that doesn't concern you? You're too good an intelligence officer for that. If there's an outbreak of Zagorsk in the territories, you couldn't build a wall high enough to keep it out of Israel. One soldier, one tourist, one kid in a settlement slipping out on a lark...that's all it would take."

"What can you tell me?"

"First things first. There are two small requests I would like to make. One, I need to have a shot at interrogating the prisoner myself."

"You want *I* should let *you* question *my* prisoner?"

"Yes, please. And second, I would like to inquire into the case of Leila Halabi. I believe my colleague, John Adler, has already been in touch with you about her."

Harel gave him a look that, if put into words, would have begun with "What the..." and ended with "...are you talking about?"

Fox saw no sign of deception in his expression. Of course, it was highly probable that the director of one of the world's premier intelligence agencies was a consummate liar. But it was at least equally likely that a certain member of another such agency, in his own country, had been less than forthcoming with him.

Emily stepped in. "The United States Peace Research

Institute, of which my hu—" she covered her slip with a cough, "—my boss is a leading supporter, has invited her to Washington for a symposium. She was apprehended at the Rachel's Tomb checkpoint one week ago, on the twenty-sixth of March, and is now being held in administrative detention at HaSharon prison."

"I have no knowledge of that."

"Does that mean whoever arrested her was not acting on your orders?" Fox asked.

"Do you have any idea how many detainees we process each day? Do you think I review each case personally?"

"This one happens to be an internationally famous educator and writer. Are you telling me no one so much as dashed off a memo to you?"

"Whether they did or not, this is an internal matter within the State of Israel."

"So you say. But when an American research institute arranges a public event, and one of our speakers disappears into Israeli detention, it becomes an internal matter within the United States of America."

"If she doesn't make it to Washington for the start of the symposium," Emily added, "of course we'll have to explain why, in front of all the television cameras. It'll be just like the time when they had to give the Nobel Peace Prize to an empty chair because China chose to lock up the laureate. Is that really the kind of publicity you want for Israel?"

"Or, alternatively," Fox concluded, "Leila Halabi could mysteriously reappear the same way she mysteriously disappeared, and we could take her to America as though nothing had ever happened.

Whichever sounds like less trouble for you."

Harel glared fiercely from one to the other, but it looked suspiciously like the glare of a cornered man. Fox returned his gaze, keeping his face neutral with a tremendous effort. Here was the head of Shin Bet, at whose name all Israel quaked, and yet it looked as though he and Emily together had succeeded in intimidating him.

"Our agents will decide," he said at last, "whether she knows anything of any value."

She most certainly does, Fox thought, *but you and she would probably define "value" quite differently.* Aloud he said, "And if she doesn't?"

"She will be allowed to return home."

"Home? Home is Bethlehem. On the opposite side of the separation barrier. Through which all points of access are locked down during Passover, correct?"

"Your point being?"

"If she has to make the trek from Bethlehem to Amman from square one, without her American escort this time, what's to prevent some overzealous kid in a uniform from apprehending her and starting this whole ordeal all over again?"

Harel made an impatient gesture. "What would you have me do?"

"Release her to us. Let us help her get her visa from the American embassy in Tel Aviv, and fly her out of Ben-Gurion."

Harel shook his head. "That's not going to happen."

"Very well, then." Fox stood up. "Good luck with your suspect. Oh, and just so you know, it took a top FBI-CIA interrogation team ten days to break her accomplice.

Considering that Passover and the Easter Triduum both begin tomorrow, I hope your agents can work faster than that."

He headed for the door. Emily rose to follow him.

Three, two, one.

"Wait," said Harel's voice behind him.

The driver dropped Emily off at the hotel before taking Fox on to parts unknown. When the car finally stopped, he emerged into the Mediterranean sunlight, squinting and blinking after so long in the darkened car. It was a few moments before he could open his eyes wide enough to see a tall, sprawling building made of pink stone. The roar of a jet flying low overhead informed him that he was near the airport again.

He passed through security at the visitors' entrance. When he presented his letter of introduction from Harel, a guard showed him the subject's Israeli passport. Name: Shira Yavin. Place of birth: Ariel. The entry and exit stamps showed that she had spent three weeks in Spain, then another three on a whirlwind tour of Europe and North America, and returned to Israel before leaving for Great Britain on a student visa a year later.

He took a seat facing a plate-glass window, and waited until a guard brought the woman from the airport. When she saw Fox, she tried to turn back, but the guard pushed her into the chair. Fox picked up the telephone receiver on his side of the window. The woman made no move to pick up hers, until the guard picked it up for her and put it into her hand. She held it to her ear and looked at Fox with a contemptuous gaze. Conducting an interrogation under these conditions was far from ideal, but he would have to take whatever he could get.

"Miss Yavin," Fox began. "May I call you Shira?"

She made no reply.

"You look exactly as TJ said you would. His description was very accurate. He even hinted that he might find you attractive, if he was inclined that way."

He was improvising. If he could lead her to believe that TJ had given up more than he really had, she might decide it was pointless to keep resisting. She looked surprised at his words, but kept her silence.

"I see you're going to give me the silent treatment," he said. "And you'll do a really good job of it, if you're as well trained as TJ was. He held out for ten days before we finally broke him. But break him we did. Now, my government is interested in you, because the first of your group's little stunts was on American soil. If you cooperate with me, then I might, just might, be able to get my superiors to persuade Shin Bet that you should be turned over to us."

She remained silent.

"You know, I used to be in American military intelligence," he continued. "Our Rules of Engagement listed twenty-four approved interrogation techniques. Now, this may be just a rumor, but I heard that the Israeli field manual has over a hundred. I'm curious how many of them they'll try on one of their own who turned against them."

She kept silent, but the expression on her face was not the stony defiance that TJ had always shown. It was the look of sad resignation that Fox had seen on the faces of too many detainees in Iraq as they were marched aboard the helicopter bound for Abu Ghraib. It was the look of someone who had already given up on life.

The horrible thought struck him that rather than face interrogation by Shin Bet, she might be planning to commit suicide.

He leaned forward. "Shira," he said in as gentle a voice as he could, "there could be a way out of this for you. I'll do all I can to help you, but I can't give you anything if you don't give me anything."

She kept her silence.

"Well, I tried," he said. "Here's a tip. If you ask them where they've taken you, and they give you some smartass answer like 'a submarine' or 'the moon,' you'll know you're in Unit 1391."

That number had the same significance for Israelis as the name "Guantanamo" had for Americans. It referred to a top-secret detention and interrogation facility, where prisoners were kept in deep isolation until they could scarcely remember that there was a world outside the prison, or any other human beings alive besides the guards.

He slowly pulled the receiver away from his ear and moved it toward its cradle, to give her plenty of time to make a last-minute statement.

She hung up.

When he left the facility, the car that had brought him there was long gone. He had to ask one of the guards to call him a taxi.

"Hotel Vista del Mar. HaYarkon Street, Tel Aviv."

As they set off, he called Emily, hoping she was

in a place where she would have reception. When she answered, Fox heard such a cacophony of shouting in the background that he could barely make out her "Hello?"

"Emily? Can you hear me?"

There was a pause. "Robin?"

"Where are you?"

"At the prison. There's a demonstration going on. Where are you?"

"On my way to Tel Aviv. I just finished up at the detention center. How's the situation?"

"Getting tense."

"Where's the prison?"

"It's right by Hadarim Interchange. But..."

"I'll be there as soon as I can."

"Robin..."

"Just tell me how I can find you."

A pause. "We're near the front of the crowd. We're in uniform."

Fox slapped his forehead. "Damn it! I didn't think to bring mine."

"That's okay. We could use someone on arrest support."

When USPRI staff were present at demonstrations or other times of tension, they wore a light blue T-shirt and matching cap, each prominently bearing the USPRI insignia: a fusion of an American flag and a dove carrying an olive branch. This identified them clearly as international observers, and usually protected them from being swept up in mass arrests. Just in case, though, one member of the team would be assigned to "arrest support," with the duty of standing apart from the others, blending in to the crowd, and being ready to contact the embassy and USPRI headquarters in case all the other members were arrested.

"No way! Do you think I came all this way just so that I could hang back and let you and Miriam risk arrest? If they take only one of us, it should be me."

"Well, I don't think my T-shirt would fit you. And the shirt I last saw on you would look strange on me, and smell even stranger."

"Emily..."

"We can work out the details when you arrive."

Fox hung up and addressed the driver. "Change of plans. HaSharon Prison, Hadarim Interchange."

The driver gave him a bewildered look in his mirror. "Are you on some kind of prison tour of Israel, or what?"

"Just drive."

When the driver turned off Route 4 at the Hadarim Interchange, the first signpost Fox saw pointed the way to the prison, as though that were the most likely destination for any visitor to Hof HaSharon. Out of the pastoral landscape of olive and orange groves rose cell blocks surrounded by watchtowers, and high fences topped with concertina wire. In front of the gate, he saw a crowd of demonstrators waving Palestinian flags, larger-than-life pictures of Leila's smiling face, and placards with slogans in Arabic and English: FREE LEILA HALABI! ADMINISTRATIVE DETENTION IS A CRIME! TEACH PEACE, GO TO PRISON?

He shouldered his way through the crowd, scanning the signs of the various groups present—International Solidarity Movement, B'Tselem, Physicians for Human Rights—until he reached the line of barricades separating the demonstrators from a row of soldiers. There, he saw two figures in USPRI kit, and a man in a yarmulke with a graying brown beard, whom he recognized from photographs.

"Emily! Miriam!" Fox ran to join them, and held out his hand to the man standing with them. "You must be Rabbi Sternberg. Good to meet you at last."

"Thanks for coming," said Miriam.

"Hey, did you think I'd come this far and miss out on the action?"

"You may be getting more of it than you bargained for," said the rabbi, directing a wary glance at the barricades.

A young Palestinian was leaning over a barricade, shouting in Arabic. The soldier on the other side held a weapon with an exceptionally wide barrel, presumably for baton rounds, tear gas canisters, or whatever type of "less-than-lethal" ammunition he was carrying in the bandolier around his midriff that made him look like a suicide bomber in uniform.

Fox was able to catch some of what the demonstrator was saying: "This is your democracy? You're sending schoolteachers to prison now?"

The soldier's disdainful expression showed no change in response to the words. Fox doubted that he understood Arabic well enough to follow them. But as soon as the Palestinian paused for breath, the soldier took the opportunity to use the few words of Arabic he did know: "*Emshi! Ibn sharmuta!*"—roughly, "Get lost, you son of a whore!"

The Palestinian's shocked look soon gave way to rage. He took a step back, and his eyes shot fire at the soldier as he reached down to pick up a rock.

The soldier raised his weapon and aimed it at the young man's face. At this range, "less-than-lethal" was meaningless. Anything fired from it at the Palestinian's head could very easily kill him.

Miriam, Emily, and Rabbi Sternberg sprang into action like well-drilled soldiers. Miriam and the rabbi stepped into the line of fire and stood back to back, Miriam facing the demonstrator, and the rabbi facing the soldier. Emily stood off and raised her hand-held video camera. One of the other soldiers stretched his hand across the barricade, trying to cover the lens, but she stepped out of his reach.

Another Palestinian grabbed the arm holding the rock. "*Walla hajar!*" he shouted. "Not one stone!"

The soldier, meanwhile, unleashed a torrent of vitriolic Hebrew on the rabbi. He listened in silence, looking like a long-suffering parent enduring yet another tirade from his wayward son.

Emily kept her video camera trained on them, and Fox snapped pictures with his cell phone. Finally, an older man in uniform approached the soldier from behind, laid a hand on his shoulder, and spoke a few words in a quiet but authoritative voice. He had three bars on his epaulet, which Fox surmised made him an officer of fairly high rank.

The soldier slowly lowered his weapon, his eyes still live coals. As the officer went on his way, the soldier unleashed one more verbal volley.

The rabbi said a few words in reply. The soldier's face contorted, and he spat on the ground between them, but he did not raise his weapon again. Miriam and the rabbi cautiously stood down.

"What was that about?" Fox asked Miriam.

"The soldier was saying, 'How could you take the side of Palestinians against fellow Israelis? You call yourself a rabbi?' And the rabbi said, 'Do not neglect to show kindness to the aliens among you. Love them as you love yourselves, because you were once aliens in Egypt.' It seems the soldier didn't take too kindly to the Torah lesson."

The Palestinian demonstrator had backed off, but his eyes still shot poison darts at the soldier. He raised his hands, with the five fingertips of his right hand holding the tip of his left index finger, a gesture that meant "You have five fathers."

The soldier evidently understood. He raised his weapon and aimed it at the Palestinian's head.

The sudden motion caught the rabbi's eye. He jumped back into position between the two, at the very instant the soldier pulled the trigger.

A black canister flew out of the barrel, trailing a white cloud behind it, and struck the rabbi in the head. He fell to the ground.

"Rabbi!" cried Miriam and Emily in unison.

For a moment, everything froze. Then, with an eruption of shouting, the crowd surged forward. With a noise like a fireworks display, more of the soldiers discharged their weapons. More canisters flew through the air, low enough that the demonstrators had to duck to avoid meeting the same fate as the rabbi. Clouds of white billowed from the places where they landed.

Fox's eyes stung, his throat constricted, and he felt a wave of nausea. For the first time that day, he was glad to have had so little to eat, since it meant there was nothing in his stomach to lose.

Emily handed him a bandanna and a can of body spray. Tear gas was designed to send the respiratory system into drowning mode, and any pungent, familiar smell—perfume, vinegar, onions—helped remind it that it could still breathe. Fox applied some spray to the bandanna and held it gently to the rabbi's nose and mouth, thinking in passing what a lucky man he was to be protected by a concentrated dose of the most agreeable smell in the world: the scent of Emily.

Behind the barriers, the officer turned back to the soldier who had discharged his weapon, and let loose another verbal barrage on him. The words were incomprehensible to Fox, but the language of military officers berating their subordinates had a certain universality.

An Arab doctor from the Physicians for Human Rights contingent rushed over to the rabbi, shone a penlight into his eyes, and called to his companions in Arabic. He turned to the Americans and switched to English: "He may have a fractured skull. We need to get him to a hospital."

Two others came running with a stretcher, hoisted the rabbi onto it, and carried him to a waiting ambulance. Robin, Emily, and Miriam squeezed in around the technicians.

There was silence as they sped down the road. Miriam broke it by saying, "Emily, tell me you got that on video."

Emily shook her head sadly. "It caught me by surprise. My camera was already off."

"*Gevalt*! Well, at least we have the story, and the

photographs. And before the day is over, we'll make sure that they get to the BBC, CNN, ABC, CBS, NBC—the whole damn alphabet!"

The ambulance took them to the Meir Medical Center in Kfar Saba. As the doctor helped the hospital staff move the rabbi into the emergency room, Fox, Emily and Miriam took their seats in a white-walled corridor with a green-tiled floor. The name "The Green Mile" floated into Fox's mind, and he quickly pushed it away.

In his heart, he prayed silently to the Great Unknowable. Emily chanted Psalm 103: "Bless the Lord, O my soul, who heals all your infirmities and redeems your life from the grave." Miriam recited the Jewish prayer for the sick: "*Mi shebeirach avoteinu v'imoteinu, Avraham, Yitzchak v'Yaakov, Sarah, Rivkah, Rachel v'Leiah, hu y'vareich et Avshalom ben...ben...*"

Finally, the attending physician appeared. His white coat was thrown, unbuttoned, over a T-shirt and jeans, as if it were a troublesome formality. He took a look at the waiting visitors, and addressed them in English.

"He'll be all right. He suffered a concussion, but no fracturing of the skull. We'll want to keep him under observation for a day or two, but if there are no complications, we can send him home and expect a full recovery."

"Can we see him?"

The doctor escorted them to the recovery room, where the rabbi was waiting with the Arab doctor who had brought them. His eyes could focus on them this time, and he even managed a smile.

Miriam knelt by his bed and took his hand. "Rabbi! How are you feeling?"

"I've had worse," he said. "But here's the awkward part: I was going to invite you all to come and celebrate Passover with us tomorrow evening, but it's looking as though they won't let me go by then. So, I know it's not exactly ideal for your first Passover seder in Israel, but I would be honored if you would join me in a celebration here."

Miriam glanced at Robin and Emily. Receiving approving nods from them, she turned back to the rabbi and replied: "The honor would be ours."

The rabbi shifted his gaze to the Arab doctor who had brought him. "Thank you."

The doctor replied with a smile. "Think nothing of it, Rabbi. We were only following your teaching."

"My teaching?"

" 'Do not neglect to show kindness to the aliens among you.' "

11

TEL AVIV—KFAR SABA
FRIDAY, APRIL 3
GOOD FRIDAY / PASSOVER EVE

The name of the Hotel Vista del Mar was not exactly a lie, but "Vista del Muddy Hole in the Ground Surrounded by Corrugated Iron" would have been equidistant from the truth. Not only this hotel, but nearly every other building in the neighborhood of the embassy seemed to be either falling into ruin or under construction. The pounding of jackhammers drowned out the sound of the sea, and the sandy, uneven streets were strewn with litter and ads for services of the kind that gave Tel Aviv its name of "Israel's Sin City." Putting as charitable a gloss on his first impression as he could, Fox supposed that the neighborhood was in transition from being an old, run-down beach resort to a newly renovated beach resort, and they had simply caught it at an awkward moment.

For all his exhaustion, sleep had been slow in coming. When it finally did, it was of the shallow kind, full of troubling dreams. He dreamed he was wandering through a huge building—possibly a museum that had once been a monastery—where galleries, corridors and colonnades led one into another in an endless labyrinthine progression. Whichever room he entered, he could hear TJ's voice coming indistinctly from the next one over. Hundreds of people were milling around, blithely admiring the works of art. He wanted to warn them, to shout that they were all in danger, but no sound would come from his mouth. He knew that if he could only catch TJ, the danger would be averted, but although he could always hear the voice from just out of sight, he could never find him. And as he ran from room to room, he always felt a dark presence following behind him.

When he woke, he felt scarcely more refreshed than when he had stepped off the plane.

He went down for breakfast to see three already at the table: Emily, Miriam, and a woman in an abaya and purple headscarf, whom he had only seen in photographs.

"Morning, Robin," said a beaming Emily. "I'd like you to meet Leila Halabi."

The variety of breads, cheeses, dips, and salads at the breakfast buffet was enticing, but Fox's appetite diminished rapidly as he listened to Leila's account of her time in prison, while Enya played surreally in the background. His stomach progressively tightened as she told of sleep deprivation, hours of interrogation, endless demands to give the names of her nearest and dearest, and constant fear of what would happen to them if she did—in other words, the same routine he knew very well from the opposing side.

It was a relief when her tale wound down and he could shift the subject slightly. "How on earth did Shin Bet come to see you as a person of interest, anyway?"

"For trafficking in a controlled substance, Mr. Fox—one called stories. We've always believed that for every story heard, an act of violence is prevented. That's why we make the Israelis nervous. If their monopoly on stories were ever broken—if the market were suddenly flooded with alternatives to the generic 'all Palestinians are potential terrorists, all Israelis are brutal oppressors'—then we might actually start seeing one another as human beings, and of course, that would be a mortal threat to state security. They're so terrified of stories that they built a seven-hundred-kilometer wall to keep them out."

Fox nodded. "You know something, Leila?" he said. "I'm starting to think that one of you is worth a hundred U.N. resolutions."

After breakfast, as they made their way back through the lobby, the young Russian woman at the reception desk called out, "Mr. Fox?"

Fox turned. "Yes?"

"Someone left this for you." She hoisted a department-store shopping bag onto the counter.

Fox turned to Miriam. "Who knew we were staying here?"

"Only Rabbi Sternberg."

He looked back at the receptionist. "Who left this?"

"He didn't leave his name."

"Can you describe him?"

She shrugged, as though recalling such details were not part of her job description. "Tall. Dark hair."

"Eyes?"

"Couldn't tell. He was wearing sunglasses."

Fox peered into the shopping bag. On the bottom, resting in the upturned lid of a cookie tin, was a Bible.

He cautiously picked it up and gave the sticky faux leather cover a gentle flex. It bent normally, with no sign that anything was concealed inside.

Unconsciously holding his breath, he carefully opened it to the page marked by a ribbon. One of the verses was highlighted. Luke 13:32: *Go and tell that fox that I will keep on healing people and casting out demons today and tomorrow, and on the third day, I will reach my goal.*

With trembling hands, he closed the Bible and put it back in the bag.

"I think we'll be checking out today," he said.

They hurried upstairs to pack, Fox asking himself over and over how their adversaries had managed to track them down. Perhaps Shira would be able to give him a clue, if he could make any headway with her today.

He paused in front of his door. "Would either of you happen to have some mints?" he asked. "I have to do an interrogation today, and I wasn't expecting so much garlic in the hummus."

Emily and Miriam exchanged a puzzled glance. "Garlic?"

"I didn't taste it at the time either, but it left a wicked aftertaste, don't you find?"

"I'll see if I have some," Emily said, with one more questioning look at him.

Fox opened the door and went straight into the bathroom to wash off the residue the book cover had left on his fingers. When he finished and straightened up, he felt a slight vertigo. He waited for it to pass, but the bathroom spun faster around him, until he had to grip the sink to steady himself. He gasped for breath and his heart pumped overtime, as though he had stepped through a magical door and suddenly found himself on a high Himalayan peak. He caught a glimpse of himself in the mirror, and his face was as red as blood.

"Emily!"

As soon as her name was out of his mouth, he collapsed to the tiled floor and lay there, convulsing.

"The Portsmouth Poisoner." That was the name the media had given him. It was fortunate that he had conducted his experiments there rather than in his little hometown of Pease Pottage, even though that would certainly have been more alliterative.

The last fifteen years, however, he had spent in neither of those places, but in the Winchester prison. He held no grudge against the Government for it. In fact, he had treasured the long, solitary hours of reading about his favorite subjects: medicine, chemistry, and toxicology. He would have been perfectly content there, except for the constant barrage of interruptions that Her Majesty's Prison Service called, with no apparent irony, "Purposeful Activity." This usually meant either hours of mindless drudgery, or tedious interviews with psychologists engaged in a futile attempt to analyze his actions. He explained to them patiently: "Looking for behavioral patterns and motivation can be useful, but only on the condition that you are cleverer than the subject of your experiment. I'm sure you can probably say that about a rat or a guinea pig, but there aren't many human beings in this world who can say it about me."

Even worse were the religious types, smug and condescending as if their visits were somehow doing the inmates a favor, who droned on endlessly about repentance and redemption. His standard response to such as those was, "Do you visit laboratories as well as prisons? Preach repentance to scientists, for the sin of experimenting on lesser animals?" He rarely saw the same visitor more than once.

The only moderately interesting one had been an earnest young lady from Oxford, who came with a sack full of books about atheism and freethought. "We know that prisons are among the most religious places on earth," she had said, "and we understand how people with a different worldview can feel isolated. And we believe wholeheartedly that faith in any kind of God is not required in order to become a good and productive member of society."

She was different, certainly, but he had been unable to resist having a little fun with her too. "If you define God as the supreme intellect, with the power to decide when and in what manner any living thing will die, how can you be sure He doesn't exist? How can you be sure that you aren't in His presence right now?"

As he expected, he never saw her again either. But to his surprise, a new visitor came in her place soon afterwards: a man closer to his own age. Unlike the proselytizers, he hadn't come with a sales pitch prepared. All he did was listen attentively. And unlike the psychologists, his reply showed that he actually understood.

"You and I both know," the man had said, "there are only two sorts of people in the world. Those who have a contribution to make to civilization, and those who don't. Those who advance the evolution of the species, and those who hold it back. There are billions of people on this planet who are infected with a virus that renders them incapable of rational thought. The only chance they have of contributing anything to the store of human knowledge is as subjects for your experiments."

Until that meeting, part of him had been dreading the end of his prison term and the beginning of what was sure to be a long and laborious search for a job that would both pay the rent and give him access to the chemicals he needed. But now, all of a sudden, this stranger was offering him the opportunity to travel first-class around the world, and experiment to his heart's content.

He applied for a transfer to Grendon, which the Government, again with a straight face, called a "therapeutic community." He said all the right things to the neophyte psychologist working his case, and within a year, he was out and ready for his mission.

First to America, to deal with a traitor to the cause. He had never imagined trying to seduce another man, but with his good looks and affable manner, he had generally been able to make anyone believe anything—a trait indispensable for finding unwitting subjects for his experiments.

And now to Israel. "Make sure my agent carries out her mission without any interference," had been his instructions. But he had watched helplessly at the Tel Aviv airport as some unknown American threw a spanner into the works. He had dreaded having to report his failure, but the reply had contained only a new mission: "Follow him, and at the first opportunity, remove him."

At first, he was afraid he had failed in that mission too. Once the American was apprehended by the Israeli police, he lost the trail. But there had been two young women with him, and it was a simple matter to follow them to his target.

All it required was patience. And fifteen years in prison had given him nothing if not that.

"Robin, are you awake?"

Fox stirred. "Emily?"

"It's me. Miriam."

"I'm awake."

He opened his eyes. He was lying in a hospital bed, with an oxygen tube under his nose and an IV drip in his arm.

"Where am I? Where's Emily?"

"You're in Ichilov Hospital. She's gone to the embassy with Leila. She wanted to be the one to stay here with you, but I vetoed that. I'm the one to get things done around here. She doesn't speak Hebrew or meet the chutzpah requirement. They'll be back as soon as their

166 | Charles Kowalski

business is taken care of."

Fox tried to sit up, but Miriam's hand met his chest and pushed him back into his pillow. "Relax," she ordered in a tone of voice that made him want to do precisely the opposite. "You're lucky to be alive."

"What happened?"

"The doctors said it was cyanide poisoning."

He struggled to recall his last few minutes of consciousness. "Did anyone else touch the Bible?"

She shook her head. "No. We're all OK."

"Where is it?"

"The police took it, of course, for forensic analysis."

"I need to have a look at it."

"Are you crazy? The book that almost killed you?"

"We were able to stop this attack because of a clue in the Bible in Thom DiDio's hotel room. If they're following the same pattern, the Bible they left for me might contain the only clue that will help us stop the next one."

"Did you not hear what I said? It's in evidence now. No one is touching it except the Israeli CSI's."

"Someone needs to go through it and look for any verse that's been marked in any way. Not the highlighted one, something more subtle, like a pencil mark under a verse number. If we waited until the forensics techs had time to spare for it, it would take days, and we don't have days. If there's anything in there, I need to find it today. I only get one more crack at the subject, and I need any little bit of leverage I can get before I go in."

"You aren't going anywhere."

"What?" Again, he tried to sit up, and met the opposing force of Miriam's hand.

"They said you need to be kept under observation for at least twenty-four hours."

"We don't have twenty-four hours! You saw what was in the Bible. 'Today and tomorrow, and on the third day, I will reach my goal.' I need to get out of here and into that booth."

Miriam rolled her eyes and exhaled sharply through her nostrils. "Any other miracles you'd like me to perform? I should maybe drop by the Prime Minister's office while I'm at it? See if I can broker a two-state solution before lunch?"

"Just look at it as a test to see whether you meet the chutzpah requirement."

Fox lay in his bed, watching the clock in an increasing state of panic. Every tick meant one second closer to the next attack, and one more second's head start that their adversaries had over them.

A male nurse came in, his white uniform tightly buttoned unlike the doctor's coat at the Kfar Saba hospital. His hair was cropped short enough to make Fox wonder whether he had recently been discharged from the military medical corps.

"How are you feeling, Mr. Fox?" he asked. His accent sounded British, perhaps from somewhere in South Central England.

"Better. Still light-headed."

"Headache?"

"A little." Fox paused. "Listen. I need to be discharged today. It's a matter of national—of *international*..."

"You'll have to take that up with the attending

physician," the nurse interrupted. "I'm just here to give you your medicine." He began preparing a hypodermic syringe.

"Is that an Estuary accent I hear?"

The nurse gave him an approving look. "Good ear."

"When did you—what do you call it—do aliyah?"

The nurse paused. "Oh, a while ago."

He hadn't corrected Fox's "do" to "make." And the answer he gave was vague enough to make Fox wonder whether he really understood that he was being asked when he had naturalized in Israel.

As he took hold of the IV bag and prepared to inject, Fox said: "Before you do that, just one more question?"

"Yes?"

"What did you use on Thom DiDio?"

The putative nurse froze, then ran for the doorway— just as Emily and Leila were coming in. It was on the tip of Fox's tongue to shout, "Stop him!" But he still had the loaded syringe in his hand, and even a slight scratch might be enough for whatever poison was inside to do its work. Fox's protective instincts won out, and he shouted instead: "Look out!"

The two of them backed away from the doorway as the poisoner ran out and disappeared down the corridor.

Emily and Leila were allowed to stay, at Fox's insistence, but the hospital placed a guard outside the door. By that time, however, all it accomplished was to give a frustrated Miriam yet another opportunity to ply her skills at arguing with Israeli security.

"You owe me dinner when we get back to

Washington," she told Fox once she was inside. "I'm
thinking Circa at Foggy Bottom. With a bottle of wine.
Make that two bottles. I don't like to drink alone."

"I take it you passed the test."

"The report from forensics says that the cover of the
Bible was coated with a solution of cyanide in dimethyl
sulfoxide. A mixture that lab techs apparently call 'liquid
death.' The DMSO, they say, explains how it could be
absorbed through your skin so quickly, and also the
garlicky taste in your mouth."

"Any markings in the pages?"

Miriam heaved a theatrical sigh. "Oh, that was the
fun part. It took me forever to persuade them to let me
have a look, and when I finally did, it had to be with a
technician watching and trying to chat me up. I'm sorry
if I didn't spend as much time or look as closely as you
might have. But I found three verses that looked as if
they might have been marked. Or it might just have
been stray marks on the paper, I couldn't tell. Anyway,
here goes." She took out a piece of paper and read from
it. "Proverbs 21:9. 'Better to live on a corner of the roof
than share a house with a quarrelsome wife.'"

The other three exchanged glances of mild
amusement. "I don't think so," Fox said. "That sounds
like either a stray mark or an indication that our boy
needs a good marriage counselor."

Miriam read the next one. "Luke 12:49. 'I have come
to bring fire on the earth, and how I wish it were already
burning.'"

There was silence as they processed this. "What's the
last one?" Fox asked.

"Romans 6:4. 'Therefore we are buried with him

through baptism into death: that like as Christ was raised up from the dead by the glory of the Father, even so we also should walk in newness of life.'"

"Baptism," Fox echoed pensively.

"The site of Jesus' baptism is in the West Bank," Miriam said.

"Or the East, if you ask the Jordanians," Fox countered. "And neither of them feels like a likely target. You would want a high concentration of people, preferably indoors. TJ talked about 'the main reservoirs.'"

"Mr. Fox?" Leila said. "Look at the rest of the verse: 'We are buried with him.'"

Emily looked at Fox. "Death and resurrection."

"The Church of the Holy Sepulchre," all four of them said in unison.

As soon as the name was spoken out loud, it seemed blindingly obvious. On the Saturday before Easter, the church would see thousands of visitors throughout the day, as Catholics, Protestants, and Orthodox Christians took turns holding their services there. The miracle of the Easter Fire—in which the Orthodox prelate carried an unlit torch into Jesus' tomb, where it would supposedly be lit with miraculous flame—drew thousands of pilgrims from around the world. And if it became the site of the next attack, all of them would unwittingly take the Zagorsk virus back to their home countries and spread it among their families and church members. It would make the Washington attack look like a practice run.

As soon as Miriam performed her miracle and secured

his release, Fox caught a taxi back to the detention facility at the airport. His arrival caused some consternation among the guards, who clearly had not been expecting to see him again. He waited as they reread his letter of introduction from Harel, argued among themselves, and made telephone calls. Finally, a sullen guard appeared and escorted him back to the visiting booths, where he waited until a guard on the other side brought Shira. Again, she recoiled when she saw him, but at the guard's insistence, sat down and picked up her receiver with a defiant expression.

"Did you sleep all right last night?" Fox asked her.

She made no reply.

"So how many of their tricks have they tried on you so far?"

She said nothing, but her eyes suggested that sleep deprivation had probably been one of them.

"Tell me, Shira, do you ever read the Bible?"

Silence.

"Maybe you'll recognize this verse: 'Therefore we are buried with him through baptism into death: that like as Christ was raised up from the dead by the glory of the Father, even so we also should walk in newness of life.'"

She gave no response.

"You've made it clear that you aren't going to come right out and tell me when and where your group is going to strike next. But do I get three guesses?"

Silence.

"The time, I would say, is probably Easter Sunday. As to the place...well, since your group is from Britain, I'm thinking maybe Canterbury Cathedral?"

No reaction.

"Well, I was just warming up with that one. How about the site of Jesus' baptism, on the Jordan River?"

No reaction.

"Okay, one more guess. The Church of the Holy Sepulchre."

No reaction. Either she was very good at suppressing her facial expressions, or she didn't know, or all of his guesses had been wrong.

"If I guessed right, then the game is pretty much up. The security forces all around Jerusalem will be on high alert. So, if you're feeling any particular sense of loyalty toward your mission, then you might as well know it's already been compromised. However, you might still have the chance to prove yourself useful. If you'll tell us more about your group, the United States might have a word to say in your favor."

Her eyes remained motionless.

"Shira," he said, "believe me when I tell you I'm trying to help you here. And believe me when I tell you you're going to need it. I spent the morning listening to the stories of a friend of mine, a Palestinian woman who was just released from Israeli prison. It was all I could do to keep my breakfast down. And she was only there for a week, partly because she had some influential Americans pushing for her release, and partly because Shin Bet eventually realized she had nothing to tell them anyway. Neither of those will be true in your case, and I don't think the Israelis will be any gentler to a turncoat from their own side than they were to her. Would you like me to tell you what she told me?"

She gave a defiant toss of her head. As she did, her hair flew back to reveal something that it had been concealing the last time he saw her: a welt under her chin, near her left ear.

Fox took a closer look at the mark, then leaned back in his chair.

"Is it the violin or the viola that you play?" he asked.

She kept silent, but her surprise was visible.

"Maybe you've heard this riddle," Fox went on. "How are a violist's fingers like lightning?"

The corners of her mouth turned down in a way that suggested she knew the punch line—"They never strike twice in the same place"—and was not amused.

"I know, those hotshot violinists always like to make the viola the butt of their jokes," he continued smoothly. "But in the hands of a skillful player, there's a warmth and depth to it that a violin just can't match. What's your favorite piece?"

He gave her an opening to reply. When she declined it, he continued: "My personal favorite is Mozart's Sinfonia Concertante in E-flat. It's always sounded to me like a love duet between the violin and viola, with all the rest of the orchestra cheering them on. Have you ever played it?"

She gave a slight nod.

"Was that one of the pieces you played with the Divan?"

Her eyes widened in surprise. She quickly squelched the expression, but Fox's guess, based on the stamps in her passport, had been confirmed. The West-Eastern Divan Youth Orchestra recruited promising young musicians from all over the Middle East, including both Israel and the Palestinian territories. Before embarking on their international concert tour, they practiced intensively in a city chosen for its history of peaceful coexistence among Christians, Jews, and Muslims: Seville, Spain.

"Call me an idealist," Fox went on, "but I've always felt that music was one of our greatest hopes for peace. That if you truly had music in your soul, there was no way you could knowingly and willfully harm another human being." He leaned forward and lowered his voice. "Unless, of course, you had suffered something so terrible that it cast a shadow over everything else."

Her lips twitched, and Fox waited, scarcely daring to breathe. Finally, they opened a crack, and out came two barely audible words.

"Not me."

"Not you?"

"There was someone else who suffered far worse."

"Who?"

"Someone who could have done more for the Middle East with his music than our leaders could in a hundred years with their talk. Someone who deserved to have his name known by the world."

"He still can," Fox said, "if you make it known."

She gave him a disbelieving look, as if to say: *How could I possibly do that now?*

"If you disappear down some Israeli memory hole," he continued, "then of course, you'll never be able to share his story with the world. But if you answer my questions, then I may be able to arrange for you to tell it to the people who need to hear it. Or at the very least, you can tell it to me and I can pass it on."

Her mouth closed again.

"So what you did was for revenge?"

She shrugged. "I suppose you could say that."

"Did you ever ask yourself whether that was really the way he would want his memory to be honored?"

"He would want that the world should know the true price tag of Zionism."

"Meaning what? More senseless death? More women and children killed?"

"Made to realize how sick they really are. The symptoms of their infection made easier to see."

Fox looked into her eyes, a revelation dawning. "Is that what you thought you were doing? Just making them sick?"

Her resolute expression faltered. Fox pressed on: "Did you really not know what was in that canister, and what it does? The Zagorsk virus. A hybrid of smallpox and a particularly nasty form of encephalitis. Not just a painful but temporary illness, if that's what you were led to believe. Two out of three cases terminal, the other left with permanent brain damage. No one infected would ever have recovered."

Her mouth opened and her breathing accelerated.

"Shira," Fox said, "you can make this right. Tell me where and when the next target is."

She shook her head. "I don't know."

"Shira..."

"I don't know! Our missions were secret. None of us knew what the others were doing."

"Who do you mean when you say 'us'? You, TJ..."

"Peg, Aidan, and Ahmad."

"Last names?"

"We only ever used first names among ourselves."

"What about Rashid?"

She shook her head. "I don't know a Rashid."

"Last name Renclaw."

"Sorry."

"All right. What can you tell me about the other three?"

"Peg and Aidan were both from Ireland. Ahmad was from Pakistan."

"How did you all first meet?"

"We were all in OAF."

"Oaf?"

"O-A-F. Oxford Atheists and Freethinkers."

"What does that group do?"

"We discuss books and films, invite guest speakers to campus, do outreach work to help people break free from the tyranny of organized religion."

"I'm guessing bioterrorism isn't one of the activities listed in the group's charter?"

She shook her head. "There was someone I met through that group. He had graduated several years earlier, but he had been president while he was a student, and he still hung out with the group a lot, sort of on the fringe. I often saw him at parties. And at one of them one day, he took me aside and asked me whether I had ever dreamed of taking action that went beyond just words."

"What was his name?"

"Chris."

"Last name?"

She shook her head.

Fox scribbled a wire diagram on his notepad. Now, more of the players were on stage: TJ, Shira, Peg, Aidan, and Ahmad, all answering to this Chris. But there was still someone waiting in the wings. Where did Rashid fit in? Was he part of a different cell under Chris's direction, operating independently of this one? Or did Chris report to him?

"Shira, I really want to help you out. But can you imagine what my contacts in America would say if I called and told them that they need to look for a Chris from England, a Peg and an Aidan from Ireland, and an Ahmad from Pakistan? How many millions do you think that covers?"

"I've told you everything I know, I swear!"

"Well, you've given me something, at least. But it'll take a lot of persuading for the Israelis to extradite you, and whether my contacts will be impressed enough to give them the push they need is anyone's guess."

There was a long pause, as Shira's lips twitched, straining to hold in words that were struggling to get out. Finally, they made their escape:

"I can identify them. If I saw them, I could point them out to you."

Fox set down the receiver and turned to a guard. He needed to call Adler, but the guards had taken his cell phone when he came in. "Excuse me. I need to use my cell phone to call my colleague back in the States."

He gave Fox the kind of look that a security guard at a mental institution might use on a raving patient.

"Is there a public phone I can use, then?"

The guard motioned Fox to follow him, and led him to a pay phone. He peered at the instructions on the telephone and tried to make sense of them. "Do you know how I can make an international collect call?" he asked. "Reverse charges?"

His escort only shrugged. With a sigh, he punched

in his credit card number from memory, wishing he had thought of keeping an expense ledger.

There was silence as the signal made its way across the Atlantic, until a voice answered in Washington. "Adler here."

"Hello, John. This is Robin Fox."

"Robin!" came the incredulous reply. "Did I read your message right? Are you in Israel?"

"You did and I am."

"What the hell are you doing there?"

"Well, let's see. Since arriving here, I've foiled the next attack, helped the Israelis arrest the suspect, survived an attempted poisoning, and learned how slow your office has been at following through on your promise of helping us find out what happened to Leila Halabi. Sorry I haven't called before now, it's been kind of busy. But here's the scoop. The subject's name is Shira Yavin. Israeli citizen residing in Britain, undergraduate at Oxford. For the head of her outfit, I only have a first name, Chris. Okay so far?"

There was a pause as Adler took down the information. "Okay, keep going."

"I'm at a detention facility near Ben-Gurion right now, and I've just had an interview with her. Our best candidate for the next target is the Church of the Holy Sepulchre, Jerusalem, sometime tomorrow. And our subject has offered to ID the agent. Could you make arrangements for her to do it?"

The silence went on long enough that Fox started to wonder if they had been disconnected. Adler finally broke it with, "Do you have any idea what you're asking?"

"Well, let's think this through. There are about five

people in the world who can recognize the members of this group on sight. One is in Washington enjoying his Fifth Amendment rights, three are still at large, and one is here with me offering her help. I think we'd be smart to take her up on it."

Adler was silent for a moment. "I need to get my superiors to make some phone calls. I'll call you back on your cell phone, probably later this evening, your time."

"Okay. But the church opens at dawn tomorrow morning. They'll need to talk fast."

Why is this Passover different from all other Passovers? Fox demanded ruefully of the universe. Why is it that on other Passovers, I don't have the chance to attend a seder in Israel—and now that I do, it feels as though there's a ticking bomb under the table?

They were back at the common room of the Meir Hospital in Kfar Saba. Fox sat with Emily, Miriam and Leila at a table prepared with copies of the *haggadah* at each place, and in the center, the seven foods symbolizing the deliverance of the Israelites out of slavery in Egypt. Fox always told his students how the most effective rituals involve all the senses, like the Catholic mass— sight of the beautifully decorated church and vestments, sound of music, smell of incense, touch of a neighbor's hand, taste of bread and wine. The Passover feast, incorporating sound, movement, touch, and taste, was another case in point. A history lesson made edible.

"We're all set to take Leila back to the States," Miriam said to Fox as a shaven-headed, bespectacled orderly set cups of grape juice at their places. "Washington via

London tomorrow afternoon. And you? Do you know what you're doing?"

"Hardly ever."

As if on cue, Fox's phone vibrated. He excused himself and stepped out into the corridor.

"Robin Fox."

"Robin," came Adler's voice. "Congrats, or something. In terms of favors owed, I think you've single-handedly tipped the balance from Israel to us and back again within twenty-four hours. But it's all arranged. I'll fly in tonight and meet you there tomorrow, along with Agent Birnbaum from the Jerusalem station. Where are you staying?"

"I'll text you when I know."

"Well, wherever it is, try to get a good night's sleep. If we want to have the place under surveillance before the first Mass, we'll have to be there at 4:30."

Fox returned to the cafeteria in time for the recitation of the Kiddush. *Blessed are You, O Lord our God, King of the Universe...*He could only follow the first few words, but just being there and listening to the chanting sent an electric current through him. They may have been in a hospital cafeteria with lime-green walls rather than a temple, but there was no question that they were on holy ground.

They all sat and leaned to the left, in a symbolic imitation of dinner guests in antiquity reclining around the table, commemorating the journey of the Jewish people from being slaves in a foreign land to being served in their own homes.

Fox raised his glass to Emily on his right and Miriam on his left. "*L'chaim.*"

They raised their glasses to their lips.

"STOP!"

Leila's voice rang throughout the hall. Some of the guests were so startled that they spilled their wine onto the white tablecloth. All heads turned to shoot her an incredulous look.

She pointed to the door. Lurking outside, watching the festivities through the window, was the orderly who had served the wine. And now that Leila pointed him out, Fox realized that he had seen him before on two occasions. He had progressively less hair each time, but the face was the same.

Fox dropped his cup onto the table and leapt from his seat. As a red stain spread across the white tablecloth, Fox ran out the door. The impostor orderly pelted down a ramp and around the corner to the Green Mile. By the time Fox had rounded the same corner, his quarry had disappeared into one of the side corridors.

Fox did a quick search from one to another, and then ran outside. He saw ambulances and taxis parked at the curbside, and a lottery kiosk where plastic frogs covered with numbers beckoned him to try his luck. But that, it seemed, had run out: the poisoner was nowhere to be seen.

Fox, Emily, Miriam, and Leila quickly packed into the rental car, and set off for Jerusalem. Miriam grumbled about having to drive on a holy day, but Fox pointed out that considering how much more skilled she was at Israeli-style driving than the rest of them, it probably counted as *pikuach nefesh*—an acceptable bending of religious rules when human lives were at stake.

"How the hell did he know?" Fox wondered aloud once they were on the highway. "I checked the news reports about the attack. None of our names were mentioned in any of them. How did he know that we were involved?"

"The wonders of YouTube?" Emily suggested. "All it would have taken is for one tourist at the airport to see all the commotion, catch it on video, and upload it. Voila, you're an instant celebrity."

"Even so, how would he have recognized..." He sank back in his seat and pressed his hands to his temples. "Oh, hell. Of course, everyone in this OAF group must know my face. Because of that damned debate..."

Emily grimaced, remembering. "You mean ambush..."

"...with Ray Dickinson," the two of them finished together, exchanging a wry glance.

A few years ago, Fox had received his first speaking invitation, and in his excitement, accepted at once without doing a thorough background check of the group that issued it. Once at the venue, he saw to his horror that he would be sharing the spotlight with Professor Ray Dickinson of Oxford, one of the world's most outspoken atheists—who, unlike him, had been fully briefed about the nature of the event. Fox had finished a very poor second by anyone's measure, and his humiliation had been televised for all to see. Even Dickinson, after the debate, had conceded privately that he found the setup "rather unsporting," but his sense of sportsmanship had not extended to showing his opponent any mercy on stage.

Miriam steered expertly through the maze of roads surrounding Jerusalem's Old City and brought them to a Palestinian family-run hotel near the Damascus Gate. Their Passover dinner ended up consisting of kebabs and flatbread, in an enclosed garden restaurant fragrant with the apple-sweet scent of shisha pipes. The requisite bottle of wine—real this time—was also on hand, and Fox drank liberally from it to calm his nerves.

He supposed it qualified as a miracle that, even with the influx of pilgrims during this combined Holy Week and Passover, Miriam had been able to find two rooms anywhere in Jerusalem, let alone in the same hotel. She and Leila took one, leaving him and Emily in the other.

Fox's first glimpse through the doorway was of rough-hewn stone walls, which gave the room a subterranean feel, but the starkness was relieved by the colorful patterns on the curtains and duvets. It looked like a desert monastery redecorated by an Ottoman pasha. There was a little fish-and-shell fountain set into one wall. Fox had no idea what it was meant for, but the Catholic in him had to resist the urge to dip his fingers and make the sign of the cross.

As Emily entered the room, Fox hesitated at the threshold. She turned and looked at him, reading his mind. "Come on, Robin. It's not as though we've never slept in the same room before."

"A hostel dormitory shared with a dozen other backpackers? Not exactly the same thing."

"No, not exactly. This time, I'll only need to worry about *one* man snoring."

Fox sat down on his bed, and succumbed to a sudden fit of the shakes. An inner voice, which sounded eerily like his old drill instructor, chided him: *Pull yourself together, Fox! You've been in Afghanistan and Iraq. This is not the first time you've been a target.* But that time, they had all been targets together, thousands of them, just by virtue of the uniform they wore. This was the first time it had been personal.

Emily sat down next to him and draped an arm around his shoulder. "You all right, Robin?"

He took a deep breath, and let it out in a shuddering sigh. "I'm sorry, Emily."

"For what?"

"I came here to protect you. And I put you in danger instead."

Her other hand joined the first one, and began to knead the muscles in his shoulders.

"So that was your reason for coming here, then? To save me?"

Her voice gave no clue as to whether she found this an enchanting feat of gallantry, or whether her feminist sensibilities were about to rear up and bite him for daring to doubt that she could take care of herself.

"Well, that and some other little things, like foiling a terrorist attack, getting intel about the next one, seeing Leila finally free…and of course, the chance for some in-depth field research on the Israeli health care system."

She chuckled. Her strong fingers sought out the pressure points on his shoulders.

"You haven't lost your touch," he said.

"Shall we do this properly? I get equal time, you understand."

"Deal."

He lay face down, and her fingers worked his

shoulders and down his spine. As healing warmth began to penetrate deep into his muscles, his mind started to drift, tossed on waves of fatigue, dissipating adrenaline, and a quantity of wine that might have exceeded the traditional four cups of the Passover seder. Images rose up and fell away in his consciousness, with present sensations, memory and imagination all blending together.

Of the same fingers easing the knots out of his shoulders in hostel rooms, after many a long day of backpacking.

Of chocolate-fueled dorm-room conversations that ended with the birds singing to welcome the dawn.

Of how it might be to come home to this every evening. To have her smile be the first sight that greeted his eyes in the morning.

Of a lock of her hair brushing his face, and her voice whispering in his ear, "Feeling better now?"

Of turning over to face her, and reaching up to touch her cheek.

Of her face, almost imperceptibly slowly, drawing closer to his.

Of their lips touching. Tentatively at first, as if by accident. Then gently and tenderly. Then with passionate urgency, as he took hold of her and pulled her tight against him.

Of her hair cascading down to make a fragrant curtain around their faces, shutting out the outside world, and leaving it to melt away for all he cared.

12

JERUSALEM
SATURDAY, APRIL 4
HOLY SATURDAY

The alarm on Fox's cell phone vibrated at 3:30. It took him a moment to remember where he was, and then a jolt of adrenaline brought him wide awake as he struggled to bring his vague memories of the previous night into focus. Headlines swirled into his mind, like the spinning newspapers in old movies, proclaiming the worst-case scenario: SEX SCANDAL AT USPRI. PROGRAM OFFICER IN AFFAIR WITH RESEARCH FELLOW. CHIEF SUPPORTER IN CONGRESS CUCKOLDED.

He looked over to the other bed, where Emily was asleep in a sleeveless satin nightgown. She stirred slightly, but her eyes stayed shut.

By the end of the day, she would be on a plane back to Washington. Fox hated to leave without a word, but he was equally reluctant to wake her—and what would he say if he did? "Goodbye, Emily, I'm off to try to catch a terrorist—and oh, before I go, I have to ask: did we or didn't we?"

He zipped up the bag containing the few belongings he had brought with him, took one last regretful look at her sleeping face, and headed into the lobby.

Adler was waiting there, along with a woman with dark, curly hair, dressed in jeans and a sweatshirt that made her indistinguishable from any tourist in Jerusalem.

Adler stood and extended his hand. "Morning, Robin."

"Morning." Robin shook his hand, and did the same to the woman who must be Agent Birnbaum, exchanging no introductions that might be overheard.

Adler cast a glance around the lobby, taking in the framed Palestine pound note from the British Mandate, the brochures for alternative tours to Bethlehem and Jericho, and the display case full of books with titles like *Occupation Diaries*.

"What's a nice American like you doing in a place like this?" he asked.

Fox ignored his quip. "Are we ready?"

They traveled on foot, the only real option in the Old City. They passed through the Damascus Gate and walked past the shuttered shops of the Souk Khan es-Zeit toward the Church of the Holy Sepulchre. Even at this early hour, there were several Palestinians coming and going. Fox noted that the most popular article of clothing among boys and young men was a knock-off Gap sweatshirt emblazoned with the letters FOX.

Jerusalem is giving me a royal welcome, he thought

wryly. *Just as it did for Jesus. And everyone knows how quickly His wore out.*

For such a major pilgrimage site, the Church of the Holy Sepulchre was remarkably well hidden. As they navigated the labyrinth of souks, their only clue that they were getting close was a row of shops selling icons, rosaries, and olive-wood nativity scenes. They passed under an unassuming archway into the parvis, the courtyard at the entrance to the church. Metal detectors had already been set up at the church entrance, along with cameras to photograph everyone coming in, and a portable cabin from which they could watch the monitors and try to identify any suspects.

Fox had visited the church before during his global wanderings, and come away empty. The gloomy, labyrinthine interior, and the profusion of overwrought icons and ornaments that smothered the presumed holy sites, had made him feel more trapped than transported. When he ducked under the low arch into the aedicule supposedly housing Jesus' tomb, and saw the Latin inscription in brass reading HE IS NOT HERE, his irreverent thought had been, *No kidding.*

Birnbaum scanned the parvis with her eyes, taking in the doorways, windows, and rooftops. Fox watched as she approached one of the police officers standing guard, pointed at the wooden ladder leading from a balcony over the church entrance to a window above, and spoke to him in imperious Hebrew. The police officer, and all his colleagues within earshot, laughed as though she had made the best joke of the week.

When she made her tight-lipped return, Fox gave her a sidelong glance and asked, "Are you by any chance new to Jerusalem?"

"What makes you say that?"

"I'm guessing you told them that ladder was a security risk and should be moved." Taking her silence as confirmation, he went on, "No wonder they laughed. That's the Immovable Ladder. It's been there for more than two hundred years. If any of the denominations that share custody of this church wanted to move it, they would have to get the approval of all five others. It's practically impossible to move or change anything at all in this church. When the roof started to fall into disrepair, they argued and argued until it was at the point of caving in before they could finally agree on whose responsibility it was to fix it."

Birnbaum pointed at the scaffolding and tarpaulins on the roof. "It seems they finally got enough of a consensus to start doing something."

Fox nodded. "Miracles do sometimes happen. Even in Jerusalem."

They entered the portable cabin. Shira was already there, her eyes on the screen that showed the faces of pilgrims coming through the security checkpoint. When the church opened at 4:30, images began flashing across the screen, one after the other, along with a light that lit up whenever anyone presented a passport from Britain or Ireland.

The first Mass of the morning began and ended. No matches.

"Keep in mind," said Adler, "that they could have cut their hair, permed it, straightened it, dyed it. They could be using wigs, colored contacts, all kinds of disguises."

"I'm aware of all that," Shira assured him.

Early morning became midmorning. They settled into a routine: keep the station open for fifty minutes, then close it for ten to give Shira a break. Fox ran to one of the open-air restaurants in the souk for cups of Turkish coffee.

Morning gave way to noon. No matches.

"Remember, if you don't find her," Adler reminded Shira, "then as far as the United States is concerned, you're worth nothing."

"John, please!" Fox said. "She's under enough stress already."

Birnbaum said nothing, but her mere presence increased the air pressure in the room to a crushing level.

By one o'clock, Fox was beginning to feel distinctly uneasy. He had never been to the Holy Fire ceremony, but from pictures and videos, he had an image of how the parvis would look in the run-up to the event: full of expectant crowds with unlit candles ready to receive the Fire, waving flags, beating drums and chanting, "We are Christians, have been for centuries and will be forever!" At the moment, though, even though there were plenty of pilgrims coming and going, there was nothing to suggest this was anything but an ordinary day.

"Where is everyone?" Fox wondered aloud. "The fire is supposed to be lit at exactly two o'clock on Holy..."

He had been about to say "Saturday," but he suddenly clamped a hand over his mouth to prevent the escape of another word beginning with the same letter.

"What?" Adler asked.

"We're in the wrong place."

Birnbaum gave him a shocked look, and whirled on

Shira. "I knew it! I knew it was a mistake to trust you!"

"Agent—" Fox tried to intervene, but she was too enraged to hear him.

"Once a traitor to Israel, always a traitor to—"

"*Agent!* Can I talk to you for a minute?"

With a smoldering glance over her shoulder at Shira, Birnbaum followed Fox outside into the sunlit courtyard.

"You didn't make a mistake," he told her, "and neither did she. The mistake was mine."

"What are you talking about?"

"I'm an idiot. I should go back to the Religious Studies department right now and turn in my resignation. The Holy Fire ceremony happens the day before *Orthodox* Easter. Which is a week later than the Catholic and Protestant one."

Birnbaum was silent for a moment. "Next week?"

"Next week."

"So...there's nothing special happening today?"

"The Catholics had their Mass this morning. There'll be other services going on as usual, but no more fire than on any other day."

As soon as the words were out of Fox's mouth, the windowpanes above their heads shattered. The two of them ducked and covered as glass shards rained down around them. Flames surged out of the windows and door, along with thick clouds of black smoke and the screams of thousands of pilgrims as they frantically converged on the single narrow exit. The Immovable Ladder, dislodged from the balcony, clattered to the courtyard.

"What the hell?" Birnbaum cried, pressing herself against the wall as the fleeing crowd began to surge through the parvis. "What happened?"

Fox was frantically searching his mind for possible answers to the same question. He was sure they had checked every pilgrim coming into the church. How could the saboteur have escaped their detection?

His gaze swept the parvis, and fell on a narrow doorway in the corner.

Without a word of explanation to Birnbaum, he shouldered his way across the fleeing crowd to the door. He ran through it, up two narrow staircases, and through two chapels before emerging into the sunlight of another courtyard, this one on the top of the roof.

Fox knew this place by reputation only: the Deir es-Sultan Monastery, a community of Ethiopian monks built on the roof of the church. All around him were free-form dwellings of rocks and plaster, where the only straight lines and right angles were in the doorways. He could have been in some ancient town in Ethiopia rather than among the rooftops of Jerusalem, except for the dome in the middle of the courtyard looking down into one of the chapels, and the black smoke that now billowed out of it.

A monk in a white robe and turban saw Fox, and pointed toward an arched doorway on the far side of the courtyard. Fox waved his thanks and charged through. He looked down the cobbled street beyond and saw a man running down it. The coveralls he was wearing would have looked entirely unremarkable on any construction site in the world, except for one thing: they had a fresh-out-of-the-package look, as if they had never been worn before.

Fox charged after him. If the suspect got to the end

of the street and down the stairs, he would merge into the crowd in the souk, and Fox would lose him again.

As he rounded a corner, though, he ran straight into a phalanx of firefighters and rescue workers running the other way. They reminded Fox of the Charge of the Light Brigade, surging into battle against impossible odds. With the narrow, winding streets and innumerable doors and stairs on all approaches to the church, there was no way for fire engines or ambulances to reach it. The only real way to fight the blaze and rescue the injured would be by helicopter.

The suspect doubled back, facing Fox for the first time. It came as no surprise that the face was one he had seen before: Kenneth Oldman, the poisoner.

Fox tried to cut Oldman off, but Oldman drew a knife from his belt and brandished it. Fox had no doubt that the point would be envenomed.

Oldman ran back the way he had come, Fox hard on his heels. As the firefighters turned and squeezed through the narrow gate into the monastery courtyard, Oldman ran straight ahead, through an arch that a sign identified as the entrance to the Church of St. Helen.

Fox followed behind. He looked around the chapel, with its vaulted wooden ceiling and Coptic icons, and checked the pews, but found no one hiding among them. He crossed the nave and cautiously stepped through another doorway opposite the one through which he had entered.

Beyond the doorway was a rough-hewn stone staircase descending into subterranean darkness. The ceiling was so low he had to duck, and the air was so humid that the moisture condensed on the walls and trickled down to form pools on the steps. He heard the sound of dripping water echoing in a cavernous space somewhere below.

The narrow passage opened up into an underground cistern, a cave filled from wall to wall with a deep pool of water. The stairs continued down to a landing, and then to the water's edge. Oldman was out of sight, but Fox knew he had to be waiting around the bend. There was nowhere else he could go without diving underwater.

Fox took off his jacket, and took one quick, cautious peek over the stone banister before flinging it down where he judged Oldman's head to be. He ran down a few more steps and vaulted over the banister, just as Oldman was shaking the jacket off his head.

Oldman lunged with knife in his hand. Fox dodged the thrust and caught Oldman's wrist.

There is a pressure point, Fox's unarmed combat instructor had taught him, on the back of the hand where the thumb and forefinger meet. If you hit it accurately, from the proper angle and with sufficient force, your opponent is guaranteed to drop his weapon.

It was a technique that a karate black belt might have a reasonable chance of executing correctly. Fox, despite his years in Japan, was not one of those. Oldman kept his grip on the knife.

Fox blocked a punch from Oldman's other hand, and then slammed the hand holding the knife into the wall of the cave. He thought he felt Oldman's grip loosen. He tried it again, and the knife clattered to the steps.

Fox snaked his other arm around Oldman's, took a grip on his collar, and forced him to his knees. Oldman's free arm swung at him, but Fox remained out of its range.

"Kenneth Oldman." Fox's voice resounded in the cave like that of a judge about to deliver the final verdict. "The Portsmouth Poisoner."

Oldman scoffed. "It's your lot who are the poisoners. Religion poisons everything."

"Where is the next target?"

"In your arse."

Forgive me, Fox prayed silently, *for using this sacred space for such a profane purpose.*

He pushed Oldman forward into the cistern and held his head under the water, tightening his hold as his captive struggled and splashed.

Civilians who voluntarily subjected themselves to waterboarding, usually to prove that it scarcely qualified as torture, lasted an average of fifteen seconds before they changed their minds. Hardened combatants captured in the field could sometimes hold out for as long as thirty-five. Forty was considered the upper limit. Fox counted ten before pulling his captive up again.

"I'll ask you again: Where is the next target?"

"I'd tell you...to go to hell..." Oldman said between his gasps, "except there isn't one, is there?"

Fox pushed him under again. Twenty seconds this time.

"One more time," he said when Oldman resurfaced. "Where is the next target?"

"If I were you...I'd be more worried...about that lady friend of yours."

Fox pushed him under again. Oldman's free hand reached desperately for his own neck, but he was unable to break out of Fox's lock.

Ten...twenty...thirty.

As Fox pulled Oldman up, he saw that the grab at his throat had not been an attempt to escape. He wore a chain around his neck, part of which now rested in his mouth. He spit it out, along with the broken, bloody remains of a glass capsule.

Fox's grip slackened. An involuntary "Oh, God!" escaped him.

Oldman grinned. "There is no God," he said. "So he can't...say..."

Before the Portsmouth Poisoner could finish his sentence, his own medicine claimed him.

Fox sat on a sofa in the American consulate in Jerusalem. The wide window offered a fine view of the courtyard, but he could only stare dully at the coffee table.

Every time he blinked, he saw flames pouring out the window of the church, and frantic pilgrims squeezing the breath out of one another as they converged on the single narrow exit. All his intelligence-gathering work had done nothing to prevent it.

And when he thought of the incident at the cistern, he wanted to throw up and then take a scalding shower. He had been assured that the cistern had not been contaminated, but when he remembered what he did to Oldman, he felt the way he imagined a woman might if she woke up in the bed of a man she hated, or a recovering alcoholic might if, after ten years of sobriety, he woke up with a hangover and no memory of the previous night. It was as though all the distance he had tried to put between himself and Iraq, all the amends he had tried to make for his role in that giant war crime, had been erased at one stroke—without even a single piece of useful intelligence to show for it.

Adler and Birnbaum, grim-faced, sat down across the table from Fox. "Seven killed in the blast at the Holy Sepulchre," Adler reported, "and five more trampled to death in the rush to escape. The burn units of all the local hospitals are completely overwhelmed. The only silver lining is that the propane ignited before it built up enough to do even more damage."

"Propane?"

Adler nodded. "Colorless, heavier than air, and one of the most volatile gases you can get. And no need to worry about smuggling it into the country, there are plenty of domestic sources for it. Since roofers often use it to heat their materials, there might even have been a tank all ready for him right there at the construction site. All he had to do was find a way to introduce it into the church, where there would always be candles burning ...and run." He heaved a sigh. "Well, Robin, if it's any consolation, you were right about the time and place after all."

Fox shook his head sadly. "I can't even claim that. This was a diversion."

"What?"

"He made a flash and a bang..."

Birnbaum interrupted. "A dozen dead and hundreds more burned. You call that 'a flash and a bang'?"

"Those aren't the kind of stakes Chris plays for. A dramatic explosion, some deaths, some injuries...and there it stops. His weapon of choice is more insidious: a virus that keeps on perpetuating itself. And you remember what TJ said about church buildings. If he

198 | Charles Kowalski

and Chris are on the same page, he's not interested
in destroying them. What he wants is to make people
so afraid of an invisible threat that they won't set foot
in one. I'm starting to think our Portsmouth Poisoner
might have been improvising."

Adler gave him an incredulous look. "The holiest site
in Christendom, the day before Easter, with the Israeli
security forces on high alert...and you're saying it was a
target of opportunity?"

"Whatever it was, it wasn't Chris's style."

Adler was silent for a moment. "If you're right, and
this was a diversion, what was it a diversion from?"

Fox thought back to the verse marked in the Bible.
"*Therefore we are buried with him through baptism
into death: that like as Christ was raised up from the
dead by the glory of the Father, even so we also should
walk in newness of life.* Chapter 6 of the Letter of Paul
to the..."

He drew in a sharp breath.

"*Romans.*"

Adler and Birnbaum exchanged a glance. "The
Vatican?"

Fox nodded. "Tonight is the Great Vigil of Easter.
The day for baptisms. Baptism, death, and resurrection."

"You're sure he means today?" Adler asked. "Not
tomorrow? Not Easter Sunday?"

Fox nodded. "The Vigil may not be as big a
production as Easter Sunday, but it's indoors. A higher
concentration of the virus in the air, and a better chance
of getting the Pope and the College of Cardinals within
reach. If I were planning an attack on the Vatican, it
would be my choice."

Adler looked at his watch. "Well, we'd better get a move on, then."

Fox glanced at his own watch. "What do you mean? There's no way we can get there in time."

Adler took out his cell phone and keyed in a number. "Oh, ye of little faith."

An hour later, they were in a car heading west on Route 1 to Tel Aviv, with Birnbaum in the back seat keeping watch over the handcuffed Shira. After another hour on the road, they arrived at the smaller of Tel Aviv's airports, which Fox knew as Sde Dov, although the sign at the gate identified it as Dov Hoz. Few places in Israel, it seemed, had only one name.

Among the jumble of helicopters and small private jets on the tarmac, a Gulfstream V was waiting for them. Adler and Birnbaum ushered Shira aboard, with Fox following behind.

Despite the warmth of the sun, a cold sweat broke out on Fox's palms. His heart beat faster and his breath came in gasps. He hesitated at the bottom of the air stairs, and leaned on the handrail.

Adler glanced back from the door, then descended the stairs to where Fox stood. "I never pegged you as a nervous flier."

Fox shook his head. "This is a rendition plane, isn't it?"

"It was once, yeah." Seeing Fox's reaction, he continued: "What's the matter? Do you have some kind of conscientious objection to flying on it? If so, just say the word and we'll run a search for available seats on

Expedia. You can catch up with us in Rome when it's all over. Or Washington. Up to you."

Drawing a deep breath, Fox took a tighter grip on the handrail, and pulled himself up onto the first step.

The Gulfstream, at first glance, fit the Hollywood image of a top-of-the-line business jet, albeit one getting on in years: leather-upholstered reclining seats, glossy faux-wood-paneled galley and tables, paisley-patterned carpeting. But the passengers it had carried during its years of service, Fox knew, had not been corporate executives. They had been captives, for whom the luxurious flight would be a surreal interlude, like an extravagant last meal for the condemned, before they arrived at their secret destinations to meet their secret fate. No matter how many times the cabin air passed through the environmental control system, it would still be heavy with the smell of fear.

Birnbaum cuffed Shira to the seat farthest to the rear, next to the lavatory, then joined Adler in the front of the cabin. Fox, who had been given no seat assignment, hesitated for a moment, then sat down across the aisle from Shira.

The plane took off. Fox waited until it reached cruising altitude, then went forward to where Adler and Birnbaum were having a conversation in spook-speak, full of crypts and acronyms so obscure to an outsider that it might as well have been a secret code. "Excuse me for interrupting, but does the prisoner really need to be cuffed?"

"That's the protocol."

"I don't think there's much she can do up here. If you're worried, can't you cuff her again before we land?"

Adler thought a moment, then nodded to Birnbaum. With a sigh, she got up to unlock Shira's cuffs. Fox took the aft-facing seat opposite her.

"You were talking earlier," he said, "about someone who suffered worse than you."

She paused for a moment, then spoke. "His name was Nabil. From Edward Said Conservatory."

"Someone you played music with?"

She nodded, and looked out the window at a distant memory. "How can I describe what it was like to hear him play? He could take an instrument that had only ever known how to march, and teach it to dance."

"You knew him well?"

She nodded. "We were duet partners. He was from Marda, and I'm from Ariel. That tells you something right there, doesn't it? We were practically next door, but if it hadn't been for the Divan, we would never have met."

"Ariel." Fox tried to conjure a mental map of the West Bank. Ariel was a settlement built deep in Palestinian territory, connected to the Green Line by an isthmus of restricted land that cut off Marda and other nearby villages from the county seat of Salfit. The whole enclave was often called "the Ariel Finger," which seemed a perfect description of what Israel was giving the Palestinians.

"I didn't build it." A defensive edge crept into her voice, as though Fox had unwittingly transmitted his thoughts when he said the name. "I was born there. It was the only home I ever knew."

"Go on. You were telling me about Nabil."

"In those forty days with him, I learned more than

in all my life until then—not just about music, but about his life. How he had to leave before dawn every morning to get to his classes, and sometimes have to wait so long at the checkpoint that he only made it in time for the last hour. How he would practice while standing in line, and became a local celebrity. How some of his friends and family told him he was wasting his time: 'Our struggle for freedom comes first, then we can make music.' But he would answer them: 'Do you think the world will support our struggle for freedom, if they don't know we can make music now?'"

He and Leila would get along well, Fox thought, then mentally edited his tense. This story, he was sure, would not have a happy ending.

"When our tour was over and we had to say goodbye, I couldn't stop crying. I'll never forget his parting words to me: 'I'll see you again when the wall comes down, *habibti.* In the meantime, keep making music, with all your heart. The world needs to hear something beautiful from our part of it, for a change.'"

"Kind of him to say 'our.'"

"Too kind. When I came back, I couldn't call it 'mine' anymore. There was no place in Ariel I could look without wondering whose land had been stolen for it. I couldn't even bear to walk by the waterfall in the park. Just the sound of it was like a perpetual 'sod you' to our neighbors down the hill who had to ration their water. I had always believed what they told me in school, that Ariel had been built on a pile of bare rocks. But now I felt that it had been built on a pile of bare-faced lies."

"Home wasn't home anymore."

She nodded, and swallowed hard. "And then I heard

the news. A couple of my classmates had taken a hike outside the settlement, and some Palestinian boys threw rocks at them. For that, some settlers went down into Marda and killed the first six people they saw." Her free hand shook with anger. "The news report didn't even give the victims' names. But I made it my business to find out."

There was a moment of silence. Fox broke it by saying, "The world lost a great treasure."

She looked out the window and blinked back tears. "He could have been Palestine's answer to Itzhak Perlman. If there were any justice in the universe, he would be on stage at the Royal Albert Hall right now with a Stradivarius in his hands. But they didn't know, and they wouldn't have cared. To them, he was just one more Arab. Or one less. Just part of the...*price tag*."

She wiped away the tears that had defied her efforts to suppress them. "The day I found out, it would have to be Yom ha-Atzmaut, Independence Day. Everyone else was happily hoisting their flags and firing up their barbecue grills, and the very sight of them made me sick. And to make matters worse, my parents always insisted on reciting the Hallel on that day, 'to thank Hashem for the gift of the Land of Israel.' As soon as they said the first words, I felt as though a noose were tightening around my neck. I couldn't even open my mouth to join in. Of course they wanted to know why. And when I told them, my father backhanded me and knocked me to the floor. 'For this we let you go to Europe? So you could become a traitor to Israel?' After that, I couldn't bear to stay there for even one more day."

"So you left for England?"

"Yes."

"And eventually made it into Oxford. And met Chris, TJ, Peg, and Aidan."

She nodded.

"You didn't mention Kenneth Oldman. Was he part of your group?"

Shira shook her head.

"But you knew him?"

"I only met him once, through our prison outreach."

"Prison outreach?"

"That program has been around for a couple of years now. We visit prisons, distribute books, set up pen-pal exchanges. Our president once said, 'The infected have always known that in prisons, they have a captive audience in every possible sense. Inmates get the Bible, the Qur'an, the Bhagavad Gita shoved down their throats day in and day out. Her Majesty's Prison Service will become one giant petri dish for the God virus unless we're in there providing some vaccination.'"

Fox recalled his ill-starred debate, where Professor Dickinson had boasted at great length about the disproportionately low number of atheists in prisons. Apparently, OAF had decided it was time to change that.

"Oldman started to say something rather odd, before he was...interrupted," Fox said. " 'There is no God, so he can't say...' and that was as far as he got. Do you have any idea what he meant?

Shira shrugged and shook her head.

"Where did the rest of you do your training? Your preparations?"

"Chris was the only one who knew. The rest of us rode with him blindfolded."

"Did you see what kind of car it was?"

"A BMW. Red."

Fox made a note. "How long did the trip take, from Oxford?"

"About an hour."

"Were you driving through the city, or the countryside?"

"The city."

"What happened when you reached your destination? Like, did you park on the street, or in a garage? Did you hear much noise from outside? Go up or down any steps? Were there any windows that you could see out of?"

She shook her head. "No windows, they were all boarded up. We parked in a garage, went up a flight of stairs, and only took off our blindfolds when we got to the room above. That's all I ever saw."

Fox finished taking down the information. "What were you studying at Oxford?"

"Microbiology."

"I assume that when you matriculated, you had a goal in mind besides biological warfare?"

She shot him a look. "I wanted to become a doctor. I thought that maybe, if I changed my citizenship, I might someday be able to go back and work in the West Bank or Gaza."

"So what happened to that dream?"

"I met Chris," she replied, as if it were the obvious answer. "When I told him about it, he said, 'A noble goal indeed. Now, how would you like to be part of the ultimate global vaccination campaign?' I didn't know what he meant at first, but as I got to know him better, he let me in on more of his plan. 'You've seen firsthand the harm the God virus does. You come from a country created solely as an incubator for it. How would you like to help eradicate it once and for all?'"

"So religion is the whole problem," Fox summed up caustically. "And Chris offered the final solution."

She winced, then glared at him. "Tell me this. The Hashem who supposedly told us that the only way to usher in the new era of redemption is to reconquer all the land from the Nile to the Euphrates. The Allah who promises seventy virgins in Paradise to any Muslim who dies fighting us. And the Prince of Peace that you worship on Sunday before shipping guns to Israel on Monday. Are they, in fact, all the same? Or is one more real than the others? Or are they all imaginary, and it's only the guns and bombs going off in their names that are real? Tell me, which is it?"

Fox took a deep breath. He had dealt with questions like this in his classes so often, he would have thought he had his talking points as well in hand as a White House press secretary. But none of his practiced, polished answers felt remotely adequate now. Even the most loyal of press secretaries, he thought, must have moments when he wanted to grab the President by the lapels and demand, "What the hell were you thinking?"

"When I was a boy," he said, "there was a cat on my grandfather's farm. One day, she pounced on a little bird and brought it to me, still alive, but just barely. I suppose she thought I would be pleased. She had no way of knowing that I loved *all* animals. She could only see me as a giant cat, and offer me the only gift she knew how to give. I tried to tell her I wasn't happy with gifts like that, but we didn't have much in the way of a common language, and I'm not sure how well the message got through."

"That's a lovely parable," Shira replied. "But did you create cats? Did you give them claws and teeth and a taste for meat? Because if you did, and then turned round and claimed that you never wanted them to be hunters, the word for that would be hypocrisy."

Fox examined his hand. "Well, I don't see any claws," he said. "What we have instead are human brains. The ultimate dual-use technology. Unlimited power for good or evil, and free will to choose either one. For us to believe in God is a leap of faith, no question. But if you accept the possibility that God exists, you have to wonder how much more of a leap of faith it takes for God to believe in us. To put power like that into the hands of us humans, with no guarantee at all that we would use it for good? It was a gamble on the order of giving a little boy a sword, trusting that he would eventually learn on his own to beat it into a ploughshare."

Shira was silent for a while. "If what you believe is true," she finally said, "then it was a stupid experiment to try. And all the evidence would suggest that it was a failure."

"Maybe. But personally, I'm grateful for whatever it is that keeps the One in charge from pulling the plug on it."

Adler came aft. "I hate to interrupt this fascinating discussion," he said, "but there's something I need to show you."

Fox followed him to the front of the cabin and sat down in a seat facing him.

"I've heard from Israeli intelligence," Adler said.

"They managed to hack into Oldman's cell phone. Pretty fast work, I have to say. Our technical team might have been a little jealous."

"What did they find?"

"Not a whole lot, unfortunately. He covered his tracks pretty well. But there were some pictures that you ought to see."

He turned the screen of his phone to Fox. The pictures had been taken at the seder at the Meir Hospital, and they showed Fox talking with Emily and touching his plastic cup to hers.

Fox recoiled as if he had been punched in the gut. "Oh, God."

"Who is she? You never said anything about a girlfriend."

"She's not. She's..." Fox tried to think of a way to explain, and then decided Adler had no need to know.

"Let me guess: it's complicated."

"Do you know if he sent these to anyone?"

"They couldn't say. His e-mail had been purged."

Fox stared out the window and made no reply.

Adler laid a hand on his shoulder. "Hey, relax. The first time I was out in the field, I got a photo like this slipped under my hotel room door. Someone—they never found out who—just did it to let me know they were watching me, to shake me up. And boy, did it ever, but that was as far as it went. The guy who took these is dead, and your...*friend*...is safely on the way back to the States, right? And there's nowhere near enough information here to allow anyone to track her movements. So there's nothing to worry about. Let's just keep our minds on the job."

Fox kept silent. Miriam's voice replayed in his mind: *We're all set. Washington via London tomorrow afternoon.* If the Portsmouth Poisoner had overheard her, and conveyed her words to Chris, the world had suddenly gotten much smaller.

13

HEATHROW AIRPORT, LONDON
SATURDAY, APRIL 4

"O y vey," Miriam muttered, once they were far enough down the jetway to be out of the flight attendant's hearing. "World Traveler Class? Is it the rule that the bigger the name is, the smaller the seats have to be?"

"Thank you for flying British Airways," Emily quipped in a mock accent. "We understand that you have a choice of airlines, and we have done our utmost to ensure that you choose someone else next time."

"Sorry, Leila," Miriam said.

Leila shrugged. "Sometimes it takes me five hours to travel even one kilometer, if the guards at the checkpoint are having a bad day. Traveling three thousand kilometers in the same time seems almost to defy the laws of physics."

As they emerged onto the concourse, a blond man in

a white coat stood waiting by the gate, with an ID card on a red lanyard bearing the emblem of Public Health England. Next to him was a tripod supporting what looked like a video camera.

As they passed, he gave the screen a concerned glance, and stepped into their path, addressing Emily. "Excuse me, madam?"

All three of them stopped. "Yes?" Emily replied.

"I'm terribly sorry to trouble you, but the thermal imaging camera was showing just a slightly elevated temperature for you. Ten to one it's just fatigue from a long flight, but I still have to ask you a couple of routine questions. Were you by any chance in Tel Aviv this past Thursday, the second of April?"

"Yes."

"Were you in or near Ben-Gurion Airport on that day?"

"The two of us were," Emily answered, indicating herself and Miriam.

"You're probably aware, then, that there was an attempted biological attack on the airport that day?"

"Yes, I seem to remember hearing something about that."

"Now, there's no cause for alarm. By all reports, the attack was stopped, and the likelihood that any contamination escaped is almost nil. But still, the Ministry of Health is very keen to ensure that the virus doesn't accidentally find its way into Britain, or onto some transit flight. I'll need to ask you to fill out a simple questionnaire. Perhaps you already got one of these on the flight? No? Very well, here you are." He handed them each a yellow card and a pen. "And while you're in

Heathrow, just as a precaution, I'll have to ask you to put these on. Again, I apologize for the inconvenience."

He passed out surgical masks to the three of them. Miriam's nose crinkled as she brought hers to her face.

"Sorry," the man said with a sympathetic shrug. "They're treated with antiseptic. Supposed to make them more effective, but they are rather pungent, aren't they?"

They sat down on one of the black plastic benches to fill in their cards. Suddenly, Emily stopped, and gripped Miriam's arm. "Miriam," she said, "I feel..."

The man in the white coat was at her side in a moment. "What's the trouble, madam? Are you feeling ill? Here, have a seat. I'll get you to the Health Center straightaway." He eased her into a wheelchair, and rolled it toward a door under a green sign reading EMERGENCY EXIT: AUTHORISED ACCESS ONLY.

"Where—are you—taking..." Miriam's voice trailed off as dizziness overcame her too. She and Leila both tore off their masks and gasped for air. When their heads stopped spinning enough to see clearly again, there was no sign of Emily.

14

VATICAN CITY
SATURDAY, APRIL 4
GREAT VIGIL OF EASTER

Again, Fox internally berated the universe for its cruel sense of humor. Attending Easter Vigil Mass at St. Peter's had been another longtime dream for him, so when he finally got the chance, why did it have to be under these circumstances?

Fox had always had a troubled relationship with the Church of his childhood. The Church that inspired Francis of Assisi to walk unarmed into the Sultan's tent and plead for peace was the same one that sent the Crusaders to besiege Jerusalem in the first place. The Church that gave the world the mystical visions of Teresa of Avila and John of the Cross was the same one that sent the Inquisition to quash them. The Church that made Maximilian of Tebessa a saint, for choosing to die rather than join the army, was the same one that gave Fox's army unit its Catholic chaplain, with his endless bloviating about Augustine and Aquinas and the doctrine of just war. The more Fox questioned, the more he doubted, which he supposed was what drove him to travel the world exploring other traditions.

And yet, at some level, the Catholic Church still had a home in him, and he in it. Whenever he visited a medieval church in Europe, it felt like coming home to a house that had been in his family for countless generations. The music, the ritual, the seasons of the liturgical year—all these still resonated somewhere deep in his soul.

And one of the highlights of the year for him—a close second after Christmas—was the vigil of Easter. Holy Saturday occupied a mysterious place in time, suspended between the despair of Good Friday and the joy of Easter. All the earth seemed to hold its breath in hushed expectation, as if aware of the epic drama unfolding deep below its surface: the Harrowing of Hell, the descent of Christ into the lowest depths to break open the gates of Hell.

It was appropriate, in a darkly ironic way. This Easter Eve was promising to be harrowing, and if they failed in their mission, all Hell really would break loose.

The Gulfstream touched down not at Fiumicino, the main airport serving Rome, but at Ciampino, a smaller airport closer to the city center. Two unmarked cars were waiting for them on the tarmac, preceded and followed by motorcycles and black squad cars with red lightning bolts, marked Carabinieri, the national paramilitary police force. Birnbaum ushered Shira into one, and Fox and Adler rode in the other.

Even with their sound-and-light escort, traffic was so heavy approaching Rome that Fox wondered whether it might have been faster to take the train. He kept an increasingly anxious eye on his watch until they finally turned onto the Via della Conciliazione, the main approach to the Vatican. The parallel rows of street lights flanking the broad avenue made it look like an airport runway, possibly for flights to heaven.

The motorcade passed through an arched gateway, as Swiss Guard halberdiers in their Renaissance costumes stood to attention and saluted. An officer of the Vatican Gendarme Corps escorted them to the security checkpoint in the colonnade surrounding the Piazza di San Pietro, which had been set up like the one in Jerusalem, with cameras feeding to monitors inside a portable cabin.

It was seven o'clock, two hours before the Easter Vigil Mass was to start, and the Piazza was already thronged with pilgrims from all over the world: Eastern and Western Europeans, Latin Americans, Africans, and some from Asia. Some of them had been passing the time by holding their own impromptu vigils, while others simply chafed at the delay, muttering words that they might have balked at repeating in the presence of the Pope.

"We can start whenever you're ready," the officer told them, in a voice that made it clear he felt that should have been hours ago.

The cameras recorded the face of everyone entering the basilica, and conveyed them to the monitors that

Shira was watching. Half an hour passed, then an hour, then an hour and a half, with no matches.

Birnbaum lost her patience. "What the hell did we bring her all this way for, if she's not going to be any more use in Rome than she was in Jerusalem?"

The clock showed ten to nine. The Mass was about to start.

Adler sighed. "All right, then. Plan B."

And into the basilica they went, to look for another yellowjacket in another beehive.

In the beginning, all was darkness.

Then the great bronze Filarete door at the rear of the nave opened, and the head of the procession made its way through. Everyone along the center aisle leaned over the red-curtained barrier, straining to see the one point of light in the darkness: the Paschal Candle, just lit from a freshly kindled flame, its light reflected from the Pope's gold miter. An island of light in a sea of shadowed faces.

"*Lumen Christi*," the deacon intoned. "The light of Christ."

"*Deo gratias*," ten thousand voices sang in unison. "Thanks be to God."

From his vantage point in the south transept, Fox had a clear view of the baldachin, the spiral-columned pavilion over the high altar where the Pope would celebrate Mass. He kept an eye out for anything unusual, trying not to be distracted by the sculpture behind him: a bronze skeleton creeping out from under a shroud of red jasper, its bony hand holding an hourglass aloft. Its message to all mortals was clear: *Your time is running out.* Fox had to resist the urge to tell it out loud, "No need to remind me."

The procession made its silent way down the aisle. As the Pope passed by, carrying the Paschal Candle, Fox thought he saw a twinkle in his eye—possibly a reflection of the light, but also accompanied by a hint of a smile on the papal lips. Perhaps the Pope was anticipating the moment when the curtain of darkness and silence would lift, and the real celebration would begin. Then again, this Pope was rumored to enjoy slipping out of the Apostolic Palace by night, eluding the Swiss Guards, and ministering to the homeless of Rome dressed as a simple priest. It could simply be that he found all the usual Vatican pomp and pageantry amusing.

"*Lumen Christi.*"

"*Deo gratias.*"

As the procession passed, it left in its wake thousands of flickering lights, as the acolytes lit tapers from the Paschal Candle, and the congregants passed the light from one to the other. By the time the procession reached the papal altar, the dark nave sparkled as though the night sky had been turned upside down.

"*Lumen Christi.*"

"*Deo gratias.*"

Then the lights came on, and Fox could finally see the whole basilica.

Holy Mother Church was in her full festive regalia, decked out in white and gold. On the papal altar, gold candle stands gleamed on the white cloth. In front of it, white Easter lilies decked the balustrade of the exedra that housed St. Peter's tomb, silent trumpets waiting for their cue to burst into songs of joy. The solemn procession marched around it: attendants in white surplices, the College of Cardinals in their gold chasubles and red zuchetto skullcaps, and archbishops in crimson cassocks with tufted birettas.

In the center aisle, two Swiss Guards in plumed helmets stood ceremonial watch. Less conspicuous but undoubtedly more functional, several men stood in strategic places, their modern suits striking a jarring note among all the medieval and Renaissance vestments. They might be taken for ushers, but the wires running from their ears to their collars hinted at their true task.

The legend of the Harrowing of Hell said that on the first Holy Saturday, Jesus descended into the nether realms to proclaim freedom to all the captive souls, past, present, and future. How, Fox's rational mind had always wondered, was this possible? But what his brain could never comprehend, he could feel in his soul now. As St. Peter lay at rest under the papal altar, his two hundred and sixty-seventh successor took a seat directly above his tomb. Monks and nuns, in habits unchanged since the Middle Ages, captured the moment with the video cameras in their cell phones. Tonight, in this hall, a world of space and millennia of time came together into a single point.

If I could just be here as a member of the congregation, Fox thought wistfully, *how I might be transported.* But at this Vigil, he would have to be the most vigilant one of all. As the Alleluias soared up to the dome, they weighed down on his heart with the knowledge that if he failed in his mission, every one of them would turn into a Requiem.

The dome...

Fox turned his eyes up toward the cupola overhead. With no light coming in the windows, and only pinpoints of artificial light around the rim, the interior of the massive dome was shrouded in darkness, but he thought he caught a trace of movement.

As quickly as he could, he shouldered his way to the nearest Vatican security agent, and pointed. The agent sighted along his point, and they both saw the same thing: an unmistakable human figure moving quickly and furtively along the catwalk.

The agent took off at a run, calling into his microphone for the Anti-Sabotage Unit: "*Unità Antisabotaggio alla cupola! Svelto!*" Fox ran after him, down the side aisle, to a door surmounted by two cherubim, which another agent was hurriedly unlocking. As soon as he had it open, the three of them charged through it and into an elevator.

When the elevator came to a stop and the door opened, a blast of chill evening air met them as they emerged onto the terrazza on the roof of the Basilica. The dome, illuminated by floodlights around its base, rose up before him. Uneven red-brick paths, sloping up and down, wound their way among smaller cupolas. The two doors in the wall were closed and locked at this time of night, but the signs above them identified them as a souvenir shop and a snack bar, as unlikely a place as the roof of a cathedral seemed for either.

As soon as the elevator doors were open, the two security agents charged out onto the terrazza. Fox started to run after them, but then changed his mind and hung back, staying within view of the elevator doors.

Sure enough, a woman in black jeans and sweater, with red hair tied back in a ponytail, emerged from behind the octagonal pavilion that housed the elevator. Fox moved to intercept her. She turned and ran in the other direction, toward the balustrade, where statues of Jesus, John the Baptist and eleven of the twelve disciples (minus Judas Iscariot) looked out over the Piazza di San Pietro a hundred and fifty feet below.

A tall white fence stood between her and the balustrade. She pushed through a gate, which had been standing just slightly ajar, then turned and slammed it shut behind her. When Fox reached it, he found it locked, with her on the other side.

She took a step back, and gave him an amused glance through the bars.

"I take it you never learned to pick locks, Mr. Fox," she said, in an Irish accent. "Sure, 'tis a skill that can come in handy from time to time."

The two security agents caught up with them. From the helpless looks that passed between them, Fox could gather that neither of them had the key. One of them spoke frantically into his radio.

The woman kept regarding them with a gloating smile. "That man down there," she said. "He gets to live here in his own little kingdom, while a billion people around the world bend the knee to him. Would they still do that, I wonder, if they knew that where I'm going, neither he nor any of his minions can touch me?"

She backed away toward the balustrade.

Fox called after her. "What's Chris done for you, to make him worth throwing your life away for?"

"More than any man in a dog collar ever has, that's

for sure."

"What did they do to make you hate them so much?"

She grinned and shook her head. "Ah, sure. Keep me talking until the lad with the key shows up, why don't you?"

She stepped up onto the balustrade, taking her place among the twelve statues—the place left vacant by Judas.

"I'm sure Chris would be impressed by your loyalty," Fox shouted to her, "but he can't reward you for it if you're dead."

"You surprise me, Mr. Fox. I would have thought you knew the value of martyrdom."

She turned to look out over the piazza, which was rapidly filling to capacity as the crowd poured out of the basilica and the European Center for Disease Control scrambled to set up decontamination booths. Fox heard a scream from below as the first person saw her. The voice was soon joined by hundreds of others.

Fox tried one last gambit. "The fall might not kill you, you realize."

She paused on the ledge.

"If you survive, how many bones do you think you'll break?" Fox went on. "How many vital organs do you think you'll puncture? How long will you spend in the hospital before they roll you into court in a wheelchair? Which would you rather? Turn yourself in while you can still walk, or be peeled off the pavement and then arrested?"

As she stood hesitantly on the granite baluster, another security agent came running with the key. He hurriedly unlocked the gate, letting his colleagues and Fox through.

That was all the woman appeared to need to steel her resolve. She flung her arms wide, and cried at the top of her voice across the piazza:

"GOD IS NOT GREAT!"

And she began to pitch forward.

The guards caught her from behind and pulled her back down onto the terrazza. As they led her away, Fox glimpsed her face in the glow of the floodlights. The expression he saw there was not fear, nor anger, nor stoic resignation, none of the emotions he would expect to see in a newly apprehended suspect. It looked like nothing so much as disappointment.

The Piazza di San Pietro had been transformed. The field investigation team from the European Center for Disease Control had set up row upon row of white tents, illuminated by floodlights, where all the worshippers from the Mass had to be sprayed with decon solution and have nasal swabs taken to test them for exposure.

Adler had pulled all the strings he could to allow his team to be among the first in line, and to be released to continue their investigation when their test results came back negative. Officers of the Gendarme Corps now led Fox to the Palazzo del Tribunale, the Vatican police headquarters and courthouse, a coffee-colored building nestled into the meticulously manicured gardens of the Vatican interior. He had sometimes wondered what happened to criminals caught in the Vatican—whether perhaps there might be a dungeon or two left over from the Inquisition that could still be called into service when needed—but he soon learned that the country's correctional facilities consisted entirely of three small "safe rooms," which rarely saw any use other than to hold petty thieves and pickpockets until they could be turned over to the Italian police.

The woman they had caught on the rooftop sat in a wooden chair across the table from him, her eyes downcast. An icon of Michael the Archangel, patron saint of law enforcement, hung high on the cream-colored wall of the interview room as though supervising the proceedings. The police had Michael, soldiers could choose between St. George and St. Martin of Tours, and the falsely accused could turn to St. Raymond Nonnatus. What about interrogators? Did they not rate a patron saint?

He looked at the copy of her passport that the Gendarme Corps had provided. "Mairead O'Mullany, from Tramore, County Waterford," he read. "Shall I call you Peg?"

She kept her gaze on the table.

"I see," Fox said. "Like the others, you've been trained not to talk. So, if you're not going to say anything about yourself, I guess I'll have to. You're a graduate student at Oxford. It was there that you joined OAF, and met Chris, who recruited you along with TJ, Shira, Aidan, and Ahmad. Have I left anyone out? Oh, yes, of course, Kenneth Oldman."

She kept her silence.

"So, now that we have some time," he said, "maybe you can answer my earlier question. What did these people do to you to make you hate them so much?"

She finally broke her silence. "How familiar are you with the Magdalene Laundries?"

Fox grimaced. "I've read about them. Not a particularly bright chapter in the history of the Church in Ireland." These laundries-cum-asylums had originally been conceived as reformatories for prostitutes, but eventually expanded their definition of "fallen women" to include unwed mothers, rape victims, and teenage girls whose families judged them too strong-willed or simply too pretty.

"Imagine, if you will, a laundry from the days of the Industrial Revolution. Now imagine a women's prison. Now imagine a convent. Now combine the worst parts of all three, and you'll have some idea of what I went through."

"My God, Peg."

"If this God of yours really exists, and if he's the one responsible for it all, then I'll thank you not to mention his name. 'Twas his supposed servants, in the name of saving my 'soul,' who made me scrub the blood out of hospital sheets, for hours upon hours every day, six days a week, until my hands were cracked and bleeding and my legs could barely support me. 'Twas they who stripped me stark naked so all the other inmates could laugh at how fat I was. Prison would have been a pleasant change. At least prisoners know exactly how long they have before they can be free. As it turned out, I only ended up staying there for two years before that evil place finally closed. But every day of those two years, I was sure that I was going to grow old there, die there, and be buried there in an unmarked grave. And do you know why I was sent there?"

"Why?"

"Because, when I was twelve years old, I told my

parents that my priest had indecently assaulted me. Instead of calling the police, they called the bishop. The result of that conversation, for me, was the laundry in Waterford. As for the priest, he's probably preaching his Easter Eve sermon as we speak." She leaned forward and recited, in a voice brimming with bitter irony: "Thus saith the Lord: 'Let whoever boasts boast about this: that I am the Lord, who exercises kindness, justice, and righteousness in the earth, for in these things I delight.'"

"Oh, Peg. All I can say is if I had gone through such a thing myself, I would probably jump at the chance to take revenge on the Catholic Church, too. And you certainly chose a clever way to go about it. Just out of curiosity, how did you get into the cupola when it was closed for the Vigil?"

"They didn't close it until the afternoon. It was still open in the morning. One equipment locker, one tiny padlock, one lockpick, and one guard in the box who never looked up from *La Stampa*. That was all I needed. I guess no one bothered to check whether the number of visitors going up equaled the number going down." She shrugged. "Italians."

Fox had been up in the cupola once before, and recalled how the security check consisted only of a token metal detector. Even if Vatican security could have been warned to expect her, it would take a very astute guard to look at her passport and make the leap from "Mairead" to "Margaret" to "Peg."

"Here's the deal," Fox said. "My colleague is in the other room right now, talking to Shira. Whichever one gives us the more useful information, we treat as a valued asset to the investigation. The other gets left to fend for herself. Now, it's fair to tell you that in this game, Shira has quite a head start on you. She told us about your group, and offered to identify you. You can't really blame her, she has a very strong incentive. Going to prison in Italy might not be much fun for you, but compared to what you've already gone through in Waterford, you might actually find it quite mild. Going to prison in Israel would be a great deal worse for her. So, if you want to catch up with her, you're going to need to start talking fast. Now, about our friend Chris."

She looked down.

Clearly, the Prisoner's Dilemma was the wrong approach to run on her. By setting up a competition, had Fox made her decide that Shira was already so far ahead of her that there was no point in trying to catch up? Or was she more afraid of Chris than she was of the CIA?

"If you answer our questions, we can guarantee your safety," he said.

To see her look of shock at his suggestion, anyone would have thought he had just propositioned her. "Shira turned on him to save her own wretched skin. That's on her account. I never will."

So the Antichrist had his anti-Simon Peter. Fox recalled the look he had seen on Peg's face on the balustrade, sending a clear message that if she had to sacrifice her life, she would be not only willing but overjoyed to be chosen for the honor. He only knew of two forces in the world that could inspire such devotion, and in spite of everything they said in the Army, patriotism was not one of them. One was faith, and the other was love. And it looked as though Peg had, as Jorge Luis Borges would say, created a new religion with a fallible—in her case extremely fallible—god.

"I see," Fox said. "You were his...special favorite?"

She looked down and blushed, but somehow managed to beam with pride at the same time.

If Chris was capable of inspiring such devotion in her, she would be able to hold out even longer than TJ. But if she could be convinced that her love had been betrayed, *Heaven hath no rage like love to hatred turned, Nor hell a fury like...*

"All your life," Fox said, "the men who were supposed to protect you betrayed you instead—the priest first, and then your father. At Waterford, you were told that you were a miserable sinner, worthless, unlovable, so many times a day that at some level, you couldn't help wondering whether it might be true. And then, for the first time, a man came into your life whom you felt you could trust. Someone who made you feel that you really were worth something, after all."

As he spoke, her head nodded very slightly, almost involuntarily, as though it were being pushed from behind by an unseen hand.

"But there was a darker side to him, too, wasn't there? He knew how to make you feel special...but he also had his subtle ways of making you think that everything the nuns said about you might be right. He made you feel that you were the only one for him...and also that he was the only one for you. That if you were to lose him, no one else would ever love you. Is that more or less how it was?"

The invisible hand pushed her head more strongly.

"I suppose you must be curious about how I knew?"

"Well, then?"

"The thing is...ah, but maybe I'm not the best person to tell you this."

"Tell me what?"

"Are you sure you want to hear it from me?"

"Tell me!"

"Very well."

He picked up the metaphorical dice, blew on them, and rolled them.

"What would you say if I told you I heard the same story from Shira?"

Her eyes widened and locked onto his. "I'd say surely it's lying you are."

Surely it was, as far as he knew. But if it were true, it would have fit perfectly into the profile that was emerging for Chris.

"I wish I were, Peg. But the truth is, we deal with people like him all the time. I'm sorry to be the one to break this to you, but he's probably done the same thing to dozens of other women. When you're with him, you feel like you're the most important person in the world to him. But in fact, love is not something he's capable of. He's a hunter, he does this for sport. He knows where to find his prey, and he knows all the right lures to tempt them out of their hiding places. But if you let your guard down around him, then you end up as meat on his plate and a head on his wall."

She shook her head vehemently, as though trying to dislodge his words from her ears before they had the chance to penetrate her eardrums and work their way into her brain. "No. I'm not having that."

"Did he ever tell you his full name? His real name?"

"Of course."

"Which name was it that he gave you?"

She looked down, lips locked.

"He never told you, then," Fox said. "At least not the truth."

"He did."

"Then what was the name he gave you? Chris w..."

He had started to ask, "Chris what?" but as soon as his lips were in position to form the "w," a look of shock crossed Peg's face. She controlled it instantly, but it had been unmistakable.

"So," Fox said. "It was the same name that Shira gave us, then."

"What was it?" The question came out in a thin, faint voice, like that of a patient asking, "How long do I have?"

"Let's say it together. Three, two, one..."

Fox called on his theatrical training and spoke in synchronicity with her. The sound came out of his mouth barely a moment after hers: "Warndale."

Fox scribbled on the page in his notebook. Chris Warndale. Finally, he had a full name at the top of the wire diagram. But there were still some unanswered questions, mainly the role of Rashid Renclaw in the network.

Chris Warndale. Rashid Renclaw.

Like a flock of birds startled from their perches, the letters flew from the page, swooped and dived in circles, and then came back to rest. Fox could barely suppress the urge to leap from his seat and rush into the hall, waving his notebook and shouting "Eureka!" Instead, he looked back at Peg with the aplomb of a master gambler about to lay down the trump card.

"Peg, I'd like to show you something. We have a

source who admitted to selling a sample of the Zagorsk virus to someone named Rashid Renclaw." He showed her the page. "Rashid Renclaw. Chris Warndale. Try counting the letters, and you'll see that they're the same in both names."

She stared, clearly seeing the letters rearrange themselves in the same way that he had, despite willing them with all her heart to stay still.

"Now, look at this." He wrote a third name, and showed her. "They're aliases. Both of them are anagrams of *Charles Darwin*. I'm sorry, Peg, but this name is no more real than anything else he gave you."

Fox watched as a five-act play of emotions began to unfold on her face. He had seen the same pattern in other subjects about to break, a pattern strikingly similar to what psychologists called the five stages of grief. Denial, then anger, then depression. *Fine, let her take them out of sequence if she likes*, he thought, *just as long as we get to acceptance in the end. Or bargaining, that will serve the purpose just as well.*

She lay her head on the table and sobbed. He placed a packet of pocket tissues within her reach, and let her cry it out. When she raised her eyes again, they were a dangerous red.

"He has a house in some fancy part of London."

"Do you know where?"

She shook her head. "We all rode blindfolded."

"So I heard. But I'm guessing that perhaps you saw a bit more of the house than the others did?"

She grimaced at the memory that had suddenly become painful. "To get from the garage to the main house, I had to go outside for a while. But I still had my blindfold on."

"What kind of surface you were walking on? Do you remember how it felt?"

"Grass at first, then flagstones."

"What kind of sounds did you hear?"

"Birds, mainly. The odd car now and then, at a bit of a distance. 'Twas a quiet neighborhood."

"And once you were inside the house?"

"Enormous it was, to be sure. I remember that my steps echoed. I went up three flights of stairs before I finally got to..." she blushed again, "the room where I could take my blindfold off. Sure and it was a gorgeous house. Expensive furniture, chandeliers, decorations all around the walls and ceilings...very Victorian. Ah, yes, and one more thing. I had to duck. Just before going up the stairs, I had to pass through a door that was a bit shorter than I was."

Fox drew a rough sketch of the house from her description. "Does this look right?"

"Something like that."

He turned to a fresh page. "What can you tell me about Aidan?"

"From Belfast, he was. When he was a boy, his parents sent him to boarding school in England. 'Twas while he was there that he got word that his parents had been killed."

Fox grimaced. "What happened?"

"They were in the wrong place at the wrong time, nothing more. They got caught in the crossfire between Catholics and Protestants."

"You mean, between Unionists and Loyalists?"

"Whatever."

"What was he studying at Oxford?"

"He was reading biology and music."

"Music?"

She nodded. "He'd a fine voice on him, to be sure. He was working on some original compositions, like the *Big Band Big Bang* and the *Evolutorio*. He always liked to say, 'Why should the infected get all the good music?'"

Between Shira and Aidan, Fox's faith in music as a force for global peace was slipping fast.

"When did you last see him?"

"We parted ways in London. I caught the Eurostar, and he went underground."

"Did he give you any clues about where he was going?"

"No, of course he didn't tell me where he was bound for. But there was one thing he did say. 'Twas rather odd, to be sure. He said, 'And so the fool gets his revenge at last.'"

Fox copied down the words. "Is that a quote?" He wondered whether it could be from Shakespeare. It fit the meter of Shakespearean blank verse, but Fox had no recollection of reading it in any play. A fool, and revenge? *King Lear*, or perhaps *Twelfth Night?*

She shrugged. "I don't know, sure."

"Thank you, Peg. You've just helped us save hundreds, maybe thousands, of lives. Is there anything else you'd like to tell me?"

"Yes. When you catch Chris, could you give him a message from me?"

"Sure."

"Tell him I've changed my mind. I hope there really is a God...and a Hell for him to go to."

Possibly out of patriotic sentiment, Adler had booked them into the Hotel Columbus, at the corner of the Via della Conciliazione and—in a twist of the knife—the Via dei Cavalleri del Santo Sepolcro, the Street of the Knights of the Holy Sepulchre. Fox climbed up and down numerous staircases, and wandered through labyrinthine halls furnished with desks that could have come from a monastery scriptorium, before he found their room.

"How did it go?" asked a haggard Adler.

Fox briefed him. "Any word on whether any contamination escaped?"

Adler shook his head. "No indication so far, but they're asking everyone who was at the Vigil to be tested as soon as possible."

"And if they test positive?"

"Rid is getting ready to fly in a shipment of the antiserum as we speak. If it's administered before symptoms appear, it should be effective."

"Should?"

"Again, we've never had the chance to test it in the field. But we have every reason to believe it will be."

"Let's hope so." Fox hesitated a moment, then voiced the question that had been on his mind. "What's to become of Shira?"

"Agent Birnbaum will take her back tomorrow."

"Back?"

"To Israel, of course."

Fox's face fell. Adler went on, "Were you expecting anything different? She's an Israeli citizen who committed a crime on Israeli soil."

"We got her to cooperate by suggesting that if she proved useful to our investigation, the United States could intervene on her behalf."

"The key word is 'suggesting.' We didn't make any promises. And even if we had, come on! How many times did you lie to detainees?"

"Too many."

"When she goes on trial—"

"If ever!"

"—then a representative in Tel Aviv will testify that she cooperated with the United States."

"A representative in Tel Aviv? Please tell me you don't mean Birnbaum."

"Who else? She's the only one who was an eyewitness."

"Come on, John, you saw how she was acting around Shira! If she's an advocate for the defense, then the prosecution can just sit back and enjoy the show."

"What do you care? Since when are you her defense attorney? What is she to you?" Adler looked at Fox through narrowed eyes. "Would you be pleading her case so eloquently if she weren't so young and pretty?"

"John, how dare you!"

"How dare *you*?" Adler shot back. "You broke the first rule for interrogators."

"What are you talking about? I haven't violated any of the Geneva Conventions."

"I'm not talking about the goddamn Geneva Conventions! You got attached to a subject. You forgot the one thing you always need to remember: The people you work with are criminals and terrorists. Oh, I know everything they teach you about building rapport, establishing a human connection, blah blah blah...but at the end of the day, it's all an act. You can never forget that you're working with the worst of the worst."

"Right. That's what they always told us at Gitmo. And how many of those people turned out actually to be guilty of anything? One in ten, at most."

"And in this case, Shira just happens to be that one. You know that better than anyone, you were the one who caught her in the act. She's going to prison, and you can't deny that she deserves it."

"I know what they do to Palestinian women in Israeli prisons. If they do the same to their own people, no one deserves that."

"Oh, stop it!" Adler snapped. "I'm tired of always hearing you talk as if you're somehow morally superior. I've seen your service record. I know you've always said coercive methods don't work, bragged about never using them yourself, looked down your Harvard nose at anyone who did. But how many subjects did you break by telling them, 'If you won't talk to me, I'll have no choice but to turn you over to those other guys'? Look me in the eye and deny that you used that strategy on Shira."

Fox was silent.

"You see?" Adler went on. "You're a great Good Cop, Robin, but you can't do that job without a Bad Cop. You're a religion scholar, you must understand this. Sometimes the promise of Heaven by itself isn't enough. To keep people in line, you also need the threat of Hell."

"I've always felt that we would be much better off without Hell."

"That's a beautiful philosophy, Professor, but we live in the real world. And there are some people in it who just don't respond to anything else."

When Fox made no reply, Adler put an end to the conversation by turning on the television and tuning in to the first English-language network he could find, which happened to be the BBC. Fox switched on his cell phone, which had been off since he boarded the flight to Rome.

He saw that Miriam had tried to call him several times, and left multiple e-mail messages. There was also a message, with an attachment, from a sender identified only by an address that he had never seen. The subject line read, "Emily Harper."

Fox felt the sudden tightening in his chest, and numbness in his limbs, that he imagined a stroke victim must feel. A subject line bearing only a person's name was rarely good news. It usually meant that the person was either in the hospital or dead. After several attempts to steady his finger, he opened the message.

The attachment was a photograph of Emily, sprawled unconscious on a bed, with a hand at the edge of the frame pointing a pistol at her head.

The text read:

> *Dear Professor Fox: On the third day, I will reach my goal. You may already have deduced where the site will be. Be assured that if any cameras catch you there, Ms Harper will not live one moment beyond that. Cordially, Chris Warndale.*

A hole opened under Fox's heart, and his soul flew out of it, bound for some unknown place, silently screaming an unheeded message: *Take me instead! Do whatever you want to me, but let her go!*

With fingers turned to icicles, he dialed Miriam.

"Robin!" came her anguished voice as soon as she answered. "I'm sorry. I'm so very sorry."

"Miriam..."

"It was my fault. If I had just—"

"Calm down, Miriam," he said, fully aware that his advice was impossible to follow. "Just tell me what happened."

She told him about Heathrow. "Of course, I reported it to the police, and the American embassy. I've told Rick, and Nels. Beyond that, I don't know what to do."

"Take care of Leila. Stay in touch with the embassy, and let me know the second you hear any news. And pray like you've never prayed before."

He disconnected the phone, and sat down on the bed before his legs gave out on their own.

Adler turned away from the TV to look at Fox. "Robin?" he said. "My God, you're white as a ghost! What happened?"

Fox told him. Adler's reaction was stunned silence, which the BBC announcer on the television obliviously filled.

"With St. George's Chapel in Windsor Castle, the traditional site of the Royal Family's Easter celebration, still under repair from the fire two weeks ago," the voice was saying, "it was decided that Their Majesties would instead attend Easter Sunday services at Westminster Abbey. The Royal Household has declared that, despite the recent worldwide spate of attacks on places of worship, the service will be held as scheduled, amid heightened security."

Slowly, Fox rejoined the universe, and turned his

eyes to the screen. "Son of a...!"

"What?"

"*That's* what he was about to say!"

"Who?"

"There is no God...*so he can't save the Queen.*"

THE REVELATION

15

LONDON
SUNDAY, APRIL 5
EASTER SUNDAY

"**M**s. Harper, are you awake?"

Emily opened her eyes. She was in a bedroom that looked like it belonged in a Victorian house, lying on a four-poster bed among tasseled brocade pillows of every imaginable shape and size. Sitting in a chair beside her was a blond-haired man, perhaps about thirty, immaculately dressed in upscale brands. His smile was warm, but not enough to thaw the ice in his eyes. It was the smile she imagined might appear on the face of a man coming home to his family after a satisfying day's work at the concentration camp.

And she had seen those eyes before, above a surgical

mask at Heathrow Airport.

She tried to sit up, but her body responded to the command from her brain only with a few twitches and spasms.

"Relax," her captor said. "It'll take a minute for your central nervous system to come back online." He dipped a tea towel into a bowl of ice water on the marble-topped bedside table, moistened her lips with it, then clamped a pair of tongs around an ice cube. "You must be terribly thirsty. Your stomach probably isn't ready for a drink of water just yet, but this should help for now." He held the ice cube to her mouth. She hesitated a moment, then let her lips part to accept it.

"I must apologize," he went on, "for the rude way in which it was necessary to bring you here. I would much rather have made your acquaintance in a more civilized fashion, but such was the exigency of the moment."

Emily tried to calm herself and think. Like all USPRI staff working in the field, she had taken the kidnapping prevention training required by their insurers, but it was a long time ago and the memory had faded since then. Who, after all, ever really expected to need it? She reached into her memory and recited the prescribed lines.

"I work for the United States Peace Research Institute, an independent body not connected in any way with the United States government. They will not negotiate for my release, or pay any ransom."

Her captor laughed as though this were the best joke he had heard in his life. "My dear Ms. Harper! Look around you. Do I really look like the sort who would be interested in ransom? No, you're here because of your gentleman friend, Professor Robin Fox. He's been rather a nuisance to me lately, and you're here to ensure that he causes me no further trouble."

He gestured around the room. "In the meantime, I'll do my utmost to make sure your stay here is as comfortable as possible. You have an ensuite bath. You have cable television, or some books if you prefer. I don't imagine you have much of an appetite for solid food just now, but I'll bring some soup later on that should go down fairly well. Do please make yourself entirely at home. There is only one rule: When you hear the doorbell ring, I must ask you to sit on the bed, where I can see you, and wait. Otherwise, I shan't be able to come in and serve you. Do we have an understanding?"

Emily glanced at the ceiling and saw a small dome, of the kind designed to mask a surveillance camera. She nodded, trying to keep her face from showing her reaction. *Trying to condition me. Like Pavlov's dogs.*

"Please try to relax, Ms. Harper, and don't worry. I'm sure Professor Fox is a reasonable man, and he clearly cares very deeply about you. So, if everything goes smoothly, you'll soon be on your way home to America."

"And if it doesn't?"

The expression in his eyes altered slightly. Now it looked as though the concentration camp guard was getting ready to leave for work in the morning.

"That would be...regrettable."

When Fox and Adler landed at Heathrow, a stocky, red-haired, red-bearded man was standing at the gate, twitching, chafing at the wait—for them or for a smoke break, or both. Adler greeted him, and made the introductions. "Mr. Donovan, this is Robin Fox. Robin, this is Agent Liam Donovan, from MI5. Oh, sorry, you call it the Security Service now, right?"

"That's all right," he said, in an accent that Fox struggled to place, somewhere between British and Irish. "Old habits die hard, and nearly everyone in Britain still uses the old name—even us, sometimes."

Donovan escorted them to an unmarked car, rolled down the window, and sacrificed a burned offering to the god Nicotine. He joined the chaos of the road to London, maneuvering the car expertly among trucks, taxis, and a red double-decker bus emblazoned with someone's idea of a public service message: *Science flies you to the moon. Religion flies you into buildings.*

"I've briefed the Metropolitan Police," Donovan was saying to Adler, "and they've pulled out all the stops. Specialist Operations 14 and 15—the Royal Protection Command and the Counter Terror Command—have been working round the clock. Last night, they scoured the entire Abbey looking for anything even slightly suspicious. No one will be able to get in today without a pass, issued by the Royal Household after a thorough vetting, and they'll still have to be screened on entry. If there's a way to make security any tighter, I don't know it."

"What about our request to keep cameras out of the Abbey?" Fox asked.

Donovan shook his head. "We tried again and again, but the Royal Household wouldn't hear of it. They said this was a unique event—the Royal Family attending an Easter service at the Abbey open to the public—and to keep the media away was out of the question. We got them to agree to a compromise: everyone will have to check cameras and cell phones at the door except for licensed reporters, and even they will only be able to use theirs between the quire and the sanctuary. In other words, they can photograph the royals, the priests, or the choir, but not the congregation. That's as much as we could get."

Fox grimaced. "I suppose it will have to do."

"And we've got something for you. Look in the bag."

Fox opened the duffel bag lying next to him in the back seat. He saw dark brown cloth, which proved on closer inspection to be a hooded robe with a white cord—the habit of a Franciscan monk.

"A disguise?"

"There'll be lots of other Franciscan brothers there. And with the hood up, no one will be able to make out your face."

"Thanks," said Fox, trying unsuccessfully to keep his misgivings out of his voice.

"If you think it's too big a risk, I don't really see the need for you to be in there at all. We have the description you got from the subject in Rome. Everyone's identity will be checked. If this Aidan tries to get in there, we'll catch him. And if he manages to get any kind of device through security, it'll be a Devil's miracle."

"If I know anything about Chris Warndale," Fox said, "he's got more than one of those up his sleeve."

Once her captor had left her, Emily got up and examined her surroundings. The bed was so high that it had a matching step-stool to help its occupant climb in and out. Besides the bed, chair and bedside table, there was a flat-screen TV mounted on the far wall, and a bookcase full of the works of atheist philosophers ranging from Jean-Jacques Rousseau to Daniel Dennett.

The door was locked with a hooded keypad. There was one curtained window, near the head of the bed. She drew aside the curtains, but found that the window was barred, and the pane was frosted, allowing no view outside.

She went into the bathroom, where bright lights gleamed off the black and white marble tiles and gilt-edged glass. Her host had prepared thick towels, a cake of scented soap, small bottles of shampoo, even a velour bathrobe. All the amenities she would expect in a luxury hotel, but nothing that looked at all useful to help her escape.

The bells were ringing in the tower of Westminster Abbey. On the flagstones far below, a queue of worshippers extended down the street, rubbing their hands and stamping their feet against the chill of the cloudy morning.

Fox, in his borrowed Franciscan habit, hovered near the end of the line, surreptitiously surveying the scene from under his cowl. At the gate, the police had expanded greatly on the simple green sentry box that usually stood there. They scrutinized the tickets and IDs of everyone coming in, checked them against a list, and waved their metal-detector wands over each one. They inspected all bags, first with an X-ray machine and then by hand, before stashing them in a portable cabin for the duration of the service. Anyone who could smuggle any suspicious object past them, including a camera or cell phone, would have to be a master magician.

Could someone waiting in line pass a canister through the bars to an accomplice inside the fence? But the police had anticipated that. Lashed to the fence were nine-foot wooden poles with plastic mesh between them, and officers stood watch at intervals.

Fox agreed with Donovan's assessment: the perimeter looked as secure as humanly possible. But the ingenuity of their adversary, he was beginning to think, went beyond human into the realm of the diabolical.

The doorbell rang. Emily, deciding she was better off complying with her captor's request until she had a clearer idea where she was and how she might escape, seated herself on the bed. The door opened, and he appeared, bearing a bowl of steaming soup on a bed tray.

"Vichyssoise, with a bit of tomato. Careful, it's quite hot." He set the tray astride her lap. The presentation was worthy of a Michelin-starred restaurant: a gold-rimmed china bowl on a satin tablecloth, garnished with a sprig of fresh parsley, and in a glass vase in the corner of the tray, a rose.

Establish a rapport with your captor. Engage him in conversation on neutral, non-threatening subjects. Help him to see you as a human being, rather than a pawn in some ideological game.

She picked up her spoon and took a taste. "This is delicious. Thank you. Did you make it yourself, or did this house come with a live-in chef?"

He gave a self-deprecating chuckle. "My own clumsy attempt. I'm glad you find it satisfactory." He seated himself in the chair and watched her take another spoonful.

His gaze fell on her Celtic cross pendant. "You're a woman of faith, then, Ms. Harper?"

Her free hand self-consciously covered it. "You could say that."

"You have a choice, you realize."

"I know."

"So I'm curious about what makes you choose to stay in a place where they'll always treat you as a second-class citizen. Try to hold you back from becoming who you really are."

She took a non-committal spoonful of soup. "What do you mean?" *Keep your answers short and neutral. Let him talk as much as he wants.*

"The Devil's gateway. The enemy of peace. Of all the wild beasts, the most dangerous. These are some of the charming little endearments your Early Church Fathers used for the female of the species. Pick any religion you like from anywhere in the world. At best, you'll be told that you must always be meek and mild, submissive and subservient. At worst, you'll be wrapped up in a burqa wherever you go, beaten to within an inch of your life if you make a sound in the marketplace, or expected to throw yourself onto your husband's funeral pyre if he shuffles off this mortal coil before you do. So tell me, what makes an intelligent woman like you stay in this company when she doesn't have to?"

"I'm touched by your concern. But my church doesn't

exactly teach women to be meek and submissive. The husband of any one of them could tell you that."

"I understand how difficult it can be to overcome the trauma of child abuse."

"I'm sorry?"

"Having frightening myths impressed on your mind as if they were true, before you were old enough to tell fantasy from reality. I know what a painful thing it is to have your childhood worldview shattered."

"Would it shatter *your* worldview if I told you my family wasn't religious? That I came to it on my own?"

He gave her a look that mingled concern with fascination, like a researcher of exotic diseases finally seeing his first case in a live patient. "So, such a specimen really does exist. An otherwise rational adult who's deluded herself into believing there's some creature up in the sky, reading our thoughts and watching what we do in the bedroom. Who created this earth as a home for us, with all its hurricanes, earthquakes, and tsunamis. Who tells us, 'I love you. Love me back or I'll torture you for all eternity.' Have I got it right?"

"I think you meant to say 'creator' rather than 'creature.' And I might change one or two details."

"That he loves us, for example?"

"That one I'd grant you."

"How, then, do you account for the existence of the virus?"

Emily had no ready answer for that one. She took a spoonful of soup to buy time to think.

"Have you ever seen someone die from Ebola?" he continued.

"No."

"Viral exsanguination. Do you know what that means? Your internal organs melt together into a bloody soup, which leaks out all your orifices until there isn't enough blood left in your body to keep it alive. Is that a way you would care to die, if you had a choice in the matter?"

"Not particularly." She set her spoon down. She had suddenly lost her appetite for soup.

"So tell me: If this world was created by a God who loves us, then whence come these little creatures who can only perpetuate their own lives by destroying ours, in what you would probably call quite a gruesome way?"

When Emily made no answer, he continued, "You see, if you look at the world from a rational point of view, the question doesn't merit a second thought. The virus's ability to replicate has evolved beyond the host cell's ability to fend it off. No question of right or wrong, meaningful or meaningless. Nature simply works according to its laws, and no prayer, no divine intervention can stop it."

With that last sentence, the ice in his eyes melted slightly. It suddenly occurred to Emily to wonder how someone so young could be living in this luxurious house, presumably alone.

She suddenly recalled Leila's words in Tel Aviv: *For every story heard, an act of violence is prevented.*

"Did you...did you lose someone you love?"

He looked down, his face impossible to read. She kept her expression of mild concern, trying to betray none of her steadily mounting fear that she had asked a forbidden question, like Bluebeard's wife innocently inquiring about the little room in the cellar.

"I sat by my mother's hospital bed," he finally said, "day after day, watching her grow weaker and weaker from pneumonia. Of course, my father made sure she had the best medical care money could buy. And of course, he prayed. And he told me to pray. And like a child, I did, without questioning. And given my father's connections, I'm sure that all the vicars and all the bishops, all the way up to the Archbishop of bloody Canterbury, were praying for her too. And did it work? Did it save her?"

The silence in the room answered his question.

"Where was your God then, Ms. Harper?" he inquired in a soft voice that could not have chilled her more if she had heard it out of the darkness behind her when she thought she was alone in the house. "Tell me! *Where was he?*"

The sudden force of his voice, coming so soon after his near-whisper, pushed Emily back against her pillows. She could think of no answer she could give that had any chance of satisfying him.

Don't play his game. Don't try to engage him intellectually. Speak to his heart instead.

"It must have torn you apart when you lost her. I can feel how much you miss her. And how angry you were when all your prayers went unanswered."

He closed his eyes, and for a moment, Emily thought he might be on the verge of tears. But when he opened them again, the blue ice had frozen solid again. "You'd think that would be enough evidence to convince any rational person that there was no such entity as God. But my father kept blathering on about how God must have had some 'purpose' unknown to us. Well, let me ask you this, Ms. Harper: If you saw someone murder the mother of a ten-year-old boy in front of his eyes, just how much would you care what his 'purpose' was?"

"You felt that your faith had been betrayed."

"Wouldn't you, Ms. Harper? Wouldn't anyone? But my father was infected beyond all hope of recovery. He carried on praying, going to church every Sunday, and squandering his fortune on so-called 'charity.' When he last revised his will, he was planning to use ninety percent of his estate to endow a foundation. *Ninety percent* of what was rightfully mine! And I could almost have allowed it, if it had been, say, a university. He could have built one to rival Oxford or Cambridge, if he had so chosen. But do you know what he took a fancy to do instead?"

Emily kept silent, prompting him with her eyes to go on.

"He decided that the best use of his money would be to set up free clinics and dispensaries, all over the developing world. He got the notion into his head that every child born, whether in South Kensington or some village in the Kalahari, should have an equal chance at life. Can you imagine? Just what this planet needs— more mewling mouths to feed."

He paused and looked at her as though expecting her to share his indignation. It was all she could do to keep her internal reaction from showing in her face.

"And he had a long list of medical students," he went on, "from the finest universities, all ready to volunteer. Seducing the best and brightest into throwing their talents away on those whom nature had clearly marked for destruction. This is the cardinal error of your Christianity, Ms. Harper. It elevates compassion for the poor, the weak, all of nature's mistakes, to the level of virtue. When in fact, their job is to die out and free the world's resources for the strong. And the purest form of 'charity' is to help them do it."

For a moment, Emily could almost smell the smoke of burning sulfur. She struggled to think of a suitably neutral reply, and to keep her voice from giving away her true feelings. "I can see you're angry with him for spending his fortune on a cause you didn't agree with." She cast her eyes around the room and its opulent furnishings. "So what I'm seeing here is just ten percent of what would otherwise have been your inheritance?"

"This?" Her captor chuckled. "Oh, no, Ms. Harper. My father passed on before his solicitor ever saw the revised will. Most unexpected and most unfortunate."

A fanfare of organ and trumpets echoed through the nave of Westminster Abbey, adding to the thousand years' worth of sacred sound those stones had already absorbed, as the royal procession made its way over the black and white tiles. The stern-faced, shaven-headed verger, in his red and black velvet robe, led the way. Next came the Nearest Guard, the Queen's ceremonial bodyguards, in gold-trimmed red tunics and white-plumed helmets. The light flashed impressively from the blades of their halberds as they marched in step, but Fox wondered whether they understood the true nature of the foe they were facing, and how little use their medieval weapons would be against him.

The choir, in their red cassocks with ruffled white collars, filed into the tiered wooden seats of the quire.

254 | Charles Kowalski

The red-shaded lamps at each place made it look like a study for forty scholars: the thirty boys in the children's choir and the ten professional singers known as Lay Vicars.

And then came the Queen, the Duke of Edinburgh, the Prince of Wales, and an assortment of princes and princesses in their Easter finery, floral ornaments piled high enough on their hats to block the vision of anyone sitting behind them. They assumed their red velvet seats, set to one side at the foot of the sanctuary steps, presumably to remind them that they were in the presence of Someone even higher than they.

Fox stood at his post in the transept, scanning the crowd. The flat-screen televisions mounted on the pillars gave him a partial view of the quire and nave. The walls surrounding him were lined with busts and reliefs of various worthies from British history, all of whom seemed to have their eyes on him, sending a message across the centuries: "Get it right this time, can't you?"

The Archbishop of Canterbury spread his hands and began the liturgy. "This is the day when our Lord Jesus Christ passed from death to life. Throughout the world, Christians celebrate the awesome power of God. As we hear his word and proclaim all that God has done, we can be confident that we shall share his victory over death and live with him for ever."

Fox wished he could be as confident of victory as the Archbishop. He was grateful for the concealment that the cowl provided, but it hung down over his eyes and obscured his view. Presumably it was meant to shut out distractions and temptations, and keep the wearer's attention focused solely on the next step. If only he knew what that would be.

The liturgy proceeded through the readings, the sermon, and the prayers of intercession. As the intercessor started to read out the prayer concerns, Fox reached through the slit in his habit that allowed access to his pocket. He pulled out his notebook and pen, scribbled a few hasty lines, and handed the notebook to Donovan.

"When I give you the signal, could you read this out loud?"

Donovan looked at the paper. "The hell?"

"Let's just give it a try."

"We commend to your fatherly goodness," the intercessor intoned, "all those who are any ways afflicted or distressed, in mind, body or estate. Comfort and relieve them in their need, give them patience in their sufferings, and bring good out of all their afflictions."

In the ensuing moment of silence, Donovan spoke up, in a voice that resounded throughout the cathedral.

"Let us pray for all orphans who lost their parents in acts of violence, and for all children, especially those here with us today. Keep them safe from all illness, Lord, and do not let anyone do them any harm."

There were scattered whispers throughout the nave. Free intercessions from the congregation were technically allowed under the prayer book rubrics, but to offer one in front of the Royal Family and a full cathedral required a degree of boldness well outside the usual Anglican range. Fox only hoped that Aidan would understand the coded message: *We're on to you.*

The choir sang the offertory anthem: Palestrina's *Sicut Cervus.* "As the deer longs for flowing streams, so longs my soul for you, O God." The alto voices soared up to the vault, soon to be overtaken by the sopranos that sounded as though they could carry the melody all the way up to heaven, until the tenor and bass voices of the adult Lay Vicars joined in to bring them back down to earth. This was a piece that, under ordinary circumstances, could lift Fox to the sky on a white cloud, but now he wondered whether he would ever be able to listen to it the same way again.

Don't let them distract you, Fox admonished himself. *Focus on the task at hand.* But his gaze kept returning to the choir. Soon, his conscious mind registered what his subconscious must have noticed first: One of the younger Lay Vicars was holding his score with trembling hands. Even in the chill of the cathedral, he was sweating. His eyes were blinking rapidly, and darting glances out to the congregation, while all the other singers were duly dividing their attention between the sheet music and the director.

Peg's voice echoed in his ears: *He'd a fine voice on him, to be sure.*

She had mentioned that Aidan had gone to a boarding school in Britain, but not which one. If it was the Westminster Abbey Choir School, he would be eligible to rejoin the choir as a Lay Vicar in adulthood.

If Fox's theory was correct, then he had to admit Chris Warndale certainly knew how to plan ahead. He had planted a sleeper agent in Westminster Abbey. Aidan, operating in his home country, would have had no need to smuggle his weapon past security on the day itself. He would have been in the Abbey for rehearsals constantly, and had ample opportunity to plant it ahead of time.

But where could he have hidden it, so that even a thorough search by the Counter Terror Command had failed to find it?

The anthem came to an end, and the Archbishop of Canterbury gave the opening acclamation of the Eucharist. "The Lord be with you."

"And also with you," the congregation replied.

"Lift up your hearts."

"We lift them to the Lord."

"Let us give thanks to the Lord our God."

"It is right to give thanks and praise."

"It is indeed right, it is our duty and our joy, at all times and in all places to give you thanks and praise, almighty and eternal God, through Jesus Christ your Son our Lord. By his death he has destroyed death, and by his rising to life again...he has restored to...to us..."

The Archbishop's voice broke off, and he looked down, his mouth and eyes wide with alarm.

A wisp of smoke was rising from the hem of his cassock.

As he stared at the rapidly expanding brown spot from which the smoke issued, it burst into flame.

The Archbishop screamed. He jumped and whirled around in panic, which only spread the flames further. The figure behind the high altar looked like a fiery demon, spinning in a mad dance and flapping its golden wings.

Shrieks erupted throughout the congregation. The verger grabbed the fire extinguisher at the base of the steps to the pulpit.

Fox glanced back at the Lay Vicar. His breath was

coming even faster, and his face was dripping with sweat. Like everyone else, his gaze was fixed on the scene, but unlike everyone else, he was not craning his neck to see. He knew what was about to happen.

The verger pointed the extinguisher at the Archbishop's vestments.

The red cylinder flashed at Fox like a warning light. It would have been easy for Aidan to steal into the sanctuary when no one was watching, and replace the extinguisher with one that had been modified to carry a lethal load.

"Stop!" Fox shouted. "The extinguisher's poisoned!"

The verger shot a disbelieving glance in his direction, and quickly returned to his task, aiming the nozzle at the Archbishop's burning vestments.

Fox stood paralyzed. If he set foot into the sanctuary, all the television cameras in the cathedral would capture his image for all the world to see. But if he held back, the verger would unwittingly spray the virus into the packed cathedral.

The verger squeezed the lever.

Nothing happened. He looked down at the extinguisher. The pin was still in place.

Fox took a firm grip on his cowl to keep it from slipping and revealing his face, and ran for the altar.

The verger pulled out the pin, took a grip on the lever, and aimed the nozzle again.

Fox caught up to him and knocked the extinguisher from his hands. Together, they pulled the Archbishop to the floor and tried to smother the flames with his heavy brocade cope.

A moment later, a firefighter came running in from

outside, with an extinguisher of his own. Fox retreated, his cowl pulled low over his head, trying to keep his back to the television cameras.

The Lay Vicar whom Fox had been watching jumped down from his seat in the quire. He ran through the arch under the organ loft, and turned when he reached the nave.

"Don't let him get away!" Donovan bellowed.

The command was unnecessary. Several of the congregants were already converging on him. He found himself cornered between the wall and a blue-and-gold wrought iron gate, now shut.

He fell to his knees. Set into the floor below him were two stone slabs, one black and one white. He prostrated himself on the white one, lowered his face to it, and kissed it, just as the police officers seized him and cuffed his hands behind him.

"Sorry, old fool," he said, gazing fondly at the stone as they led him away.

Fox glanced at the stone. The inscription read:

CHARLES ROBERT DARWIN
BORN 12 FEBRUARY 1809
DIED 19 APRIL 1882

Fox ran down the aisle and out the door, with Adler and Donovan close behind. He reached the silver Mercedes Sprinter van parked on Dean's Court, just as the officers were pulling Aidan aboard and getting ready to close the door.

One of the officers held up a hand to stop him. "I'm sorry, Brother..."

"Brother, my ass! I'm with the CIA!"

He jumped aboard and seized Aidan by his white surplice. "Where's Chris Warndale?"

"I don't know."

"Bullshit!" He slammed Aidan into the wall of the van, with such force that his head whipped back against the metal. "He has a house in London. You know where, and you're either going to tell me or watch what I'm going to do to you."

"I'm telling you, man, I don't know!"

The van's back door opened wider to reveal Donovan and Adler.

"Fox!" Donovan called.

Fox pulled out his pen, and with his other hand, pried Aidan's right eye wide open. The left eye had gone almost equally wide with fear.

Fox held the point of the pen an inch away from Aidan's eye. "One more 'I don't know' out of you and you get an eye patch, two more and you get a white cane. Where is Chris Warndale?"

Aidan's mouth trembled, but no sound came out.

"Five! Four! Three! Two! One!"

"Now that's what I call interrogation!" Adler said.

The words pierced a hole in Fox that drained all the air from his lungs. For a moment, it was as though his soul had temporarily detached itself from his body, like a hospital patient looking down at his own inert form on the operating table. He saw himself, in the habit of the Franciscan order—one that he had always respected for its commitment to peace and nonviolence—brandishing his improvised weapon in the face of a helpless subject. Who was the true villain in this picture? If Emily saw it, how would she answer that question, even knowing it was all for her sake?

He released his hold, and lowered his pen. The terrified expression on Aidan's face, he saw, had its reflection on Donovan and all the police officers who were watching.

"I'm sorry," he murmured. "I'm sorry."

"Fox, lad." Donovan spoke in the voice of calm authority he must have learned at police academy, for use with hostage-takers and bridge-jumpers. "He's telling the truth. He doesn't know."

Fox nodded. The signs, if his mind had been clear enough to read them, would have told him the same.

"But maybe," Donovan went on, "we can take you to someone who does."

The doorbell rang. Emily straightened up in bed as the door opened and her captor entered.

"It's been lovely chatting, Ms. Harper," he said, "but I'm afraid I have some unfortunate news. Mr. Fox has not kept his end of the bargain. I'd imagine he's probably on his way here, with the police in tow."

Emily tried not to let her face show what her heart was saying: *Thank you, God.*

"Now, Ms. Harper, I know you're a woman of deep faith. But what about Fox? He's a scholar of comparative religions. Do you know what he really believes? Would his faith be as strong as yours, if it were put to the test?"

"Yes." But she was saying what she hoped rather than what she knew to be true, and she felt sure that he could hear it in her voice.

"Well, if I'm to have you both here, perhaps you'll indulge me in a little experiment." He took a flash drive out of his pocket, and plugged it into the side of the television. The screen lit up with a few lines of text.

"If you both say these words, or if you both refuse, then both of you can go free. But if only one of you says them, then the one who does will go free, and the one who refuses will die. What do you think? Will you say them?"

She read the words silently, and shook her head. "You should know me better than that."

"That's what I thought. Well, we'll see whether Mr. Fox feels the same." He removed the flash drive, and keyed in the code to open the door. "I'll be back presently to bring you your lunch. Do you have any requests? I'd like to make you something special, for the meal that might be your last."

Donovan drove Fox and Adler in the unmarked car, along A40 to Oxford. Ordinarily, Fox would have enjoyed the drive through forests and rolling hills, with stone cottages and fences that looked as though they might date back to Roman times. But all his attention now was turned toward the Great Unknowable. *Please, let Emily be all right. Please, let us not be too late.*

"Bugger me up, down, and sideways," Donovan muttered as he drove. "Here I was thinking I'd seen everything. But I never imagined I'd see the Archbishop of Canterbury spontaneously combust. How in the hell did this Chris of yours do that?"

"My best guess would be linseed oil," Fox said.

"It would have been ready to hand in the Abbey, for polishing the woodwork. Soak a few strips of cloth in it, put them into a plastic bag, and then, when you can get into the sacristy when no one's looking, cut a slit in the hem of the Archbishop's vestments and slip it in. An hour or two later, ignition."

"Good odds he was the one behind the fire at Windsor Castle, too." Donovan shook his head in disbelief. "Bloody hell. Atheoterrorists! Is no one safe now, then?"

Fox arched an eyebrow. "Had you thought it was only the religious ones who were dangerous?"

"Hey, I grew up in Belfast, all right? Over the past twenty years, I've seen public enemy number one go from the IRA, Provisional IRA, Real IRA, who the hell knew what new offshoot of the IRA back then, to the Islamic terrorists now. I used to think that if we could just do away with religion, I could sit on my arse and read the Times all day. But now comes this bloke, prostrating himself on Darwin's tomb as if he were praying to bloody Mecca..."

"*And so the fool gets his revenge at last,*" Fox recalled. "That's what he meant. Darwin's contemporaries called him foolish so often that he took to signing his letters, 'Stultus the Fool.' Maybe Aidan thought he was 'avenging' him for the offense of burying him in a church. Someone should have told him that Darwin was a deacon."

"I'll tell you," Donovan sighed, "if the old boy could see what's being done in his name these days, he wouldn't be evolving, he'd be *revolving* in his grave."

Adler was tapping the screen of his phone. "Speaking of which, I've got something on Chris Warndale. There's a blog and a Facebook page under that name, with plenty of subscribers to both."

"I don't suppose he was obliging enough to post a photo?"

"No such luck." He showed Fox his phone, with Warndale's Facebook page on the screen, and the profile picture was an artist's rendition of a DNA helix. "But look at some of the stuff he writes: 'The time for rational debate is past. Again and again, we have seen that those infected with the God virus are immune to logical arguments, popular condemnation, and even legal action. They operate outside the law and all the constraints of civilized society. And unless we wish to be tortured, stoned, beheaded, burned at the stake, or simply stripped of our freedom of thought by the disciples of idiocy, intolerance and insanity, we must do likewise.'"

"Clearly the rhetoric of a sane, rational, scientific mind," Fox commented.

"There's something about this guy I don't get," Adler said. "He went to a lot of trouble to cover his tracks. He trained his agents in counterinterrogation. And yet, he left clues for us in the Bibles. What was that about?"

"He's playing a game with us," Fox replied. "It's more exciting for him if the game is close. He fancies himself as a chess grandmaster playing against a novice. He can suggest a good next move for us, confident that he's still going to trounce us anyway. I'll bet that he's planning to boast about it afterwards to his online followers. 'I gave them all these hints, and they still couldn't stop me. Look how stupid they are, and how clever I am.'"

"Well," Donovan decreed, "he'll be eating those words before he ever writes them."

Fox looked out the window at the approaching spires of Oxford. "Say that after we've caught him."

They stopped outside a white house on a tree-lined street. When they rang the doorbell, the door opened to reveal a gray-haired figure in a blue cardigan, who looked curiously from one of them to another. It took him a moment to recognize Fox. When he did, his eyeballs threatened to jump out of their sockets and shatter his wire-rimmed lenses.

"Hello, Professor," Fox said. "Sorry to bother you on Easter Sunday, but somehow we didn't think you would be in church."

"Well, well, Mr. Fox! This is an unexpected honor. Have you come for a rematch?"

"Not exactly."

Donovan took his badge out of his pocket and held it up for inspection. Adler remained motionless and expressionless, possibly hoping Dickinson would assume that he was also with MI5. Dickinson's eyes widened again, and he took a step back.

"We'd like a word with you, if you don't mind," said Donovan.

Dickinson ushered them into a bright and spacious living room. Fox glanced around the shelves that covered the walls from floor to ceiling. Curios from the professor's travels—African masks, birds' nests, wooden horses from miniature carousels—shared space with a variety of scientific treatises, an equal number of literary works, and one whole shelf full of copies of his bestselling antitheist manifesto, *The Greatest Delusion on Earth*.

"So, Professor Fox," said Dickinson once they were seated, "is this what you Americans do when you lose a debate? Show up at your opponent's door with MI5 in tow? Rather over the top, I must say."

"Professor," Donovan said, "if you've been following the news, you're aware that in the past two weeks, there have been four incidents involving the genetically engineered encephalitis virus known as Zagorsk. A prayer rally in Washington. The airport in Tel Aviv. Easter Vigil Mass at St. Peter's, and Westminster Abbey this morning."

"Well, it's just as I've always said, isn't it? Going to church is hazardous to your health."

"You may also be aware that the suspects apprehended in each case are Oxford students, and members of OAF. You're the faculty advisor for that group, are you not?"

Dickinson shot Donovan and Adler a wary glance. "Now wait a minute. Do I stand accused of something?"

"Relax, Professor," Donovan reassured him. "No one is accusing you of anything. We just think you might be able to give us information that would be helpful in solving the case. Were you aware that any members of this group were involved in planning these attacks?"

"Of course not! If I had been, I would either have put a stop to it or reported it to the authorities immediately. I never advocated violence of any kind."

Fox stood up. "If I may?" He pulled down a copy of Dickinson's book from the shelf and read aloud. "In 1980, in a feat of international cooperation one could wish to see more often, the World Health Organization finally succeeded in ridding the world of a deadly scourge that had plagued it for centuries: the smallpox virus. And we could have done the same for polio, had it not been for a handful of imams who concocted the story that the vaccine was an American plot to sterilize Muslim men. If only viruses of the mind could be eradicated as easily as those of the body." He slammed the book shut and hurled it onto the coffee table.

Dickinson looked down at the book, then back up at Fox. "I meant, through education."

"Someone must have missed that part."

"My teachings have been twisted. Perverted!"

"Well, that could happen even to Jesus Christ, couldn't it?"

Dickinson's glare made it clear that he did not find the comparison at all flattering.

Donovan resumed his questioning: "All the suspects were on campus together within the last two years. Thaddeus James Moresby-Stokes. Shira Yavin. Mairead 'Peg' O'Mullany. Aidan Kelly. And an Ahmad, whose last name we don't know, but he's Pakistani."

"I know one Ahmad in OAF, Ahmad Ghilzai. He's actually Afghani, but his family fled to Pakistan."

"To escape the Taliban?"

"Why else? Maybe it was when they cut all the pictures out of his father's medical texts, saying that any likeness of the human form was forbidden. Or maybe it was when his mother was grabbed off the street and publicly flogged, for the heinous crime of laughing out loud while talking to a friend at the market." He turned to Fox. "Are you still interested in defending these people?"

"I was never interested in defending the Taliban, Professor, you know that. And this is hardly the time for a continuation of our debate. The leader of this group is someone who uses the aliases Rashid Renclaw and Chris Warndale."

"I've never heard either of those names."

"He graduated a couple of years ago, and still makes occasional appearances at OAF parties. We think he lives somewhere in London."

Dickinson shrugged. "Sorry. I wish I could be of more help."

"He probably majored in microbiology or something like that, and is most likely now working in medical research—someplace where he would have access to a high-containment laboratory. He was president of OAF some years ago, but probably not within the memory of any current student. John, our source in Georgia said he looked like a more handsome version of TJ, correct?"

At a nod from Adler, Fox continued: "So, blond hair and blue eyes. Flamboyantly rich. He drives a red BMW and has a big Victorian house in an upscale neighborhood of London. Highly intelligent, with an ego to match—expects admiration from everyone and reacts badly to any little criticism. Very charming, probably has a bit of a reputation as a ladies' man, but isn't the type to have stable long-term relationships. Who do you know that fits that description?"

"Who do I know that fits that description?" Dickinson repeated the question, and shrugged a shoulder. "I do not know any such person."

Fox felt the same rage welling up within him that he had in the van with Aidan. "Professor," he said in a voice of ice, "may I remind you that withholding information would make you an accessory?"

Dickinson glared at him over the rims of his glasses. "I'm aware of that. One does not withhold information from the Security Service."

"I may not be as skilled in debate as you, Professor, but one thing I've been trained to do is to spot when someone is lying. Now, I will ask you one more time. You have someone in mind. You know someone who might be the person who goes by the aliases of Rashid Renclaw and Chris Warndale. Who is it?"

Dickinson looked down and to the right. The "internal dialogue" direction. The answer was waiting at the gate of his lips, and he was debating with himself whether to open the gate and let it out.

At that point, silence was the most effective tool. Sometimes a subject would let valuable information slip just to break an uncomfortable silence, but one inopportune word could send the answer scurrying back into the deepest recesses of his brain, never to resurface. Even though every tick of the grandfather clock in the corner sounded to Fox like the blow of an axe against the branch where Emily was standing, all he could do was wait.

16

MOSUL, IRAQ
2005

Evening had turned to night. Fox was exhausted, but sleep would be out of the question with so much at stake tomorrow. He rubbed his temples, and tried to focus on the sheaf of papers on his desk. The resourceful MJ had procured several reports from the Ministry of Agriculture and the Iraqi Poultry Producers' Association, and he was now in the process of learning more about the poultry industry in Iraq than he ever wanted to know. Wearily, he ran his eyes down the long list of places that had recently placed orders for large quantities of eggs.

A children's hospital in Ramadi. A veterinary vaccine plant near Karbala. That one raised a momentary red flag, since the old regime had often used vaccine factories as cover for bioweapon sites, but Karbala was the heart of Shi'a territory, enemy country for the Sunni AQI.

Numerous schools, bakeries and restaurants in Baghdad and the surrounding area. He came to the end of the list wondering whether he was any further ahead.

As he read, he cast surreptitious glances around the gator pit, waiting for a moment when Browning, Newcomb, and Mendes were all away from their desks. Finally, around midnight, he had his opening. He picked up the phone and called the guard at the cells.

"Could you get Ibrahim ready for me, please?"

"Yes, sir."

He allowed the guard five minutes to get Ibrahim ready, then went to the interview room.

"*Assalam aleikum,* Ibrahim," he greeted him with hand over heart. "How are you feeling?"

"Better, *al-hamdulillah.* Maybe even better than you. You look exhausted. I thought sleep deprivation was something you only did to us."

"No, we do it to ourselves too. As a gesture of solidarity."

He gave a wry smile. "I appreciate that." With his face still turned toward Fox, his eyes darted in the direction of the video camera. He lowered his voice and spoke in Arabic. "And I appreciate...what you did, back in that room."

Fox kept his voice neutral as he answered in the same language: "I couldn't have done it without you."

Fox's exhortation to "Look at him!" had diverted the attention of the others for only a split second, but it had given him enough time to disconnect an essential cable. And after "Remember how you writhed, remember how you screamed," the Arabic words he had spoken next meant, "And do it, when you hear me say the word 'hajji.'"

Ibrahim had proven himself a very skilled actor. And Fox's outburst at the end, with the dramatic gesture of pulling all the cables from their sockets, ensured that no one would discover the truth. Between them, they had run a reversed version of the Milgram experiment, in which the ones who thought they were in control were really the test subjects.

Fox switched back into English. "Ibrahim, why do you choose to stay here when you don't have to?"

"Because I know you will never be happy until you beat me at chess."

"You have a family and a mosque to take care of. All you need to do is answer our questions, and you could be back with them tomorrow."

Ibrahim sighed. "So we come back to that. You want me to tell you what I know of Zuhairi."

"Yes."

"Very well, my friend, this is what I know of Zuhairi. His father fought in the war with Iran. He was always feeding the boy on his own idea of jihad. I tried to teach him a better way. You may defend yourself when attacked, but do not repay an evil with a worse evil. And to whoever bears persecution with patience, Allah promises three hundred layers of recompense, each one equal to the distance between the earth and the sky."

He sighed again. "But I failed. During the war in Kuwait, Zuhairi's father was killed. When you Americans came back to invade Iraq, he saw his chance for revenge, and ran off to join the insurgency. And now, every day, I see his mother in my mosque. She has lost her husband, and her son is gone she knows not where.

There is nothing left for her but to pray that one day, he will come to his senses and come back to her. And I have made her prayer mine, too. How, then, could I deliver him into your hands?"

"So you're just waiting for him to see the error of his ways, and come back of his own will?"

"Do you know the ninety-nine names of Allah?"

"Not all of them."

"*Al-Gaffar*, the Most Forgiving One. *At-Tawwab*, He Who Welcomes the Repentant. As his minister on earth, I must do the same."

"Do you really think Zuhairi is even capable of repentance?"

"How could I possibly know that? Only Allah can see into the hearts of men."

"Let me ask you a hypothetical question, Ibrahim. What would you do if someone in your mosque confessed to you that he had committed a murder?"

"It would not be for me to absolve him of his crime. That is a matter between him and Allah. If he sincerely repented and performed a *du'a*, then perhaps he could reduce his sentence in hell."

"But would you advise him to turn himself in to the police? Divine mercy is one thing, but wouldn't you say he would still have to face human justice?"

"Do you truly believe that 'justice' is what happens here, my friend?" He spread his hands to encompass the base. "I wish I could agree with you."

Fox took a deep breath. He was about to commit a grave breach of protocol, by telling a detainee how the information he provided fit into the larger intelligence picture. But they were running out of time, and he felt himself running out of options.

"We have credible information that one of Zuhairi's close lieutenants has gotten his hands on a sample of a deadly virus. We believe that they're planning to make it into a weapon for use against American forces. If they do, that means the contagion could spread to the American homeland. To their wives and children."

"Need I point out that he wouldn't be able to do that if you weren't here?"

"I know how you feel about our being here, Ibrahim. But we're talking about women and children back in the States, who have never done any Iraqis any harm. Does it not say in the Qur'an, 'Whoever takes one innocent life, it is though he had slain all humankind. And whoever saves one innocent life, it is as though he had saved all humankind'?"

"If you look at the context, you will see that is actually a quote from the Talmud."

"But you agree with the principle?"

"Yes, of course. But, my dear friend, do you really want to sit there, in the uniform of the United States Army, and start a discussion with me about the taking of innocent life?"

His words pierced Fox's heart.

"Do you know what the Qur'an says of such as you, my friend?" Ibrahim continued mercilessly. " 'For the Christians, We ordained the Gospel with its guidance and light. If only they would follow it, then surely We would remit their sins from them and bring them into gardens of delight. Among them are some who follow the right path, but so many of them follow the path of evil.' "

"So do you want to see more Americans die?"

"No, my friend! I do not want to see more Americans die. Neither do I want to see more Americans kill more Iraqis. Neither do I want to see more Sunnis and Shi'as kill each other. Iraq has seen enough of violence."

At that moment, a door opened. In any interrogation, the most important questions are the ones not asked aloud: *Who is this person? What does he want most? What does he fear most?* Once the interrogator knows the answers to these questions, and finds a way to play on the subject's hopes and fears, the field is won. And Ibrahim had unwittingly answered the unspoken question.

"You don't want to see any more violence."

"That is right."

"Any information you give us, we know we can trust. But if you don't give us anything, my superiors will start following any little lead that comes their way, from any source, trustworthy or not. Business rivals, jilted suitors, Shi'as with an axe to grind against Sunnis... anyone looking to settle any little grudge could give us a name, and we would have to chase it down. More false arrests and more needless killings. You could put a stop to it all."

He closed his eyes—either deep in thought, or at prayer. Fox waited silently for him, scarcely daring to breathe.

"If you found Zuhairi," he finally said, "you would kill him?"

"We would do our best to take him alive. That's what the Army teaches us: it's better to capture than to kill, and surrender is better than either." That, at any rate, was what the Field Manual said. Fox just hoped his fellow soldiers on the ground would live up to that principle.

Ibrahim fell silent again. Fox waited, trying to give the appearance of patience, when all his concentration was focused on the door: *Open up and let it out*.

"Shortly before I was detained, his mother received a gift from him. It was sent from somewhere in al-Anbar province."

Al-Anbar, where angels feared to tread. The heart of the insurgent stronghold that the soldiers dubbed the "Triangle of Death."

"And that, my friend, is all I know."

17

OXFORD—LONDON
SUNDAY, APRIL 5
EASTER SUNDAY

A sigh from Dickinson, a slump of his shoulders, and
a twitch of his mouth announced that the guard at
the gate of his lips had finally relented.

"I had such high hopes for him."

"For whom?"

"I was his thesis advisor. He was the keenest pupil
I ever had. In the classroom, in the laboratory, and in
my public lectures, he was always in the front row, eyes
always on me, hanging on my every word."

"His name?"

Dickinson's mouth twitched a few more times before
his lips opened again, seemingly in defiance of orders
from his brain.

"Theodore Gottlieb."

Donovan took down the name. "What's he doing

now?"

"He's a research fellow at the William James Laboratory, in the Dunn School of Pathology."

"Here at Oxford?"

"That's right."

"Where does he live?"

The professor shrugged. "In South Kensington somewhere, I believe. I only have an e-mail address for him. I don't know his street address."

"No matter," said Donovan. "Now that we know his name, we should be able to locate him. Thank you, Professor."

They stood up to go.

"Mr. Fox?" he said as he rose to see them off. "You must understand that he doesn't speak for all atheists."

Fox turned and fixed him with a glare. "I realize that. But if you moderates don't want to find yourselves painted with the same brush, you need to get out there and condemn your extremists a little more strongly."

Emily closed the curtains around the four-poster bed, went into the bathroom, and stood before the mirror. She ran her fingers through the long red hair that her husband admired so much.

He'll be disappointed, she thought, *but he'll be lucky enough if he gets his wife back alive.*

She took the bathmat from the rim of the tub and held it against the mirror. She made her other hand into a fist, and took a deep breath.

Just let me have some good luck today, and I'll happily take the seven years of bad.

She punched. The mirror remained intact.

She punched again, harder. The second blow made a few cracks, like a spider making a down payment on a web.

She struck again, this time using her elbow. A few fragments tumbled down into the sink.

She wrapped one hand in a towel, and used it to pick up the largest piece. With the other hand, she grasped a lock of her hair.

As they sped back to London, Donovan adroitly juggled the steering wheel, a cigarette, and his cell phone as though his job exempted him not only from traffic regulations, but the laws of physics as well.

"What made you so sure Professor Dickinson was lying?" Adler asked.

"You didn't pick up on the cues yourself? First, when I asked him who he knew that fit our profile, he repeated the question in its entirety. That's a way of stalling for time. Second, he only shrugged one shoulder. Gestures that are genuine are usually symmetrical. People who shrug one shoulder, or smile on one side of their face, are forcing it. Third, when we accused him of holding something back, he said, 'One does not withhold information.' That might just have been a British mannerism, but you must have noticed the distancing language—he was talking about what people do in general, not what he was doing at that moment. And also, he used contractions most of the time he was talking to us—'I don't' or 'I'm not'—but not that time: 'I do not know any such person.' People use uncontracted forms more often when they're lying.

Even if they're British."

Adler shook his head with an admiring smile. "All I can say is that when you left the service, we lost one hell of a weapon in the war on terror."

Donovan's phone rang. "Donovan here...You did? Brilliant...Yeah, go ahead...Hyde Park Gate? Bloody hell. All right. We'll be there within the hour. And we'll need a backup team from SO15, C-Burn equipped. Cheers."

He hung up. "We've got him. There were lots of listings for Theodore Gottlieb in London, but only one with a red BMW and a house that matched the description you gave us."

"Hyde Park Gate?"

"That's right. To rent a flat in that neighborhood costs more for a month than I make in a year. To buy one would cost more than I'll earn in my lifetime. To buy a whole house there, you have to be a Saudi oil sheikh or someone like that."

"So how did he come by it?"

"His father was the president of Goodlove Pharmaceuticals. Passed away last year, and the son inherited the whole lot. Mysterious circumstances, but no one could ever prove foul play."

"From what I've gathered about him," Fox said darkly, "he's the type who could kill both his parents, and then persuade the court to grant him clemency because he's an orphan."

Emily saw herself, lying face down on the bed, in the bathrobe her host had so graciously provided.

That was how she hoped he would see it, at any rate.

The bathrobe, stuffed with pillows, lay half-tucked into the bed. More pillows concealed the places where her hands should be, and one, with her hair draped across it, formed the head. No one who saw it with the naked eye could mistake it for her, but God willing, it would be close enough to fool a video camera.

Assuming that the monitor screen outside the door was the only one. If there was another one anywhere else, and he had been able to see her making this decoy, then all her efforts would be for nothing. But when he said "I can see you," he had gestured, perhaps involuntarily, toward the door. She only hoped she had been reading him right.

She ran a hand over her shorn head. *Well, if nothing else, it'll be cooler once the Washington summer starts.*

She heard a door open somewhere in the hall. She dropped down into a crouch and waited.

That shard from the mirror would be an effective weapon.

God, forgive me for thinking such a thing.

The bell rang. She took a breath, and tried to calm her heart.

The deadbolt clicked aside, and the door began to swing open.

Dear God, be with me now.

Her captor pushed the door open, carrying a tray.

She sprang up from her crouch and slammed her hands into the tray, driving it into his face. She shoved him aside and ran past him into the hall.

It was completely enclosed. There were no windows and no sign of a staircase. How did he get up and down? Along the walls, she saw only a full-length mirror in a gilt frame, a credence table with a large vase, and three doors. One stood slightly ajar, opening into what looked like another bathroom. The second had hinges that swung outward, meaning it was probably a linen closet.

She ran for the third door, at the end of the hall. But when she reached it and tried to turn the knob, she found it was locked.

A hand grabbed her collar and jerked her back. The other arm snaked around her throat, seizing her in a headlock.

"You ungrateful bitch!"

He dragged her back into the bedroom and shoved her backward onto the bed. He jumped on it and sat astride her, pinning her arms with his hands.

"A grievous mistake, Ms. Harper! I tried to show you proper hospitality. But if you insist upon being treated like a garden-variety kidnapping victim, then I'm entirely capable of granting your wish."

He reached into the pocket of his blazer, pulled out a pair of handcuffs, and fastened her wrists around one of the bedposts.

"I have to go and attend to Fox now, then I'll come back and settle with you." He looked up and down her body, subjecting every detail to thoughtful scrutiny, like an art appraiser examining the wares for sale at an auction.

"You know what they say about the God virus? It's often hereditary, sometimes contagious...but very seldom sexually transmitted."

Donovan's car swung by New Scotland Yard, to meet a

caravan of police cars, a fire engine, and an ambulance. Fox had envisioned British police cars as boxy black sedans marked only with a checkered tartan stripe, but these were silver, with incandescent orange and red plastered all over them in stripes, checks, chevrons, and every possible combination thereof.

The convoy made its way, sirens blaring, through the streets of London. They passed in front of Buckingham Palace, but Fox was too tense even to think about snapping a picture through the window as they drove by.

Finally, they rolled past the towering mansions of Hyde Park Gate, and stopped in front of one. The path beyond the garden gate passed by immaculately manicured shrubs, then up a few steps to the front door of a façade replete with bay windows, balconies, and gables. An architecture critic might call it a "gingerbread house," and indeed, its occupant bore a frightening resemblance to the one who had played host to Hansel and Gretel.

The SO15 officers, in blue "C-Burn" suits—Chemical, Biological, Radiological and Nuclear—with hoods and masks in place, jumped out of their Sprinter vans, carrying compact Heckler & Koch MK5 rifles. Donovan stayed behind the wheel of the unmarked sedan. Fox took hold of his door handle, but Adler stretched out a hand to stop him.

"These guys are the field agents," he said. "We're the analysts. We've done our job. It's time to let them do theirs."

"But—"

"Robin, have you ever shot anyone?"

"No."

"You say that like you're proud of it."

"I am."

"Could you, if you had to?" When Fox hesitated, Adler pressed on: "Then I don't think you want today to be the day you find out."

Fox grudgingly had to admit the truth of Adler's words.

The SO15 team passed between Corinthian columns and climbed the steps to the front door. They rang, they knocked, and when they received no answer, two officers came with a battering ram. Three good swings splintered the wood around the lock. The officers, rifles at the ready, made their way inside.

Fox had some idea how hard it must be to be the boots on the ground. But in its way, it was equally hard to be the intelligence officer on the sidelines, watching as others risked their lives while acting on information he had collected, and powerless to do anything to help them except pray that his judgment had been right.

18

MOSUL, IRAQ
2005

It was morning, and all eyes in the room were once again fixed on the live feed from the Predator. Some of the intelligence officers on the ground—those who could put on civilian clothes and blend in fairly easily with the Iraqi population—had been keeping close watch on the apartment building where Jaffari and his crew had holed up since last evening. Now, Major Browning had them on the phone as the Predator hovered over the building.

A car rolled out of the parking lot—a Toyota Corona, with the passenger-side mirror missing.

"Do you have a visual?" Browning asked the leader of the surveillance team, then shook his head as he received the reply. "He sees the driver and one guard," he reported, "but no sign of our boy."

A minute later, another car rolled out. The surveillance team gave the same report: driver and guard on board, but no sign of Jaffari.

Another minute passed, and a third one rolled out. The same report: one driver, one guard, no Jaffari.

Browning let loose a combinatorial explosion of expletives. Newcomb shot Fox a look that said, "Any more brilliant ideas?"

"He's got to be hiding in one of them," Fox said. "Can we see where they're going?"

The Predator's camera zoomed out until all three cars were in the frame, as they went in divergent directions. One headed east, on the road to Baqubah. The second headed southeast, on the main highway to Baghdad. The third headed southwest, toward Fallujah.

"Any idea which one to track?" asked Browning. "Vasily?"

"The one going east could be heading for the al-Taji plant," she said. "But the one heading southeast on the Baghdad road could be going to any of several sites, including al-Daura. My money would be on that one."

"Fox?"

Fox's mind raced. Jaffari was working for Zuhairi. Offered a weapon this powerful, Zuhairi would surely want to keep it as secure as he could, in an insurgent stronghold, close to his center of operations. And if possible, away from any sites that had already been identified.

Ibrahim had said that at last report, Zuhairi was in al-Anbar province. And Fox seemed to remember Ramadi, its capital, being mentioned on the list of egg purchasers MJ had given him.

"The one going southwest," he said.

"There's nothing that way," Stephanie objected.

"Only the al-Muthanna plant, and that was destroyed."

"You said yourself that he could be heading to a site we don't know about."

"We need a decision here, people!" Browning shouted, slamming a hand down onto his desk. "Fox! Final answer!"

Why, thought Fox, *do I have to be the one to make the call?* Because he was the senior member of the interrogation team? Or in order that, if Jaffari eluded them, the blame would fall squarely on him?

Logic was on Stephanie's side. They knew there were bioweapons facilities in the Baghdad area, at least one of them potentially still workable. But his intuition was pulling him hard in the direction of al-Anbar province.

"Southwest," he said.

Stephanie's green eyes shot darts at him.

"So be it," said Browning, and relayed the instructions over the phone.

For the next two hours, Fox trained his eyes by turns on the television screen and the paperwork on his desk, studiously avoiding eye contact with Browning, Newcomb, Mendes, Stephanie, or anyone else.

The car made its way along Route 23, past Lake Tharthar, the giant teardrop in the middle of the desert. Eventually, it turned west and rolled into downtown Ramadi, along the road the Americans referred to as "Michigan." Rather than try to learn the Arabic names for all the streets, they tended to rename them after American states—or, lamentably often, fallen comrades.

It approached a large building, or rather two buildings connected in a T-shape. From the front building, which abutted the main road, they saw several cars and pedestrians coming and going. The car they hoped was Jaffari's, however, turned into a narrow side street and steered up to the other building in back.

"Zoom in," Browning ordered over the phone. A minute later, the building on the screen came into clearer view.

"Vasily, does that look like a germ factory to you?" Browning asked.

"Sir, a bioweapons plant isn't like a nuclear reactor. There's no telltale sign that you can spot from the air and say 'That's it.' But..." she directed her laser pointer at the roof of the outbuilding, "those bifurcated plenums could be ventilation ducts for a high-containment facility."

"That sign out in front," Fox said. "Any way to zoom in on it from an angle, and see what it says?"

"It's going to say 'AQI Biological Weapons Facility,'" said Newcomb, "in big English letters. Is that what you're expecting?"

Fox had no idea what he was expecting, but kept his eyes on the screen as Browning relayed his request over the phone. The image moved, the viewing angle shifted, and the lens focused in on the sign. It read, in Arabic and English: *Ar-Ramadi Children's Hospital and Vaccination Center*.

"My God," Fox said. "What if it really is what it says it is?"

"It doesn't make sense," said Stephanie. "You wouldn't have a vaccine production plant in the middle of a populated area. You have to work with live viruses, and an accident could infect the entire town. The Soviets learned that the hard way."

"You wouldn't have a bioweapons plant there either,

for the same reason."

"Unless that was part of your strategy, to make sure the other side couldn't take it out without massive civilian casualties."

"Not good news for us either way, then."

"I say we just blow the whole thing and let their Allah sort them out," Newcomb contributed. Fox decided not to rise to it.

Colonel Matthews, the base commander, appeared at the doorway. This was a rare occasion, but all eyes were so fixed on the screen that it was several seconds before someone noticed him and rapped out, "Attention."

"Fox, you're here," he said, brandishing his cell phone. "I have the commander of a strike team out of Camp Blue Diamond on the phone. He needs to know if you're sure of your intel."

"As sure as I can be, sir."

"Let your word be either 'Yes, yes' or 'No, no,' Fox," he said sharply. "The Special Forces are standing by. Are you confident enough to send them in?"

Fox became acutely aware that he had replaced the live feed as the cynosure of all eyes in the room. He took a deep breath and said a silent prayer.

"Yes, sir."

Matthews spoke into his phone. "Affirmative. You have a go mission."

Camp Blue Diamond was just on the outskirts of Ramadi, so the journey was short. Within minutes, Humvees began to roll into the frame, taking positions at the crossroads, cutting off access to the hospital. Then came the rotor blades of two Black Hawks.

"Praise be to the Lord my Rock," Matthews intoned,

"who trains my hands for war and my fingers for battle. He is my fortress and my shield, who subdues nations under me."

Psalm 144. But Fox had a verse from a different Psalm in mind: *Lord God Almighty, may those who hope in you not be disgraced because of us. May those who seek you not be put to shame because of us.*

Suddenly, the roof of the outbuilding came alive. A door burst open and armed men poured out, taking positions at the chest-high concrete wall, opening fire with Kalashnikovs.

The Black Hawks returned fire with their M60 machine guns. Some of the figures on the roof hunkered down behind the wall. Those who were not fast enough fell backward and lay motionless.

At ground level, a mad hejira was in progress. Children were pouring out of the exits, some running, some hobbling on crutches, some offering a shoulder to those too weak to walk by themselves. Some of the larger figures stood still, presumably doctors and nurses trying to see to the safety of their patients.

A rocket-propelled grenade lanced through the air. One of the Black Hawks lurched, barely avoiding it. The trail of smoke led back to the window of one of the surrounding buildings.

Fox held his breath. It suddenly looked frighteningly likely that the feature they were watching was about to turn into a sequel to Black Hawk Down.

A second RPG shot by, this one from the opposite direction.

Browning swore. "They've got shooters in all the buildings around the hospital. Even if our boys can clear the roof and land, they'll be big juicy targets."

It soon became evident that the commander in Ramadi had come to the same conclusion.

The helicopters backed off. A shadow passed over the scene, followed shortly by a flash that momentarily turned the whole screen white. When they could see the image again, thick black smoke was billowing from the building behind the hospital.

Then the shock wave knocked down the nearest wall of the hospital building itself. The roof caved in, followed by the remaining walls. Within a minute, the entire compound was a pile of rubble, spewing enough dust and smoke to block the sun over Ramadi.

The helicopters turned and fled.

"Dear God," Fox murmured, "what have we done?"

19

LONDON
SUNDAY, APRIL 5
EASTER SUNDAY

The ringing of Donovan's phone brought Fox's attention sharply back to the present.

"Donovan here. Yes. What? My God! Just a moment."

He put down the phone and turned to Fox. "They say he's got the place wired with incendiary bombs. He's threatening to set them off unless his demand is met."

"What's his demand?"

"He wants to see you."

"What? Me?"

"He asked for you by name."

A few minutes ago, he had been eager to leap into the action. But on hearing these words, he felt as though all the air had just escaped from his body.

He swallowed hard. "All right."

Donovan spoke into his phone. "Just a minute.

He's coming."

"I don't suppose you have a spare suit?" Adler asked.

"I'm afraid not."

Reflexively, Fox made the sign of the cross. The academic in him noted that action with detached interest. A scholar of religions spends years immersing himself in different traditions, searching for the universal truth that unites them all. And yet, when danger threatens, he immediately calls on the Divine by the names he learned in childhood.

He got out of the car, climbed the steps to the door, and passed through.

The entrance hall seemed better suited to a museum than a house, with a chandelier hanging from a high ceiling surrounded with intricate moldings, and a marble-topped table supporting a bronze bust of Darwin. He passed through a pair of double doors into a living room about the same size as his entire apartment. Persian rugs on the marble-tiled floor, candelabra suspended from an inlaid ceiling, floral wallpaper, brocade curtains, chairs that looked like thrones...every square inch was ornamented, with no rest for the eyes anywhere.

The officers' protective suits made them look like invaders from the future. Their weapons were all pointed at an armchair, next to the mammoth fireplace that showed no signs of ever having been used. In the chair sat a young man, blond and blue-eyed, who looked as though he had stepped out of a recruiting poster for the Wehrmacht and into the pages of a Selfridges catalog. The glass-topped table in front of him was laid with a teapot, two cups on saucers, and a plate of biscuits. He balanced a tablet computer on his crossed knees, and on the table next to him were a remote control, a video camera on a desk-sized tripod, and a pulse oximeter wired to a clip on his fingertip.

"Mr. Fox, welcome! I'm so glad you could come! Please, have a seat." He gestured to the sofa with a delighted smile, as if Fox were an old friend who had traveled all the way from America to see him. As if it were just the two of them for afternoon tea. As if he didn't have the muzzles of half a dozen assault rifles pointed at his head.

After a moment's hesitation, Fox seated himself on the sofa.

"Do please help yourself," Gottlieb urged, nudging the plate of biscuits in Fox's direction. He hefted the teapot one-handed, filled a cup, and looked up to address the SO15 team. "Give us the room, if you please, gentlemen."

The officers remained motionless, their guns unwavering.

"Come now, gentlemen, what's to be gained by posturing? We all know you aren't going to shoot me. I apologize for repeating myself, but indulge me for a moment as I fill in our new arrival." With his right hand, he gestured to the device attached to his left. "This device will be triggered if the oximeter fails to register a pulse. I call it the next-generation dead man's switch. Tested and proven, I really must remember to apply for a patent. If triggered, it will detonate several incendiary devices around the house. I would really rather not have to use it. This house is a splendid example of Queen Anne architecture and it would be a great shame to destroy it.

But I will, if you insist upon leaving me no alternative."

The heads of the officers turned to look at the one in the lead, who nodded. With cautious steps, guns still trained on Gottlieb, they retreated back toward the vestibule.

"That's more like it," said Gottlieb. He pushed the tea saucer toward Fox, who left it untouched on the table.

"Oh, go on, go on! I assure you there are no viruses in it. After all, we Englishmen always insist on having our tea properly boiled, and there aren't many organisms on this planet that can survive that." As if to prove his point, he poured a cup for himself, and had a sip.

"What have you done with Emily?"

"That's rather a familiar way to refer to another man's wife, don't you think? I assure you, she's fine. No thanks to you, for failing to keep our gentlemen's agreement."

"I don't remember agreeing to anything."

"I could have killed the pair of you for that. But I couldn't pass up the chance to meet the man who fared so poorly in a debate with my esteemed mentor, yet still fancied himself a worthy adversary for me." He took a sip of his tea. "Well, I suppose I should say congratulations. You guessed my riddles—all but the last one."

"Suppose I told you I got that one too? What's my prize? Will you let Emily go?"

"The rewards aren't quite so lavish in this game, Mr. Fox, but at least you'll have my great admiration."

"Isaiah, chapter 23, verse 13."

Gottlieb set down his teacup. "Well done, Mr. Fox. Very well done indeed." He gave Fox the kind of benevolent smile that a chess grandmaster might when acknowledging a clever move by his novice opponent, even as the game was nearing its end and the best the challenger could hope for was a stalemate.

" 'A prophecy against Arabia.' It's the only reference to Arabia in the Bible, and it didn't take a genius to see where your next target would be. Mecca, during the Hajj."

"Well reasoned. No wonder you were able to wreak such havoc on my vaccination campaign."

"Is that what you call it?"

"Naturally. Religion is the smallpox of the mind, and I am its Jonas Salk. You know how a vaccine works, right? A milder virus protects against a more serious one. *Variola minor* kills one out of a hundred, but gives the other ninety-nine lifelong immunity to *Variola major*, which kills one in three. Significantly better odds, wouldn't you say?"

"And Zagorsk? Which kills two out of three, and destroys the brain of the third? You call that mild?"

"Well, I'm sure you remember that lovely September morning in your country, when twenty people infected with the God virus brought about the deaths of three thousand. That's a mortality rate of *fifteen thousand* percent! If we are ever to take the next step in our evolution, then this virus needs to be eradicated from the face of the earth."

"If you have such faith that the species is destined to evolve beyond religion, then why do you need to interfere in the process? Why not just let evolution take its course?"

"Because the troublesome thing about the God virus is that it doesn't usually kill its host. And when it does, it has a way of taking others along with it. But most carriers can go on infecting others over a lamentably long life. So, a more...shall we say, direct intervention was required. However, I reasoned that the hosts shouldn't mind."

"What makes you say that?"

"One of the curious properties of this virus is that it's been known to take away the fear of death. Just as the rabies virus can make a smaller animal bite a bigger one, even at the cost of its life, so the God virus can make its host march willingly into the jaws of death if that will help it propagate itself. It is, in fact, perhaps the only virus in history that the infected have willingly chosen to die rather than be cured of. And other hosts actually admire them, calling them 'martyrs'—as though there were anything remotely admirable about treating your life as worth less than an infantile delusion. What about you, Mr. Fox? Do you admire martyrs?"

"It depends," Fox replied cautiously.

"On?"

"On the cause they're martyred for."

"What would you consider a worthy cause?" Gottlieb turned his tablet around so that the screen faced Fox. "If I said I would kill you unless you said these words, what would you do?"

Fox read the words on the screen. "You must be joking. Trying to make converts by forcing people to recite some creed? Taking a page from the Spanish Inquisition?"

"That's right. Poetic justice, don't you think?"

"And if I refused, what would you gain by killing me? You think that killing people will destroy their ideas? How well did that work for Pontius Pilate? How well did it work for...do you even know the name of the man who

298 | Charles Kowalski

shot Gandhi?"

"Nathuram Godse. Lucky for India that he did his deed before that ridiculous fakir could spread his backward philosophy any further. Now, would you say these words if I told you I would let Ms. Harper go free if you did?"

Fox hesitated. "You should know that when dealing with lunatics like you, I always assume every word out of your mouth is a lie until proven otherwise."

"A useful policy, I'm sure. Now, would you say them if I told you I would kill her if you didn't? Would you insist upon testing my honesty in that case?"

Fox took another glance at the screen, as his mind searched frantically for ways to stall for time. "Why is it so important for you to hear me recite this creed of yours?"

"Because your sort, Mr. Fox, are the most dangerous of all."

"I beg your pardon?"

"You preach understanding and tolerance among different religions. You believe yours is the path to peace, do you not?"

"I do."

"Do you know what the Soviets found when they tried to weaponize the Ebola virus? They couldn't make it into an effective weapon, because it worked too well. It killed its hosts before they could spread it very far. You see the paradox? If it were less deadly, it would be more dangerous."

Gottlieb leaned so far forward that the cord on the pulse oximeter strained alarmingly. "You, Mr. Fox, are helping the virus mutate into its most insidious strain.

Reconciliation among religions is the last thing our species needs. If the Christians, Jews and Muslims want to kill one another, then by all means let them. That's what we call 'natural selection.' But you spread the lie that if only different strains of the virus could coexist, the host would be healthy again. Utterly illogical, of course, but people believe you. They need to know that you have finally recognized this virus for the menace it is."

Gottlieb leaned back again. "I saved one last little bit of Zagorsk solution, in a canister in the guest room now occupied by Ms. Harper." He poised his finger over the remote control. "With a touch of this button, I can release it. Unless you say the words. In five..."

Just say them. A few words, spoken under duress. They mean nothing.

"Four."

Yet how many throughout history have willingly faced prison, torture and death rather than say them? Do you have that kind of courage?

"Three."

If it were only your own life on the line, that would be a different matter. But if you make the wrong call now, Emily will be the one who suffers.

"Two."

"Stop!" Fox closed his eyes and heaved a deep sigh. "You win. I'll say it."

A triumphant grin spread across Gottlieb's face. "You've restored my faith in humanity, Mr. Fox." He reached for the video camera. "You're going live."

Emily started as the television screen on the wall

suddenly came to life. She craned her head to see the screen. Like a supernova, her heart swelled with radiant heat when she saw Fox's face—and then, on hearing the first words out of his mouth, imploded into a cold, dense lump drifting in empty space.

"After careful consideration, I have concluded that the human race has been deluded by religion for far too long. The theory of God cannot be proven on any rational grounds. And the practice of religion is responsible for virtually all the evil in the world, and no good that could not be better achieved by other means. The time has come for Yahweh, Jesus, and Allah to join Ra, Zeus, and Odin in the dustbin of history, and for humankind to evolve into a new age of reason."

The screen went black, along with the rest of her world.

Fox slumped back in the sofa with a long exhalation, as though trying to expel from his lungs all the air that had been contaminated by contact with the words he had just spoken. He had seen the same attitude many times in subjects who had just broken down and told the interrogator everything they knew. But he had never known, until that moment, how it felt to be on the other side.

Gottlieb switched off the camera. "Perfect on the first take. Thank you, Mr. Fox. You might have had a successful career in television. As it is, once this video is uploaded to the Internet, all the world will know that the brilliant religion scholar Robin Fox had what I believe is known as..."

As he spoke, he set down the tablet, and his right hand reached under his blazer.

"...a deathbed conversion."

He drew out an automatic pistol and aimed it at Fox's head.

Fox ducked and twisted, as the shot burst out.

He hurled the contents of the teacup into Gottlieb's face. Gottlieb cried out in pain and raised a hand to wipe away the scalding liquid.

The SO15 team came running back into the room. Gottlieb, still wiping tea from his eyes, dived out of his armchair.

As he did, his finger slipped out from the clip of the oximeter. A long, urgent beep issued from the machine.

Fox saw Gottlieb seize the remote control from the table, point it at the fireplace, and press a button. The brick firebox slid aside, revealing a passage behind it.

Gottlieb ducked under the mantel. Once he was through, the firebox started to slide back into place. Fox threw himself into the opening, wedged himself against the frame, and tried to brace it.

Then, as if a dragon imprisoned under the house had suddenly awoken, flames erupted from the heating grilles set into the floor. In an instant, the living room became a box with four walls of fire.

The SO15 officers instinctively ducked and covered. A blast of air slammed into the unprotected Fox with the force of a hurricane and the heat of a crematorium. He fell to the side, and the firebox slid back into place, shutting him into the space behind it.

Fox was at the foot of a spiral staircase. He heard Gottlieb's steps ascending. As quickly as he could, while still moving quietly and staying out of sight, he climbed up one flight of stairs, then a second. At each landing was a steel door.

Above him, the footsteps came to a stop. He heard the sound of a mechanical bolt sliding open. But by the time he reached the top of the stairs, the door had closed and locked again.

All the doors probably operated by remote control, and Gottlieb carried the controller. But surely there must be a manual switch somewhere, for emergencies? He felt his way around the edges of the door.

The overhead light flickered. If the power shorted out, what would happen? Was this a "fail-safe" system that would release him, or a "fail-secure" one that would trap him inside? Fox had a terrible feeling that he knew the answer.

He found a button recessed into the steel door jamb, and pushed it. The bolt slid aside.

He swung the door open and stepped into a hall, empty except for a credence table displaying an antique vase. The secret door was concealed by a full-length antique mirror on the other side. There was only a faint haze of smoke hovering near the ceiling. This floor was evidently sealed off from the rest of the house, with the secret stairway the only access. This might buy some time, but Fox wondered how much protection it would be against the gases that would slowly be filling the air: carbon monoxide and hydrocyanic gas, a colorless, odorless blend of car exhaust and Auschwitz.

He saw four doors, one of them standing slightly

open. One of the remaining three was locked with an electronic keypad, and had a video monitor next to it. It showed Emily, handcuffed to a bedpost, as Gottlieb stood beside her, pistol in hand.

Fox cast a frantic glance around him. His eyes fell on the door standing ajar, which opened into a bathroom.

He ran in and opened the medicine chest. It contained an assortment of antique health-care products that had probably been there ever since the house was first built: amber medicine bottles with yellowing labels in Latin, perfume bottles of all shapes and colors, and for some obscure purpose, a mortar and pestle. But after a moment's searching, he found what he needed: a bottle of talcum powder and a make-up brush.

He ran back to the locked door, tapped a measure of powder into his palm, brushed the keypad with it, and gently blew away the excess. The fine white dust clung to the residual skin oil on four keys: 1, 5, 8, 9.

From ten thousand possible combinations to twenty-four. Much more manageable, but still, working through them by brute force would take minutes, and Emily's life was being measured in seconds.

1985? Gottlieb could easily have been born in that year. Fox keyed in the number.

The light flashed red.

Maybe his birthday was January 9? Written the British way, that date would be 9/1/85. Fox entered those numbers in sequence.

The light flashed red again. 1/5/89 and 5/1/89 yielded no better result.

Theodore Gottlieb. Also known as Chris Warndale and Rashid Renclaw. Both of which are anagrams of

Charles Darwin.

What were Darwin's dates? Fox struggled to remember what he had seen on the slab at Westminster Abbey that morning. Panic made it hard to concentrate, and he suspected the gases were beginning to muddle his mind as well. Had Darwin died in 1895? No, Fox was fairly sure it had been earlier than that.

But not before he published *The Origin of Species*. From Gottlieb's point of view, that would be the turning point of history, infinitely more significant than the birth of Christ. If he were to become dictator of the world, he would probably create a new calendar and proclaim that as Year Zero. The exact date escaped Fox, but there was only one combination that would yield a year during Darwin's lifetime.

He keyed in: 1859.

The light flashed green.

Whoever You are, help me now.

He shoved the door open, seized the vase from the credence table, and hurled it into the room.

A shot rang out, and the vase shattered. From the direction of the sound, and the shards as they scattered, the shot had come from his left.

Dive-roll in the direction of the shooter. The second shot will usually go high.

It was every bit as clumsy a maneuver as would be expected from someone who had been out of the service for so many years. If his drill instructor saw his performance, he would probably let all the other recruits have a good laugh at his expense, and then sentence him to a few dozen push-ups. But when Gottlieb fired again, he did in fact overshoot.

Fox staggered to his feet. He had closed up most of the distance between himself and Gottlieb, but he was still a good two paces away.

Gottlieb shifted his aim to Emily. "One more step and she dies."

The scene before Fox's eyes shook as if he were seeing it through a hand-held video camera. The gymnastics had made him dizzy, and the gases were undoubtedly making it worse.

"If we don't get out of here," he replied, "we'll all die."

"Well, I find that far preferable to living out my days in some prison cell. And unlike you, I won't find death a disappointment. I know exactly what to expect. Nothing to hope for, nothing to fear. Simple oblivion."

"But then," Emily said, "who's going to tell your story?"

Gottlieb glanced at her. Fox shifted his weight and moved his foot as far forward as he dared, before Gottlieb's gaze returned to him. One more step to go, in this deadly game of Red Light, Green Light.

"You may not care if you die," Emily went on, "but do you really want your story to die with you? Who's going to tell it, if you don't?"

"MI5 and the American government, that's who," Fox said, picking up her theme and running with it. "The two of us will be honored as martyrs. As for you, it won't be long before your name is forgotten. If anyone remembers you at all, it will just be as 'that atheist nut job who burned his own house down.'"

"But if you come out alive," Emily went on, "you get to tell the story yourself, in front of the TV cameras, with all the world watching. Imagine how many would rally around your cause. I wouldn't even be surprised if you got your share of marriage proposals."

His gaze dropped down, as he seemed to consider this, but only for a fraction of a second before it snapped up again.

"A commendable attempt, Ms. Harper."

But Fox had seized the moment and taken the final step.

Step in and sideways, out of the line of fire. Grab the wrist with one hand, and strike the face with the other. Turn the weapon back on the attacker, pry it out of his hand, and kick to control distance.

Now Gottlieb stood with his back against the wall, and Fox held the pistol.

"This is for Thom," he said. "Oh, and Peg says she hopes there really is a Hell for you to go to."

He took aim at Gottlieb's head.

A gasp came from Emily.

He automatically glanced in her direction. From the horrified expression on her face, anyone would think he was pointing the pistol at her, rather than the one who had abducted and threatened to kill her. He saw the scene reflected in her eyes: Robin Fox, conscientious objector, teacher of peace, seeker of the universal truths common to all the world's religions, which included the commandment "Thou shalt not kill"—pointing a pistol at an unarmed man.

Robin. A voice that sounded like Thom's echoed in his mind. *If you do this, don't say you're doing it for me. You know me better than that. And I thought I knew you better than that.*

The hand that held the pistol wavered.

If I pull the trigger, he thought, *I'll kill two people. Theodore Gottlieb...and the Robin Fox I've always tried to be. The one everyone thinks I already am.*

He aimed the gun over Gottlieb's shoulder, and fired.

The windowpane shattered. It would release some of the smoke and gases, but even without the bars, it would have offered no way out for them, and no way in for the fire brigade. It faced the enclosed garden behind the house: a sheer drop of three stories, to a flagstone patio treacherously strewn with wrought iron tables and chairs.

Keeping the gun trained on Gottlieb, Fox backed around the bed, until they stood on opposite sides. Emily raised her hands, and squeezed her eyes shut in anticipation. Fox took his eyes off Gottlieb just long enough to fire a careful shot that broke the handcuff chain.

But when he swung the gun back in Gottlieb's direction, there was no one there.

Before Fox even had time to wonder where he had disappeared to, a hand grabbed his ankle and pulled it out from under him. He fell to the floor and lay on his back. Gottlieb, from his place of concealment under the bed, pinned Fox's arm to the floor and pried the gun out of his hand.

As Fox pulled his arm free and got back to his feet, Gottlieb's head and torso emerged from under the bed. Supporting himself with one arm, he took aim at Fox with the other.

Emily jumped in between them, and looked Gottlieb in the eye.

"You don't believe your mother is watching you, do

you?" she asked.

Gottlieb held the pistol steady, and made no reply.

"You don't believe you'll see her again one day, and have to account for how you lived your life," she went on. "There's no such thing as a soul. Everything that made her who she was, was in a gray lump of tissue inside her skull that's long decomposed. That's what you believe, isn't it? There's no place in the universe where any part of her still lives. Except in here." She knelt down and touched his head. "In the memories in your brain, and the DNA in your cells. Now let me ask you this: Could she shoot me?"

Fox and Emily began to take small steps backward. Gottlieb kept the gun trained on them.

"If you pull that trigger," she said, "you betray her genes in you. You'll wipe the last trace of her off the face of the earth. *Forever.*"

They backed up, Emily still shielding Fox's body with hers. Gottlieb kept them in his sights, but made no move to pull the trigger.

They passed through the door and pulled it shut. Emily pressed a random key on the keypad to slow Gottlieb down.

The smoke was so thick in the hall that the farthest they could see was the blistering, peeling wallpaper on the walls. Fox and Emily coughed, and struggled to see through tears as the smoke stung their eyes.

"You know a way out?" Emily asked between coughs.

Fox shook his head. "The hidden staircase I came up is sealed off at the bottom. We'll have to find another way."

"I got out of the room once, but I couldn't see any

stairs or anything like..."

The door at the far end of the hall shuddered. The wood around the doorknob splintered, as the blade of an axe poked through. What was left of the door swung open, and a helmeted, gas-masked figure emerged, in the black and yellow turnout gear of the London Fire Brigade.

"Take her!" Fox said, and gave Emily a push toward the firefighter.

As she crossed the floor, it groaned under her weight. The firefighter caught her by the arms just as the section she had traversed collapsed behind her, sending a cascade of boards down to feed the fire below. Smoke and flames welled up from the hole.

Fox stepped back from the blaze, shielding his face with his hand, and felt the muzzle of a gun at the back of his neck.

"Stupid are the merciful!" came the sneering voice from behind him.

Fox raised his hands, then spun around and seized the gun arm. Both of them fell into coughing spasms, but Fox kept his hold on Gottlieb's wrist, and Gottlieb kept his hold on the pistol. They circled around as they struggled. Slowly, using the last of his strength, Fox succeeded in turning the gun around so that the muzzle was pointed at Gottlieb.

"Now that—Ms. Harper—isn't watching—" Gottlieb squeezed the words out between his paroxysms, "are you going—to kill me?"

Fox fell into another fit of coughing, using all his will to maintain his grip on Gottlieb's gun arm, and keep his eyes open despite the sting of the smoke.

"I've never—killed anyone," he gasped when he could speak again. "And you—don't deserve the honor —of being the first."

He pried the weapon out of Gottlieb's grip, and tossed it toward the hole in the floor. Gottlieb lunged for it, lost his balance, and toppled over the edge.

The scream that issued from the inferno below, Fox knew, would haunt his nightmares for the rest of his life.

He collapsed.

The chandelier above his head became a kaleidoscope. It spun around as its branches multiplied, and its crystals flashed rainbows through the smoke. It was hypnotic. He could go on staring at it until his eyes closed for the last time.

Whoever You are, he said to the Great Unknowable, *into Your hands I commend my spirit.*

20

BETWEEN THIS WORLD AND THE NEXT
BETWEEN TIME AND ETERNITY

Fox had always heard that in your last living moment, your life flashes before your eyes. He had often wondered how that would work. Would it appear all at once, like photographs neatly lined up on a table? Would it be sequential, like a montage from a movie, condensing an entire lifetime into a fraction of a second? Or could it be seen across space and time together, like movies playing on a hundred different screens simultaneously?

What he saw now was none of those. Not a gallery, nor a movie, but a single frame, filling his entire field of vision. And what it showed was Emily's face, in such minute detail that he could count her eyelashes.

It had been a short life, but one full of blessings. And all the most precious memories were moments he had shared with Emily. If the ancient Greeks had it right, and he would have to cross the river Lethe and be cleansed of all memories of this world before his shade could proceed to the next, he would say "No, thanks," and elect to spend eternity on this side of the riverbank rather than give up a single one of them.

Of regrets, he also had more than his share. And the uppermost was that he was about to go to his grave without ever having told her, *I love you.*

21

LONDON
SUNDAY, APRIL 5
EASTER SUNDAY

"Robin?"

Fox opened his eyes. Emily sat by his bedside, in a plush white robe identical to the one he was wearing. She reached out and took his hand.

"Emily. Thank God."

Her self-inflicted haircut had been retouched by a professional stylist, and although he could never have imagined it, the end result suited her remarkably well. But then, he thought, any style would.

"You look great."

She smiled, and patted her hair with her free hand. "Like it? I was thinking of auditioning for Peter Pan."

He was lying in a huge bed in an equally huge bedroom, with a wall-mounted television screen big enough for a home cinema. Donovan and Adler sat near the foot of his bed, in brocade-upholstered armchairs not too different from the one the Queen had occupied at Westminster Abbey. He could have been in a five-star hotel, except for the oxygen tube under his nostrils.

"For a moment there, I thought I was in heaven," Fox said, "except that you gentlemen aren't dressed for it."

"You're in the Ambassador Suite at the Cromwell Hospital," Donovan said. He took an admiring look around. "A long call from the National Health Service hospitals, I must say."

"Just so long as they understand that I'm not actually the ambassador. I'm an ordinary American, and our idea of health insurance is a card that says 'Get well soon.'"

"I shouldn't worry about that," Donovan replied. "You're to have the best care Britain can provide...by order of no lesser authority the Royal Household. You helped save the lives of the entire Royal Family, not to mention the extinguished Archbishop. I shouldn't be surprised if you were offered a knighthood."

"Sir Robin?" Emily tried the title on him for size.

Fox laughed and shook his head. "That's just too Monty Python."

"Besides," said Donovan, "as an American, I'm sorry to say you couldn't claim the title of 'sir.'"

"Just as well. I got enough of that in the Army to last a lifetime."

"I'm sorry to break this to you," Donovan said, with another glance at the opulent surroundings, "but they say you can probably be discharged soon. What's next for you? Would you like to stay in England for a while, to help us wrap things up? Acknowledge the accolades?"

Fox shook his head. "I need to get back to work. I've

missed enough classes already. I can only hope that saving Western civilization doesn't ruin my chances for tenure."

That reminded him of the one remaining loose end. It wasn't only Western civilization that had been under threat.

"Ahmad is still out there," he said to Adler. "The Hajj isn't until October, and now that we have Gottlieb and the rest of his team, there's no telling whether he still intends to carry out his part in the plan. But still, you'll make sure the Saudis are properly forewarned, right?"

"Yes." Adler looked at him and nodded. "Yes, of course. So, as soon as they say you're ready to go, we'll have a brief session with the press, and then catch the next flight back to Washington. How's that?"

"Sounds good."

"And you may not be able to join Her Majesty for tea at Buckingham Palace," Donovan added, "but I should think we all definitely deserve a pint at Buckingham Arms."

22

OVER THE ATLANTIC OCEAN
SUNDAY, APRIL 5
EASTER SUNDAY

Another business class flight, this time courtesy of the CIA, on British Airways direct to Washington. The beef-and-Stilton pie was better than Fox had expected, and this time, he had no compunction about sampling from the wine list. Yet, strangely, he felt as little able to relax and enjoy the trip as he had on the way to Tel Aviv.

It was over. Gottlieb was dead, and all but one of his minions were in custody. Ahmad was still at large, but it was only a matter of time before the authorities tracked him down.

What, then, was this nagging unease in Fox's chest that he couldn't shake? He recalled the last time he had had to ask that question, about a mission that by any conventional measure was a success.

I've never killed anyone, he had said to Gottlieb. But

full disclosure would have required him to add: *At least, not directly.*

In his mind's eye, he stood once again in Colonel Matthews' office, facing his commander across the marble-topped desk inherited from Saddam Hussein.

"The report is in from our boys in Ramadi," Matthews was saying. "They recovered enough evidence to verify that your analysis was exactly right. They found equipment for producing biological agents at scale, empty mortar shells, and machines for filling them. And Saif al-Jaffari has been confirmed EKIA."

Enemy Killed in Action. Fox wondered why he couldn't just say "dead."

"Was there any contamination of the surrounding area, sir?"

Matthews shook his head. "All he had was a small sample of the virus. They hadn't even begun the production process. No health risk detectable."

Fox dreaded asking the next question. "And the hospital really was a hospital, wasn't it, sir?"

He nodded. "They investigated that. It seems that Zuhairi offered the hospital some kind of deal: AQI gave them funds from their Saudi sponsors to renovate it and put in new equipment, in exchange for letting them set up shop out in back. Well, they choose that strategy, they get what's coming to them. Those that sow the wind shall reap the whirlwind."

"Do we know how many civilian casualties there were, sir?"

Matthews shrugged with an abstracted look, as though Fox had just asked him the population of New York—a detail that at some level he felt he ought to

318 | C h a r l e s   K o w a l s k i

know, but was of no great consequence if he couldn't call it to mind at the moment. "A couple dozen, maybe."

"Children, sir?"

"Yeah, most of them, probably."

Fox bowed his head.

"Yes," Matthews went on with a sigh, "when al-Jazeera and the Stateside networks get their claws on it, there'll be a crapstorm, no way around it. But here's what's important to me. One of our highest priority targets is dead. A biological attack on American forces— which could have started a terrible epidemic back in the homeland—has been prevented. AQI's germ factory is ashes. And all this was done without a single American casualty. You have the right to be proud of what you've done, Captain. I see a Bronze Star in your future."

"Thank you, sir." Fox tried to look suitably pleased, but the attempt fell flat.

There was something else Matthews needed to know. "Sir, it's my duty to tell you that I've decided to file for conscientious objector status."

Matthews looked up in surprise. "Why is that?"

"You can read the details in my application, sir." He had listed numerous reasons, and Matthews had just unwittingly given him another: He felt he had to do something before he reached the point where he could watch the deaths of dozens of children, and see only a PR problem.

Matthews gave a resigned nod, as if to say that the decision disappointed him, but he still respected it.

"Fox."

"Sir?"

"You did your job. And you did it very well."

"Thank you, sir."

At least, thought Fox, *he didn't call me a hero.*

He looked to his right, where Emily was sleeping. The Celtic cross pendant around her neck gently rose and fell with her breathing. Her face was turned toward him, her eyes closed, her lips parted. It would have been a clear invitation to kiss her, if she had been conscious.

They had lived through more together in the past week than most married couples do in a lifetime. And here, between continents, in an indeterminate time zone, thirty thousand feet above reality, it was easy to entertain the illusion that the world belonged only to the two of them. But as soon as their wheels touched the ground, it would be his duty to let Rep. Frederick Paxton, D-MD, reclaim his rightful place at the center of her life. He had always tried not to begrudge the Congressman his good luck. At the same time, he found himself wishing that the pilot had taken the scenic route across Asia, the Pacific, and the entire North American continent, rather than this shortcut across the Atlantic.

Emily stirred and opened her eyes. Fox felt a momentary flush of embarrassment that she had caught him staring at her.

"Robin," she said in a dreamy voice. "You owe me."

"What?"

"You never gave me my back rub. Before I finished with you, you were already snoring."

Fox smiled, and sighed internally with relief. "Sorry. I'll make it up to you when we get back to Washington. I hope I didn't keep you awake."

She shook her head, closed her eyes again, and turned her face away.

He looked to his left, across the aisle, to where Adler was engaged in some prodigious snoring of his own. The stranger in the window seat next to him was rummaging through the amenities kit for earplugs.

"Yes," Adler had said, when Fox had talked to him about alerting the Saudis to a possible attack on Mecca. Then he had looked at Fox, then nodded, then said, "Yes, of course."

He hadn't looked Fox in the eye until after he spoke. His gestures followed his speech, when in a sincere person, they would usually appear together. He had reiterated his answer with a "Yes, of course." Three affirmatives were much less convincing than one. And then he had quickly changed the subject. All the signs were pointing in one direction.

He had been lying.

As soon as they cleared customs at Dulles and emerged into the arrivals hall, an explosion of flashbulbs greeted them. In the midst of all the reporters stood a tall figure in a blue suit and red tie. When he saw them, he spread his arms wide. Emily broke into a run and leapt into them. They embraced and kissed, as all the camera lenses turned to point at the reunited couple.

A photographer stepped in front of Fox, snapping away and blocking his vision. It was just as well.

Eventually, the cameras retreated to make room for microphones. "Today is a great day," the Congressman said. "My heartfelt thanks to the British police and

Security Service, our embassy in London, and the United States Peace Research Institute. Once again, the staff has shown great courage and resourcefulness in their mission of protecting America's interests without violence. May it continue to grow and expand, until the day when a Secretary of Peace sits on the Cabinet! I owe an unending debt of gratitude to all of them...especially Robin Fox! Robin, thank you for bringing this wonderful woman home to me!"

He extended his hand. As the reporters parted to let him through, Fox came forward to take it. The Congressman clasped Fox's hand in one of his and Emily's in the other, and lifted them high as another storm of flashbulbs erupted around him. He looked for all the world like an Olympic gold medalist acknowledging the silver and bronze winners, or a stage star inviting the supporting cast to join him in the curtain call.

23

WASHINGTON, D.C.
MONDAY, APRIL 6

Fox was back at work, trying to focus on his classes, and attend to the necessary paperwork for making up the ones he had missed, with his mind still reeling from the whole experience. Jet lag did not help matters at all.

As he sat in his office, staring blankly at a form he was supposed to be filling out, the conversation with Adler still kept running through his mind. He knew it would leave him no peace unless he did something about it.

He locked his office and headed downstairs without greeting Mirage, for fear that she would have another message from someone who needed him to do something. His feet automatically carried him to the intersection where they always paused to ask him whether he wanted to turn left, toward USPRI headquarters, or right, to catch the Metro home.

He stopped for a moment, and then kept going

straight to New Hampshire Avenue, turned left, and walked up to a marble-and-glass façade with a green flag flying above it. Embossed in gold in the wall next to the door was a palm tree above two crossed scimitars, and the words: EMBASSY OF THE KINGDOM OF SAUDI ARABIA.

The next time his phone rang, Fox had no need to check the screen to know who it was. He inhaled deeply for two rings, exhaled for another two, and answered.

"Robin Fox."

"What in the..." came an explosive voice from the other end. He held the receiver a few inches away from his ear, and waited for "...did you think you were doing?"

"John. Always a pleasure to hear from you."

"What in the nine circles of hell gave you the idea that a civilian consultant like you has any business messing around in diplomatic affairs of this level?"

"What's the problem, John? All I did was double-check to make sure the Saudis got your message. You know how easy it is for these things to get buried in bureaucracy. Stovepipe organization and all that."

"Do you have any idea what a serious matter this is?"

"If you think you can charge me with a crime, then you're most welcome to send the police over to arrest me. I already know all about the right to remain silent."

Adler was silent himself for a moment, but the sound of his breath would have done credit to the fiercest of dragons.

Fox's voice became ice to Adler's fire. "Or did the message actually get sent in the first place? Could it be that you weren't planning to tell them? That you were just going to stand by and let it happen?"

Silence.

"Give those damned hajjis a taste of their own medicine? Let them know what it feels like to be the target of a terror attack? Still thinking we have a little score to settle from September 11? Is that what you had in mind?"

"It's not like that. What kind of monsters do you think we are?"

"You tell me, Adler. What kind of monsters are you?"

"It worked."

"What are you talking about? What worked?"

"The antiserum. They administered it to everyone at the Vatican who had been exposed. And in the follow-up test, not one of them tested positive for Zagorsk. Since then, Rid has been cooking it up on a huge scale."

"On a..." Fox broke off as Adler's meaning slowly began to sink in. "So. A biological attack on Mecca, by a secular Afghani operating out of Britain, no connection to us. And then America gets to ride in on a white horse and save the day. Talk about winning hearts and minds. Is that what you were thinking?"

There was silence on the other end. As the full ramifications of Adler's plan became clear to Fox, he felt a chill and a wave of nausea together, as if he were going to vomit ice water.

"And what would you have demanded in return?"

More silence.

"How very convenient. Potential outbreaks of Zagorsk all over the Muslim world, and the only known cure is an American trade secret. You could ask any government to do anything you wanted, and they could hardly refuse. A blackmailer's paradise on a global scale."

There was another pause. Then, "If one word of this gets out..."

"I know what the consequences would be, and believe me, I don't want to see them any more than you do. If I were you, I'd be more worried about the consequences of your secret staying in. The consequences for your soul."

Adler was silent long enough that it became apparent he had nothing further to say.

"John."

"What?"

"Peace be with you."

Adler hung up.

A wave of applause swept through the auditorium at USPRI headquarters. From the lectern, a beaming Leila nodded graciously to acknowledge it. Fox joined in enthusiastically, and glanced to either side of him to share a smile with Emily and Miriam.

As the applause tapered off, Leila kept the microphone. "I should give special thanks," she added, "to three people without whom I would not be standing here today: Miriam Haddad, Emily Harper, and Robin Fox. And at this time of year, it seems appropriate to honor a very special Jewish gentleman, born in my hometown, who may have been the first-ever teacher of nonviolent resistance in occupied Palestine. So, to all my Christian friends: Happy Easter!"

The panelists and USPRI staff adjourned to Circa at Foggy Bottom, where Fox and Emily regaled Miriam

326 | Charles Kowalski

and Leila with their stories from London. When Fox got to the part about the Archbishop of Canterbury, the waiter, with timing worthy of a master magician, arrived with his flaming crème brulée.

After dinner, the group dispersed, leaving Emily and Fox walking toward the Metro station together.

"It's a beautiful evening," Fox said. "Do you feel up for a walk around the garden?"

"Sure."

They passed through the Sheen Hok Gate into the Dixon memorial garden, and strolled among the flowers in silence for a while.

"You know something," Fox said.

"What's that?"

They walked past a sundial. *Time began in a garden*, the inscription informed them. Right, Fox thought ruefully. Back when there was only one man and one woman in the world, with no further complications.

"You know something," he said again.

"I like to think I know a few things," she replied, "but I don't know which one you're talking about."

He took a deep breath.

"Back in Gottlieb's house, after the firefighter took you, and I blacked out—at that moment, I was sure that my life was over. And the one thing on my mind was..."

His voice trailed off.

"Was?" she prompted.

He took another deep breath and tried to calm the pounding of his heart.

"Was..."

Now or never.

" 'Now I'll know.' I've spent all these years studying

the world's religions, learning all the different ways they envisioned life after death. And now, here I was, about to discover it myself. The culmination of all my research. I didn't feel any fear at all. In fact, it was the most exciting moment of my life."

Coward, coward, coward! You faced a poisoner, an armed madman, a fire, the wrath of the CIA, even the drivers on Israeli highways...and now, at this *of all moments, your courage fails you?*

"So," she said, "are you disappointed that you'll have to stay in this world a while longer?"

"Well, it does have its compensations." He was just bold enough to add: "You're one of them."

She turned to him with a smile. "I'm glad you feel that way. Because there are a lot of people who would have been very sad if you had chosen to pursue your research to the end. I'm one of them."

They came full circle, back to the gate. She turned to him, wrapped her arms around him, and held him close.

Ah, with moments like these, who needs Heaven?

She released him partway. They stood, arms lightly holding each other, forehead touching forehead, nose almost touching nose. The slightest inclination of the head, just a degree or two in either direction, would clear the way to a fearsome, forbidden, fabulous point of no return.

They kissed.

One chaste little peck on the right cheek, and one on the left. Their lips were the identical poles of two powerful magnets: bring them close enough together and they would connect, at any point but that one.

"See you tomorrow?"

"Definitely."
"Good night, Robin."
"Good night, Emily."
She went home to her husband. He went home to meditate.

Acknowledgments

First and foremost, heartfelt thanks to Susan Brooks of Literary Wanderlust, for making this book a reality. Also, many thanks to the literary guardian angels who kept me going through the long journey: Leo J. Maloney for his extraordinary kindness to a fledgling author. Sean Vogel for his valuable comments on the manuscript, especially on military matters. Gloria F. Boyer for editorial guidance. Ruth M'Gonigle for her cover design. Peter Greene of the Adventure Writers Competition for being incredibly generous with his graphic design and filmmaking talents. And finally, Edith Hope Bishop for her constant encouragement and companionship.

Thanks to Anna Baltzer for her guidance on Middle East issues, Rabbi Ilene Schneider for Jewish traditions and customs, and Imam Muhammed Rasit Alas for Islamic theology (and Turkish Delight). Any errors or misrepresentations that remain are my own fault.

Dr. D.P. Lyle for medical advice. Jennifer McQuiston and Nitesh Parmar of the Center for Disease Control and Prevention, Christie Cullinan of the FBI, David Barker of the British police, and others at agencies that may or may not exist for any information they may or may not have provided. Again, for any errors or creative liberties (such as bringing the HIG to the Hoover Building rather than the off-site facility where they work in real life), the responsibility is mine.

R. Martin Rogovein for Israeli cultural information. The staff at the Meir Medical Center and St. Peter's Basilica for their help with location research. Elaine Hepburn and Chetan Rama for their hospitality in London.

While writing *Mind Virus,* I referred to books, articles and websites too numerous to list, but I would like to acknowledge certain authors without whom this book could not have been written: Friedrich Wilhelm Nietzsche, Richard Dawkins, Sam Harris, Christopher Hitchens, and Darrell W. Ray for inspiration. Matthew Alexander, Tony Lagouranis, Chris Mackey, Joshua E.S. Phillips, Erik Saar, and Justine Sharrock on the life and work of military interrogators. Paul Ekman, William L. Fleisher, Nathan J. Gordon, Pamela Meyer, and Joe Navarro on interrogation and deception detection techniques. Ken Alibek, Richard Preston, and Amy E. Smithson on biological weapons in the former Soviet Union and Iraq. Maxine Kaufman-Lacusta (and the contributors to her book *Refusing to Be Enemies*), and Mark Frey on nonviolent resistance movements in the Middle East. Asma Afsaruddin, M. Amir Ali, and Imam

Shamsi Ali on Islamic peace philosophy. Marietta Jaeger for her personal story of forgiving the unforgivable.

And finally, many thanks to my very patient family, for believing in me.

About the Author

Charles Kowalski is almost as much a citizen of the world as his fictional character, Robin Fox, having lived abroad for over 15 years. *Mind Virus* won the Rocky Mountain Fiction Writers' Colorado Gold Award and was a finalist for the Adventure Writers' Competition, the Killer Nashville Claymore Award, and the Pacific Northwest Writers' Association Literary Award. Charles currently divides his time between Japan, where he teaches English at a university, and his family home in Maine.

Made in the USA
Coppell, TX
16 April 2020